Fear of Drowning

Fear of Drowning

Susan White

The Acorn Press
Charlottetown
2019

ACORNPRESS

P.O. Box 22024
Charlottetown, Prince Edward Island
C1A 9J2
acornpresscanada.com

Edited by Penelope Jackson
Designed by Matt Reid
Printed in Canada

Library and Archives Canada Cataloguing in Publication

Title: Fear of drowning / Susan White.
Names: White, Susan, 1956- author.
Identifiers: Canadiana (print) 2019006949X | Canadiana (ebook)
2019006952X | ISBN 9781773660257
(softcover) | ISBN 9781773660301 (HTML)
Classification: LCC PS8645.H5467 F43 2019 | DDC C813/.6—dc23

Canada | Canada Council for the Arts | Conseil des Arts du Canada

The publisher acknowledges the support of the Government of Canada
through the Canada Book Fund of the Department of Canadian Heritage
for our publishing activities. We also acknowledge the support of the
Canada Council for the Arts for our publishing program.

To Kathy. Our 2011 cross-Canada adventure
included a Thousand Islands day cruise, where the seed
for this book was dropped and began to germinate.

Fear of Drowning is the back-and-forth unfolding of the stories of six generations of women connected by blood or circumstance. Those women, by birthdate:

Marion Kingston Randolph: Born 1877, died 1941

Lillianne McDonough Randolph: Born 1899, died 1998

Cordelia Randolph (Kingston): Born 1901, died 1993

Clara Randolph Pasternak: Born 1918

Leah Pasternak Jacobs: Born 1946

Hilary Jacobs Thompson: Born 1973

Rivers Thompson: Born 1999

You don't drown by falling in the water;
you drown by staying there.

—Edwin Louis Cole

Lillianne
1993

When I was a child, shadows were a mystery to me. At certain times my shadow might tower over me, when in another light it would crouch and bow before me as a servant bows to his master. The past, like overlapping dark shadows, was as much a mystery to me as the formations of my childhood shadows. The past was always present, always bidding me to delve deeper to bring the shadow of my memories into a brighter and more discernible light. In these, my final days, the shadows of my past were as dark as the blackest ink, but still I tried to illuminate them.

I refused to move from this house. Before accepting that, Clara kept up her gentle but forceful persuasion, trying to get me to sell and move into a nearby seniors' home. Her reasons seemed sound enough but were in such opposition to all I cared about. This house held my past, and that was what kept me going. In many ways, it was this house that kept me afloat all the years I was so far away from the protection of its red brick walls. This house was the lifeline that kept me from drowning, kept Lillianne McDonough from disappearing, and I intended to keep a firm hold on that lifeline.

I rose from the chair and walked away from my writing desk. At this same desk my father had sat reading the telegram that changed everything. Even at the young age of six, I knew the words on the paper were important words; words that were upsetting my father and words that later brought my mother's anger.

*

"Does she think we can just drop everything and come to California at her beck and call?"

"She has no other family, Claire. But I can go alone."

"She would like that, wouldn't she? Getting you away from your poor, unworthy Canadian bride. She has been scheming to do that for the last ten years. Has she even considered getting on a train and coming here? How has she not done that in the last six years? Has she no desire to meet her only grandchild? I will not drag Lillianne on a long train ride to see a woman who has shown no interest in her existence. And now she sends a telegram begging you to come when a sprained ankle lays her up."

I seldom heard my mother angry, and her tone startled me that day. She scooped me up into her arms and comforted me when she saw me standing in the doorway. She kissed my cheeks in the way that always made me giggle. For years afterwards I would press my eyes closed and remember the feeling those kisses gave me, followed by the delight of her beautiful smile when her rapid kisses brought my laughter.

"You are my beautiful girl, my precious treasure, my lovely Lillianne." She said those words to me a million times and I hear the echo of them still. On countless nights in the years that followed, it was the echo of those words that carried me through the dark, frightening loneliness.

*

"This desk was your grandfather's, Clara, and it has always sat right here in this front room, and I will not allow you to move it."

"But, Mother, we could move the desk into the next room if

we brought your bed down and set it up here. If your bed were in this bay window, you would get the early morning sun, and you must agree not having to go upstairs would make things easier if you insist on staying here alone."

"This was Father's office, and his desk has always sat right here between these two windows. I would perch myself on the top stair and look down at the people who sat and waited for him in the front hall before he called them in. When I came back to this house, this desk was sitting right in its spot, even though much of the other furniture had been stolen or vandalized. This desk is going nowhere, and I am still perfectly able to walk up and down the stairs."

I ran my fingers along the curve of the roll-top desk. Clara had mentioned moving my bed down to this room several times. I was still the decision-maker in this house and would not let my daughter's constant nattering get to me. What *if* I were to collapse on the stairs? What *if* I were to die on the trek up to bed? To die in this house would not be the worst end I could imagine. Dying in a narrow bed in a room at the Briarlea Nursing Home would be much worse as far as I was concerned.

*

"This is your bed, Lillianne."

The large room at the orphanage had at least fifty narrow metal beds. Each bed was covered with a flat pillow and a grey wool blanket with one stripe of a reddish-brown colour that looked like blood.

*

My bed at home had been big and so far off the floor I needed a step to climb up into it at night. It had a soft and bouncy mattress, silky sheets, a puffy comforter, and many pillows. I sank into that glorious pile every night when Mother and Father tucked me in, performing the bedtime ritual that began with a bed lunch Mother would bring to me on the beautiful silver tray.

"Five generations of McDonoughs owned this tray, and your mother gifted it along with a huge heap of guilt, reluctantly allowing her son to take it from his ancestral home."

"You make too much of her words, Claire."

"Do I, Frederick? You do not hear the poison in her words or feel her barbs? Or does she save those exclusively for the woman who stole her darling son?"

I remember the bed lunch on the last night. Mrs. Price had made my favourite cranberry scones and Mother had buttered a scone for me, putting it on one of her best rosebud china saucers. In a small bowl beside the saucer was a spoonful of strawberry jam. There had also been hot cocoa in a china cup.

"Frederick, she's asked for this tray back. Can you believe the nerve of asking us to return a wedding gift? Do you suppose her coffers have become so depleted that she has to sell a silver tray to stay afloat?"

Mother adamantly refused to return the tray.

"This is Lillianne's special tray. I have been bringing her bed lunch on this tray since she was old enough for her big bed."

I asked Mrs. Price about the tray the next night, but she could not find it. The tray was gone and I cried silly tears for it, not knowing the volume of tears that would follow.

As I watched my parents preparing for their trip to San Francisco, I kept dragging my small carpet bag from room to room, pleading with Mother to pack my things and take me along.

"We will not be gone long, darling. Father and I must go to tend to Grandmother McDonough. With any luck, we will be successful in persuading her to travel back home with us so she can convalesce here."

I had no idea what *convalesce* meant, but I did know from the conversation I'd heard earlier in the day that Mother didn't really want my grandmother to come to our house. Nevertheless, no amount of pleading could convince Mother to pack my tapestry travelling bag. The next day I stood in the doorway sobbing as I watched my parents get into the big black car that had come for them.

In 1906 I'd seen very few motor vehicles, and for the longest time I blamed that black motorcar for all my troubles. The first few days were difficult, but nothing compared with what was ahead for me. Mrs. Price tended to my needs, and even though the care she provided wasn't the loving attention my parents gave me, I knew it was just for a few days. My beloved parents would be back.

My parents arrived at my grandmother's home on Post Avenue late on the night before the early morning quake that occurred in San Francisco on April 18, 1906. It was days before word found its way to our home in Odessa, Ontario. Thousands of people had been killed in the earthquake, and Frederick and Claire McDonough were two of them. I lived every one of the eighty-seven years following that terrible spring day in the shadow of that dispatch.

*

"Mother, why are you sitting in the dark?"

With the sudden glare of the overhead light, I could see by the mantel clock that it was seven o'clock. I had not even realized I'd been sitting for hours, deep in remembering the St. Vincent de Paul Children's Home. There was no point explaining to Clara just how often in the last few weeks I had found myself transported back inside the formidable stone structure that was my home for nine years. I had never been able to talk of those years except very briefly to Clifton on those first heady days when I thought his love was to be the release I so desired.

"I'm going to open a can of soup for your supper, Mother. I wouldn't have to worry about your meals if you would consider moving into Briarlea. Wouldn't you like to be fed three nutritious meals a day by a staff paid to care for your dietary needs?"

"Did you know I learned to cook over an open hearth? I lifted cast-iron pots weighing nearly as much as me when I first arrived at St. Vincent de Paul's. Even when the large cook stoves were added, we little ones were given tasks far more difficult than children these days could even imagine. I don't think you even washed a dish until you were well into your teens. I probably didn't do you any favours. No coddling by the Sisters of Providence, I can tell you."

Clara gave me the same look she always gave me when I referenced her spoiled upbringing, then left the room. I could hear her clanging the pots in the kitchen. I returned to my train of thought.

*

Mrs. Price kept me for three weeks after word of my parents' death reached us. Her voice faltered when she explained to me she was unable to stay any longer and could not take me with her when she returned home. She packed my small bag with a change of clothes and a few of my most treasured possessions. She laid out my cream-coloured chiffon dress. I loved its frothy layers of ruffles, but I cried as I put it on, thinking of the day Mother had brought it home to me. I was crying even more as I pulled on my ten-button boots and covered my dress with my garnet-coloured melton-cloth coat and donned my matching hat.

If I'd known how thoughtlessly my precious clothes would be discarded, I might have chosen a less favoured outfit. It wasn't just my clothes, of course, but the very life I knew that would be cast aside, and had I known that, my quiet crying would have been wailing and I wouldn't have followed Mrs. Price so unceremoniously out the door of my beloved home into the back seat of the waiting motor car and then later onto the platform at the train station. I would certainly not have fallen into an unworried sleep during the train ride to Kingston.

But I quickly realized no amount of wailing or any other show of emotion would sway the sisters from their strict and precise attention to settling me into the residence I found myself in on May 12, 1906, just a few days before my seventh birthday.

Firstly, I was instructed to change into a starched white blouse, its cuffs frayed and discoloured; a tight, scratchy, pinstriped jumper; grey tights; and scuffed brown loafers a size too big for my feet. I was then marched into a room where my blond curls were unceremoniously cropped close to my head. I held in my tears as I watched one of the women sweep my curls into a metal dustpan and throw them into the dustbin. The curls fell on top of the velvet hair ribbon Mrs. Price had tied into the large and showy bow I'd worn so proudly, thinking myself almost as pretty as my beloved mother.

*

"Come out to the kitchen and have your supper, Mother. I think you drifted off again. I hope you're taking your medications properly. You seem to be in a bit of a daze lately. That's another worry I wouldn't have if you would go to Briarlea. They take over all your medical care."

"I am not over-medicated, if that's what you think, Clara.

I always remember to take my vitamins and that one pill Dr. Dawson gave me on my last visit, although I don't remember exactly what it's for. I hardly think I'd be better off with bossy people treating me as if I haven't got a brain in my head. I'll stay my own boss as long as I'm able, thank you very much. And as far as I can see, it doesn't hurt anyone if I sit and do nothing all afternoon long. I would think you'd be happy I was saving on the light bill by sitting in the dark. I have no intention of being marched off to an institution. I had my fill of that, I can tell you."

"But you've never really told me, Mother. You sometimes make reference to the years you spent in the orphanage, but other than the fact that every one of your novels has an orphaned character looking for her way back home, you've never really shared your past with me."

"A literary reviewer now, are you? I've kept it all pretty much to myself, I suppose. Never saw the point of letting you know about those years. I tried my best to give you the life I didn't have. Why bother you with the troubles of my past? No amount of talking about it changes anything."

"Oh, Mother. Do you know how many times you have told me how hard you tried to give me the life you didn't have? I have probably imagined your childhood as far worse than it really was. Sometimes I wished I had been dropped at the doors of St. Vincent de Paul myself. You made me feel like I was never good enough. I was never the brave, determined girl that you were. I am a seventy-five-year-old woman with my own deep losses and heartbreaks and accomplishments—but I'm not the great, long-suffering Lillianne McDonough."

"I don't have the energy for your dramatics, Clara, and I won't apologize for your insecurities. And I suppose your father has nothing to account for? I suppose he did everything right?"

"I've never said that, Mother. I would just once like you to really tell me about your childhood without making me feel like I was a spoiled, entitled brat who was never thankful for anything. It's not my fault my parents didn't die in a natural disaster. I'll be back tomorrow. Maybe we can sit and have a conversation without this old fight cropping up."

As Clara bent to kiss my forehead, tears glistened in my eyes. What she'd said was true. I had always been hard on her. She had never been an easy child, and her resentment at being separated from her beloved father was always an open wound. Had I done my best? Had my obsession to get back to my girlhood home been the fuel driving all my choices? How easy it had been to write characters to mirror my deepest emotions instead of sharing them with the people I loved.

"I love you, Clara, my beautiful girl, my precious treasure. Don't give up on me. I appreciate you coming by. Maybe tomorrow we can just sit and talk."

﹡

My first thoughts as I woke early, before pulling back the bedclothes and making myself get up, were layered and somewhat convoluted. What if my grandmother had not sent the telegram? What if she had never tripped on the bottom step and twisted her ankle? What if I had gone with Mother and Father? That was at the core of all my emotional floundering, which seemed not to have lessened even with the passing of almost nine decades. I still found myself going back to the crucial questions: What if they had not gone to San Francisco? What if I had gone with them? My life was forever changed because after receiving the telegram from my grandmother, my father booked train passage for my mother and himself and left me behind.

What if the telegraph had never been invented? If my grandmother had mailed a letter instead and the receipt of it was delayed by even one day, my parents would not have been in San Francisco when the earth moved and sections of the city were levelled.

This was to be a long and tiresome day if I continued to mire myself in a web of useless thoughts. What if the train Mrs. Price and I caught that day had left the tracks? What if she had taken me home with her? What if I'd not taken employment at the Prince George Hotel?

Possibly my reluctance to share my deepest thoughts with Clara had more to do with my inability to truly see my life. Had I, like she said, simply used the cloak of my misery to gird myself from any real introspection? Was getting back to being the darling daughter of Frederick and Claire McDonough my motivation for all the choices I made?

I put my bare feet on the cold floor. They looked ancient, the skin almost opaque and the nails claw-like and frightening. The veins running up my legs looked like lines of ink on parchment paper. Where would I begin if Clara were to sit and patiently listen to my ramblings? Could I ever begin to tell her how even in this decrepit body I feel still like a young girl? I still longed for the freedom of my youth and the first stirring of love I had for her father. At eighteen I felt I finally had some hope of reclaiming what had been stolen from me at the St. Vincent de Paul orphanage.

I never intended to make Clara believe I was heroic, strong, brave, or in any way better prepared for the difficulties of life than anyone else. I was simply trying to hold on, to not let the rush of misery drown me, submerging me in the sorrow of losing oneself. Even after all these years, is that what propelled me?

Perhaps some simple and true remembrances, some honest and unembellished facts, would free me once and for all. If Clara would allow me, I would attempt to voice what I had fiercely protected for so long.

I took my silk robe from the hook on the back of my bedroom door. Perhaps I would write today. My publisher had asked me to write a foreword for the re-release of my first novel, *Beyond Wind and Whitecaps*, and maybe I could get back to the story I started months ago.

The character I created in the pages of my debut novel was brave and determined. The dramatic turn her life took when she found herself stranded on an island in the St. Lawrence River was not exactly my story, but parts of it mirrored my own experience. I had considered taking the small boat and rowing off the island when after six weeks the Randolphs had not returned. During those weeks of solitude I began writing the story that later became my first published work. So many dreams resurfaced the summer I spent on Randolph Island. So many dreams, and so much heartache once I realized Clifton would not be my saviour.

To tell Clara everything about that summer would be cruel. Her father, grandmother, and beloved aunt Cordelia held such a place of esteem for her, and I didn't intend to alter that. I would try, however, to tell her some of what she'd asked to hear. Possibly someday I would find the courage to tell her everything. I'd begin by telling her of the years leading up to my first encounter with Marion Randolph and the split-second decision I made that changed the course of my life, and certainly formed Clara's.

I looked in the bevelled mirror of my dressing table, trying to tame the unruly mess of white hair. The reflection that gazed back at me was a stranger, certainly not the face that had looked back at me over the years, the face so closely resembling my mother's. I picked up the small oval frame on my bureau that held the only photograph I had of my parents.

❊

My narrow bed at St. Vincent's was in the room assigned to the six- to eight-year-olds. Beside each bed was an upturned tobacco box, and in mine were all my possessions, my four folded pairs of undergarments, and the second pair of tights. My own clothes had not been given back to me, and the only other possessions I was allowed to keep were my framed photograph and the small black notebook I had taken from my father's desk minutes before leaving home.

I had not taken a pencil from Father's desk, and it was months before I was able to steal one and hide it with the notebook under my pile of clothes. After that I tried every night, before the lights were turned out, to write a few words in the notebook. The first few pages were covered with my childlike attempts at printing "Lillianne Elizabeth McDonough" over and over again.

❊

Walking slowly down the stairs, I gazed at the framed photographs and awards on the wall, tributes to my literary career. The words written in my stolen moments before sleep during my years at St. Vincent de Paul had set my course. I held tightly to the dream of becoming an author and making my own way. Randolph money carried me along until I was able to make a living at my typewriter. My writing gave Clara the life she had. Why did she feel such resentment toward me?

The kettle boiled, and as I filled the teapot, Clara came in carrying a brown paper Tim Horton's bag. Sitting down across the table from me, she buttered two muffins, seemingly ready to hear more.

I didn't wait to begin. "The nights were the worst. It was never silent. A room of fifty lonely little girls makes a noise all its own. It wasn't always crying, but even the sighs or the quiet moaning held such eeriness. Most nights, a girl was suffering from a beating, and it was easier to listen to crying when it was Sister Mary Alice's strap that caused it. But it was harder to listen to the moans of misery when they so closely resembled my own gnawing pain."

"You were beaten in the orphanage?"

"Oh, yes. Typical of the times. It came in waves, almost as if Sister Mary Alice was controlled by the phases of the moon. A misdemeanour that one day would get you a harsh tongue-lashing might another day earn you several forceful lashes with her leather strap. I think the worst beatings were when she simply chose you to be the orphan she despised the most that day.

"*You think yourself quite special, don't you? You think those blue eyes and your blond curls make you something precious. A fancy name and rich dead parents don't make you any better than the rest of these pissants.*'

"*Pissants* was one of her favourite insults. She had a string of them, but *pissants* always struck me as the funniest. But she really pounced on you if you laughed while she was delivering her speech declaring your worthlessness.

"*Bladderskite* was another one she favoured. We tried our best to seem invisible around her. If you did your work and kept your mouth shut, the others didn't bother you at all. It was Sister Mary Alice who took such pleasure in our misery."

"What kind of work did they make you do?"

"Wasn't much we didn't do, really. We certainly earned our keep. Served me well in the long term. We were trained in all the finer points of housekeeping according to the volumes of *Cassel's Household Guide*. We didn't see many whalebone corsets, but we knew how to launder them. Laundering was the bread and butter at St. Vincent's. The sisters profited from the scores of homeless girls available to them at the time. They had the contract for laundering the bed linens for the prisons and all the hospitals. We rose early, and after our daily cleaning jobs we went right to the large laundry facility. We worked long hours, just as hard as any indentured servant of the day."

"In *Beyond Wind and Whitecaps* a little girl was scalded in a large vat of lye soap. Did that really happen?"

"It did. Her name was Velma, but it didn't happen just the way I wrote it. God love her, she died a few hours later. I'm sure what really happened was better for the poor thing than the way I wrote it. Lye soap is unforgiving, and Velma's agony at least was short.

"But I don't want to drone on about the misery of my years at St. Vincent's. Like you said yesterday, I have always used references to those days as a yardstick for the gratitude you should feel for your own childhood. I never meant to imply that my suffering set me apart or gave me some great wisdom. I suppose it must seem like I wore my childhood as a badge of honour. Perhaps I did. But I can honestly say that for years I gave it very little thought. Maybe it was in the rereading of *Beyond Wind and Whitecaps*, or maybe I've just become a pathetic old woman with nothing but the past to ruminate over. Whatever it is, I cannot seem to escape the walls of my childhood prison.

"I suppose calling it a prison only adds to the drama of it, but in reality I got quite accustomed to life in the care of the

Sisters of Providence. Providence. The dictionary definition of *providence* says 'God's care and help; Care or preparation for the future.' Given the chance, I could have certainly renamed that order.

"I find myself consumed with the memories of those years, and I feel trapped by them. I know that sounds ridiculous when I am probably living my last few months, and dissecting my past will in no way alter my future. I feel the need to forgive myself, though."

"Oh, Mother. I don't even know what to say to that. I've been your harshest critic, too hard on you in many ways. You must know my hurtful words have been more about my own shortcomings."

"That's kind of you to say, but I do have some things to answer for. Not what you may think, either. I am going to keep going with my ramblings, and maybe I will get to the crux of the matter. Unless you have somewhere else to be, please just humour a poor old woman."

I held out my teacup for Clara to fill and continued. "There were happy times. We stuck together for the most part. There were some nasty girls, but most of us watched out for each other. Gloria could do amazing impressions of all the nuns. We would fall into peals of laughter when she did her version of the tirades we heard daily.

"'*You pissants have nothing to snivel about. You are lucky to have been given a roof over your head. Do you think the meals you get here are anything like the meals in the poor house or in the Anglican Parish home? You have fallen into the care of God's most faithful servants, and everything you receive here is an undeserving gift from a God who turns a blind eye to your sin and your black, evil souls.*'

"After scrubbing every coal-covered surface in that nasty

old building, we knew our bodies were black and filthy, but we were never convinced our souls were. Over and over we would remind ourselves who we were, where we had come from, and who had loved us before we became unloved and unworthy. The girls who had been left as infants did not have that, and if anything set us apart from one another it was that.

"I feel the guiltiest about that now. Believing myself to be the beloved daughter of Frederick and Claire McDonough may have kept me from accepting the love of others."

"What do you mean? Are you referring to Father?"

"No, not entirely. I clung so desperately to the notion of who I was that I didn't bother to find out who I could have become." I paused, winded. "I'm done for now. Exhausted and it's not even noon. Perhaps heavy medication would be a better option. This soul-searching is completely unravelling me. I'll have a nap and then maybe this heaviness will have gone."

"I'll stay. I thought I might even spend the night if that's okay."

"Of course. I would enjoy your company. We spend so little time together. It seems since Leah moved, the only time I see you is when you come for a quick check-in. I suppose you have to keep the others informed that the old girl is still alive."

"Go have your nap, Mother. You're getting cranky, and I was quite enjoying the softer side of you."

I smiled wryly. "The side I reserved for strangers, you mean. The ones I loved the most often got the opposite view."

*

It was midafternoon when I came back downstairs. Clara had a lovely lunch prepared, and I sat in the dining room eating it while she bustled about, dusting and rearranging the bric-a-brac that covered the surfaces. I resisted the urge to instruct her to pack up the useless clutter. China, crystal, porcelain figurines—a lifetime of accumulating becomes valueless as you reach the end of your days.

When I'd finished lunch and regained some strength, I continued my story. "On my sixteenth birthday, I realized the life I'd settled into during the last nine years may not have been so bad. We can grow accustomed to anything, even a toothache, as they say. My life changed abruptly when I was brought into the Mother Superior's office and told of the change in my circumstances. I had been aware, seeing older girls leave, that there would come a time when I would be sent out into the world.

"I was given a pile of folded garments, which consisted of a starched white blouse, a grey gabardine jumper, a woollen coat, Oxford shoes, and some new undergarments. One of the more motherly nuns spoke kindly as she showed me how to tightly wind my hair, which had grown long, into a respectable bun. She pinned the loose tendrils and fastened it with a clip. Sister Mary Alice stood across the room, and not missing her opportunity to bring some piety to the proceedings, began her discourse.

'*Don't expect your good looks and slender figure to pave your way through life. Hard work and godliness will be your best assets. Your training and your affinity for good hard work will be your best providers. You will leave with a reference letter and the good name of the Sisters of Providence. Make sure you mention my name when you present yourself to Sister McCleary at the Holy Name of Jesus Parish on the Old Kingston Mills Road. On our word, she will find you domestic employment. We have done our part; now the rest will be up to you.*'"

Clara looked taken aback. "Were you frightened? I cannot even imagine at sixteen being sent out to work for strangers. Hilary wouldn't even go to a friend's house overnight when she was sixteen. Do you remember how timid she was?"

"Funny how single children tend to be overly attached to their mother's apron strings."

"I detect the sarcasm in your voice. It was a month before my sixteenth birthday when I convinced you to allow Aunt Cordelia to pay for my passage to accompany her to London on the *Carinthia*."

Choosing to ignore Clara's remarks, I continued. "On the day after my sixteenth birthday, I was delivered to a mansion on Ontario Street and found myself in the employ of the Higgins family. I was given another narrow metal bed, but this time in the dark and damp corner of a small room in the cellar. I sobbed that night, desperately missing the familiar sounds of St. Vincent's. I would have even welcomed a thrashing from Sister Mary Alice, and thought that many times over the next fifteen months.

"I was the youngest of a staff of twelve and was given the most disagreeable tasks. My payment was 'in kind,' which was anything but kind on the part of the head housekeeper, Mrs. Gillis. I worked from sunup till late into the night; the Higgins household was a bustle of social activity. But the drudgery of working long hours was far better than the misery of my cold and damp sleeping chamber when the fall and winter months came. I would huddle on the wide top step in the back stairwell on the especially cold nights."

"That's terrible. Was there no place you could turn for help?"

"Back then, a young girl with no family was lucky to have work. There was no social welfare. The Catholic Church had done its part in housing me for nine years, and I didn't see any alternative to my circumstances. I kept my mouth shut and did my work.

"But the hunger was even worse than the cold or the loneliness. I was only offered leftover food after all the family, guests, and other staff had eaten. The abundance in the Higgins larder was not for my sustenance. In fact, it was a loaf of sourdough bread that was my undoing. It had supposedly been left on a rack in the pantry, and when it went missing I was accused of stealing it. If my denial wasn't convincing enough, the loud growls of my empty stomach should have proven my innocence.

"But I was let go without ceremony, and with theft on my record, the sisters at the Holy Name of Jesus wanted no part in procuring my next placement. I was put out on the street at seventeen with nowhere to turn. Now I was in real trouble."

"Is that when you started working at the Prince George?"

"Shortly after that, but I was on the street for a few nights, sleeping under stairs and in doorways. On the third morning as I approached a delivery boy unloading a wagonload of produce at the back door of the Prince George, I ran into the woman who would become my benefactress. Rosemary Donavan was a fiery, quick-witted, redheaded Irishwoman who put the fear of God in me in a way even Sister Mary Alice's leather strap did not. She had lived through the sinking of the *Empress of Ireland*.

"She had been housekeeping staff on that luxurious ship, and if she hadn't been bringing fresh linens to a stateroom on the top deck when the *Storsad* hit the bow of the *Empress*, she would likely have perished below, as did so many. The ship went down in just fourteen minutes, and her quick plunge into the frigid waters accounted for her good fortune; that and the lifeboat rescuing her from those waters before she succumbed to the cold or drowned.

"In that lifeboat was a man named Wilfred Thompson, part owner of the Prince George Hotel in Kingston, Ontario, and a week later Rosemary was put in charge of Prince George's housekeeping staff. Her quick assessment of my predicament that morning steered my course.

"'A strong, healthy girl who can put in a day's work has no call to be living on the street. By the look of you you'll be needing hot water and some soap, and your hair a good combing. Tonight you'll sleep in a bed like a decent girl, not in the dirt like a rapscallion.'

"So in the summer of 1916 I found myself employed at the Prince George under the supervision of Rosemary Donavan. I had my own room in Rosemary's comfortable home on Brock Street. I didn't know why she took such a liking to me, and for a while she was the closest thing I had to family. But things are not always as they seem, and that was a bitter truth I learned from Rosemary Donavan. I was young and so naive.

"For nine months I worked long days, exhausted and happy to return to the comfort Rosemary provided, and I can honestly say I never paid much mind to the comings and goings at night in Rosemary's Brock Street home. I also never questioned just how an Irish housemaid could afford such a grand home and furnishings, not to mention her impressive wardrobe and expensive jewellery. Perhaps I just believed I had finally been returned to the privilege I deserved, being the beloved daughter of Frederick and Claire McDonough. I was soon to find out just how wrong I was on that account.

"The house and Rosemary's luxurious life were not acquired with the salary of the head housekeeper at the Prince George Hotel. The currency that provided such luxury was explained to me on the eve of my eighteenth birthday.

"'Did you not realize the other girls in the house contribute by accepting visits from some of Kingston's finest gentleman? But I am not without conscience or compassion, Lily, and I would not allow a young lady to be ravished before her eighteenth birthday.'

"I was speechless and heartbroken. As she spoke, I realized she was no different from the Sisters of Providence, just better dressed. She had fooled me into thinking she cared about me when she, too, just wanted a service I could provide. I did not exist. Lillianne McDonough ceased to exist when my parents left me behind and never returned."

"Oh my God, Mother, the woman was running a brothel?"

"Don't sound so shocked, Clara. There is and always has been much evil hidden behind masks of respectability. You've been sheltered from the seedy side of life."

Clara frowned. "Just because I wasn't offered up for prostitution doesn't mean I haven't seen my share of greed, lust, and the dark side of humanity. Surely you can't believe I've lived a charmed, untouched life of privilege."

"No, of course not, dear. I didn't mean to dismiss your suffering."

"Keep on with your story. It was Grandmother, wasn't it, who helped you escape?"

"Oh yes, Marion Randolph provided a way out for me, but, of course, she had her own reasons for hiring the orphaned girl she found at her disposal."

Marion
1883

Some might say that a three-year-old child does not have the capacity for clear recollection. I would argue that point; my memory of the minutes I sat alone on the shore were vivid. I knew as I sat there shivering that Mother was not going to join me, her final efforts having gotten me to the sandy place where I could stand and walk out of the wide river. But she'd been swept out to deeper water, and I couldn't even see her head now. I called for her, and my cries brought the others.

The first to come was Mr. Henderson. I didn't know his name at the time, but Father had taken me to his shore a few days earlier to show me the huge fish tethered to a large anchor. The sturgeon was longer than Daisy's calf and it took three men to lift it onto the back of the wagon.

"Where is your mother?" he asked. I had no words to answer but simply pointed out to the blue expanse, still expecting my mother to rise from the water and walk toward me. She would hold me and stop my teeth from chattering. She would wrap the warm grey blanket around me and carry me home. I knew the blanket was spread out underneath the picnic basket sitting where the grass met the sandy shore.

We'd brought the blanket for our picnic. Mother said I could play a while longer while she set out the food. I had helped Mother pack the basket. I had put two yellow transparent apples on top of the other food before covering the basket with a red checkered cloth.

"Where is your mother?" he asked again, and I pointed, remembering the stick I had been pretending was the *David Weston*. Mother said we would go on the *David Weston* soon. We would catch it at the Bedford Wharf and sail to Indiantown. Grandfather would pick us up there and we would visit my Granny in the city. I was watching the stick and imagining being on the deck of the *David Weston*, waving back to Father. The rippling water and the breeze had caught the stick and I'd stumbled in after it.

By the time the others arrived I was crying, and now not from the cold but from the realization that my mother was not coming out of the water. Mrs. Fullerton wrapped me in her coat, and even in my confusion I remember wondering why she was wearing a heavy coat. It was still summer, even though Donald, Victoria, and Roland were back in the schoolhouse. That is why Mother and I were having this special day. *"Not many beach days left,"* Mother had said as we packed our picnic. *"We'll be back in time to make Father's tea."*

"Who will make Father's tea?" I cried. I had asked many other questions, but it was as if no one could hear me. *Why are you carrying my mother? Why is she lying on the beach? Why will she not get up?*

"Marion Kingston. Pay mind to what you are doing."

The sharp voice of Mrs. Lanigan jolted me out of my trance. The mindless job of polishing the ornate silver tea service had set my mind wandering. Looking at the table, it appeared I had spilt some of the silver polish, which would no doubt result in my wages being docked. That thought struck me funny, as what I was being paid could hardly be considered wages.

Free labour, as far as I could see it. Father's new wife had dragged me along when she took summer employment, and Mrs. Lanigan, the head housekeeper, had no trouble finding tasks for me to do. It appeared the city folk who spent their summers in this big house on the shore near Bedford Wharf could not manage without several servants to do their bidding, even if one of them was just a six-year-old girl.

Lillianne
1993

Clara sent me into the living room while she cleared the table and did the lunch dishes. I pulled the afghan up over my legs and waited for her to finish and come in. I was anxious to return to my reminiscing. When she sat on the chair across from me, I started right up as if there'd been no interruption.

"Three weeks before Rosemary's harsh announcement, I was assigned exclusively to the service of an American woman who'd taken residence in the hotel's finest suite. Marion Randolph burst into the Governor's Suite as I was just finishing making up the elaborate linens on the king-sized bed. I turned and saw an ample woman dressed in a fine royal blue brocade suit, a mink stole draped over her shoulders, and a large hat adorned with a peacock feather perched upon her head. She struck me as a comical character, but her tone and forceful demeanour were not the least bit humorous.

"Her first instructions were to the bellboy who had followed her into the room, somehow managing her two large steamer trunks, her upright wardrobe trunk, and several travel bags. She removed her hat and threw it on to the bed, directing her next string of demands at me.

"*Young lady, retrieve my grooming set from this bag and do something to save this coiffure from the destruction inflicted by having this horrid hat on my head since daybreak.*'

"I didn't for one second consider ignoring her request. I quickly opened the tapestry bag she was pointing to and pulled from it a sterling silver case, which held the grooming set. I approached her timidly, having little confidence in my hairdressing abilities.

"'I will need my teal dinner gown from the dresser trunk. Perhaps if it hangs a while it will not need to be steamed. I do assume, however, if steaming is required, this establishment provides such a service. Speaking of service, I will require a girl to attend to my needs for the duration of my stay. I suppose you will do. Inform your supervisor that Mrs. Clifton Randolph will be employing you exclusively. I expect you to return immediately once you have done so.'

"Her words caught me off guard, and I quickly scooped everything into my cart, preparing to leave as her last instruction so forcefully demanded.

"'My hair first, young lady, and before that take out my dinner gown. I have not happened upon an imbecile, have I?'

"In the next few minutes I fixed her hair as best as I could, hung the teal gown in the closet, and laid out her toiletries while running a hot bath. I was brought up to speed on Mrs. Clifton Randolph the Third. She explained that she had just arrived by train from New York and would be staying at the Prince George for three weeks until May 19, when her husband and two of her children would come from their home in Chicago. Her oldest son would also join them from New York, and together they would take a vessel to their summer home on Randolph Island which she described as being unrivalled in its splendour.

"I hurried out the door minutes later to find Rosemary and tell her of Mrs. Randolph's request. I had concluded that Mrs. Randolph was a woman who was accustomed to getting everything she wanted."

"She was determined," Clara interjected. "Not without compassion, though. I was almost grown up before I saw the vulnerable side of my grandmother."

Part of me bristled to hear the degree of tolerance Clara had for her grandmother, when her patience and understanding for me always seemed to be in such short supply. I did not voice that, though; I was enjoying the several hours we had managed to spend together without confrontation.

I completely agreed with Clara's assessment of Marion Randolph. I came to realize my mother-in-law's vulnerability and even came to feel compassion and a certain fondness for her—although I never let her know that. I tried over the years to keep my negative feelings about her from Clara, but I likely failed at that just as miserably as I failed at everything else.

"So for three weeks I was at the beck and call of the bossiest woman I had ever met, and she had told me just about every detail of her life. I found that even with her abrupt and demanding manner, she was funny, warm, and really quite likeable. I would rise every morning quite anxious to see what another day with Mrs. Clifton Randolph the Third would bring.

"Your grandmother was born Marion Kingston, the youngest of four children. When she was three years old her mother drowned. Soon afterwards, her father remarried a woman several years older who had grown children and no interest in raising all of his, but they kept Marion, while the others were sent to Saint John to live with their grandparents.

"'I learned every possible household chore at a very young age,' she would say every time she instructed me to do the simplest task."

"That's funny," Clara interjected. "Gran would always lecture on the way linens were to be folded, silver was to be polished, and the proper setting of a table. I used to wonder why she cared when she always had several people to do those tasks for her."

"There is much more I could tell you in that regard, but I'm going to try to stay on track. My memory is bad enough without jumping all over the place. I'm going to keep telling you about the first weeks working for Marion Randolph before I get to all that followed. The first few weeks set the stage. Being in the room the day she arrived cast the die for what happened from then on.

"It was the morning after Rosemary's announcement, the day of my eighteenth birthday, when I rose early and made my way to the Governor's Suite to help Mrs. Clifton Randolph the Third dress, pack, and prepare to meet her family at dockside. To say I had put in a restless, troubled night would be to put it mildly. I had spent hours trying to grasp what staying under Rosemary's roof held for me. I knew that the duties Rosemary had so clearly explained were to begin right away and I would be given no choice in the matter.

"I don't think your grandmother even noticed the state I was in when I arrived that morning. She was caught up in the excitement and anticipation of the day ahead. She fired a continuous stream of demands at me, and before long we were exiting the hotel. With the help of the bellboy I got all her luggage across the street and down to the harbour. I remember standing beside her in the brisk early-morning air. As I wrapped my coat around me tighter, I could feel the small oval frame I had slipped into the bodice of my uniform before leaving my room. I'd felt the need to have my parents with me that day.

"I'd tried several times to tell Mrs. Randolph about the burden I was carrying. Somehow I felt she would listen and perhaps even offer a solution. Even standing on the dock shivering while Mrs. Randolph fired orders at the crew of the boat, I kept trying to find my voice, to find the words to ask her to help me out of the predicament I found myself in.

"It was your father's voice that distracted me from my worries.

"*Mother, must you natter on like a fishwoman?*'

"I turned and saw a young man approaching us. He was tall, pale, very thin, but handsome. He was followed by a girl a few years younger decked out fashionably in a fitted coat that cascaded down to a full skirt, trimmed with a large fur collar that was turned up and hit the brim of an elaborate fur-trimmed hat. She looked like a young version of her mother. Behind them a boy of about eight or nine was bounding toward us with enough energy it seemed he might bounce right off the unrailed edge of the dock. A dignified and well-dressed man took up the rear and caught up with the young boy, settling him considerably with a mere clasp of his hand to the boy's shoulder.

"*Charles, your mother does not need to see her youngest son tumble into the cold waters of Kingston Harbour. I know you've got pent-up energy after that long train ride, but we'll be on the island soon, and you'll have the entire summer to run and play. I'm quite looking forward to it myself.*'

"The man then turned his attention to his wife, embracing her and engaging in an affectionate kiss. I felt my heart skip a beat. It reminded me of the affection I recalled seeing between my parents.

"*Have you brought the staff with you, Clifton?*'

"*What kind of a greeting is that, Marion? You have not seen me or the children for weeks. Are we not the faces you have been longing to behold?*'

"*Of course I'm glad to see you and the children, Clifton, but these last few weeks have been taxing, and I was counting on Mrs. Rogers and Peggy, at the very least, to accompany us to the island.*"

"*None of them saw their way clear to join us this year. Mrs. Rogers has suffered terribly with her arthritis, and her husband's health is not good. Peggy got another job for the summer, although she didn't tell me that directly. As it was, I had to leave without engaging anyone. I am sure we'll manage, dear. Let's just have a good old-fashioned holiday and not try to keep up the social expectations that would require a full complement of domestic help. The children are old enough to do for themselves. I am sure we will be just fine.'*

"Marion Randolph reached out and hugged each of her children before returning to face her husband.

"'I am distraught with this turn of events, Clifton. It is a huge job to clean and prepare the house for the season. I cannot possibly be expected to spend the entire summer isolated and living like a pauper. We must keep up some of the social requirements. We will be invited to the neighbouring islands and cannot shun our social responsibilities. I cannot possibly manage without any help.'

"It became crystal clear to me: I would offer to accompany the family and work the summer on Randolph Island. I would simply not return to Rosemary Donavan's home. I would be well out of her reach if I were to leave with the Randolph family. I spoke up quickly before losing my nerve.

"'I will go with you, Mrs. Randolph. I have not run an entire household before, but I have all the skills necessary. I would be pleased to do my best, and as you know I am not afraid of hard work.'

"'Perhaps that is the solution, Lillianne. Would you not feel obligated to give your employer notice? We sail right away, and you would have no time to return for your things.'

"I put my hand to my heart, pushing on the oval frame between my breasts. *'I have nothing worth going back for. I would be very pleased to find myself in the employ of an upstanding American family. That, I am sure, would be to my advantage when looking for future employment. I can sacrifice the blemish leaving the Prince George without notice might leave on my employment record. Please consider employing me.'*

"I wondered if my words sounded to her as desperate as they did to me. If she refused, I would have no other choice but to return to the future Rosemary would fashion for me. Mrs. Randolph accepting my offer was my only hope."

"Obviously Gran hired you, and, as they say, the rest is history."

"History, all right, but with lots of dips and dives. Little did I know as I plotted my escape from Kingston that I was walking into another trap." I paused. "That sounds unfair, but it was so much more complicated than I imagined. I will tell you about the trip to the island, but I'm not sure it is entirely fair to delve any deeper into the mess I stepped into that day. Some of it I don't think is my place to tell you."

"If I don't hear it from you, who else would tell me?"

"Your father and your Aunt Cordelia would have a different perspective, I'm sure, and might not tell it the same as me. Your grandmother, God rest her soul, had good intentions, and I do not want to sully your memory of her. Your grandfather was oblivious to it all, I think, but even if he had known, he would probably not have opposed his wife. As far as blame or placing any guilt, we all could take our share."

Marion
1888

I stared at the fancy birthday cake Mrs. McCready had just finished decorating. We were expecting a large crowd arriving by riverboat this afternoon for the Simms's thirteen-year-old daughter's birthday party. I had arrived before dawn, and along with the other staff had cleaned the large house from top to bottom. I had no call to even be in the kitchen but seemed drawn to the beautiful cake sitting on the crystal pedestal. All day during the hustle and bustle and constant talk of Miss Dorothy's birthday celebration, I felt a gnawing pain. My eleventh birthday earlier in the week had gone completely unnoticed. Not even a mention of it.

No doubt if Father were asked, he would not even know my age, let alone my birthdate. It had always been Mother who kept those facts in order. She would go all out to celebrate our birthdays, even when money was scarce. For my third birthday, she made an angel food cake. She had walked to Mrs. Fullerton's and got the six eggs she needed. I walked with her and she'd let me carry the basket up the laneway. She had skimmed the cream off the milk can and beat it until it stood high atop the cake. I remember the first sweet taste.

I remember my present, as well. She'd made me a pinafore from the colourful flour sack Mrs. Kimball had given her. She starched the ruffles and I felt like a princess wearing it. I wore that pinafore long after it fit me and cried uncontrollably when Winifred cut it up for dusting cloths. It always seemed even crueller when she forced me to use those squares. God forbid she lift a hand to dust or do anything else, for that matter. That's what she kept Marion for.

"You're not getting anything done standing there gawking."

"How many eggs did you use?"

"What business is that of yours? Three, if you need to know. Don't let on like you have any idea what it takes to make a fine cake like this. I've worked for the Simmses for thirty-seven years and have made this recipe for every birthday. Now get out of here and check with your mother to see what else needs doing."

"She is *not* my mother."

"Get out of here, I said. You have a lip on you. I've a mind to tell Winifred to leave you home for the rest of the summer."

I walked away, knowing the hollowness of that threat. Where else could Mrs. High-and-Mighty McCready get a slave like me for fifty cents a week?

Lillianne
1993

"The sailing was horrific. The nausea hit me before the anchor was lifted, and I found myself retching over the bow. I was grateful we were far enough away from the dock or Mrs. Randolph might have sent me back to shore. I am sure she had second thoughts on bringing me as she watched me lose my breakfast over the rail."

Clara suddenly stood and left the room. A bathroom break, I thought, and I couldn't blame her for needing a reprieve. She hadn't said one negative word, though, and our time together had been more pleasant than usual. Maybe she was more interested in the past than I thought. I wondered, however, if she wanted the complete truth.

Clara returned to the room and settled back in the chair directly across from me. "Aunt Cordelia took me shopping as soon as we got to New York. From the window of our incoming train I'd seen the RMS *Carinthia* looming large in the harbour, so the shopping excursion along Fifth Avenue once we were settled in the St. Regis only added to my excitement. Our purchases replaced the clothing you had packed for me, and Aunt Cordelia instructed the hotel staff to distribute my discarded outfits to the poor."

"Oh, really?" I asked, acting surprised.

"I don't know what made me think of that. The talk of sailing,

I suppose. It was a very special time for me, a turning point, really. I left Odessa a child and returned a young woman."

I chose not to make a comment. I took a deep breath and continued with my own recollections.

"The boat put down anchor a distance from the island and the next hurdle was getting onto the scow. The bags, furniture, several trunks, and many crates were transferred onto the barge. Mrs. Randolph and Cordelia were assisted into a rowboat and for a moment I thought I would be, too.

"'I certainly hope I don't have to share my seat with the hired girl. I swear if this thing capsizes and I'm tossed into this frigid water—'

"'Oh, hush up, Cordelia,' Clifton called down to his sister, then turning to me said, 'Don't pay any mind to my sister. She can be quite full of her own importance but is really quite harmless. A good dunk in this cold water might do her a world of good.'

"I tried not to think what a dunking in the water would do for me if I were to slip off the rung of the ladder as Clifton stepped closer, instructing me to take his hand as he helped me onto the scow.

"'The water is much calmer closer to shore, and you will be fine seated in the middle of this barge.'

"Once on the scow I settled myself on a large trunk as Charles burst into a dramatic rendition of 'Fifteen Men on a Dead Man's Chest,' with an extra punch on 'Yo-ho-ho and a bottle of rum.'

"'What is a bosun's pike?' Charlie stopped singing long enough to ask.

"'Let's just say the mate did not enjoy being fixed by the bosun's pike, nor did the bosun fare well, being brained by the marlinspike, and nor did the cookie particularly enjoy his throat marked be like.' Clifton lifted his brother and threw him over his shoulder as together they belted out the end of the last verse.

"I sat, clutching the handle of the trunk and watching the two brothers, praying they would not plunge into the sullen swell in the midst of their tomfoolery."

"You remember all of this?" Clara asked.

"I do. Some things are forever etched in my mind, like the closeness and affection between those two brothers. I became very fond of that little boy, which made what happened months later so unbearable, and also served to cement the memories of the short time I had with him.

"In the midst of all this racket and fun we approached the island, and I saw for the first time the house that would be such a part of my life. The buildings of my past loom so large in my thoughts lately: the red brick of this house, the dreary, foreboding limestone structure of my childhood prison, and the white clapboards of the grand house I gazed upon on that day from my perch on the barge. Perhaps a part of me already knew as I looked up at the grandeur of the Randolphs' summer home that within those walls my fate would be set."

"That sounds dramatic. Although whenever we sailed close to the island when I was a child, my first look at the house filled me with such joy. It always felt as if I was coming home, and when we sailed away from it the last time, a part of me stayed behind. Maybe that house did hold some magic."

"The house and the island cast a spell on me. I gazed up at the large house with its four dormers and its towering turret on the dark roof, its white clapboards and sky-blue shutters framing the mullioned windows, the large glassed-in sun porch, the wraparound veranda, the hexagon gazebo.

"I should have been daunted by the realization that I would be responsible for maintaining such a grand house, as I waded in the knee-deep water and then walked along the shore and up the wooden stairs to meet Mrs. Randolph on the veranda. She began a long list of tasks.

"'Lillianne, I want those trunks and crates unpacked right away and a fire laid in the stove in the summer kitchen immediately to take the dampness out. The woodshed is behind the house, but I expect Mr. Tibbetts has likely filled the wood box. I will want a cold-plate lunch served as soon as possible and will advise you on the menu once I've looked over the provisions. The entire house will have to be aired out, swept, and dusted, and the beds made up in every room. The water cistern in the back porch must be filled from the well house, and fill the tank in the gas cook stove so there will be hot water for my bath this evening.'

"I set about my tasks and did not stop on that first day until almost midnight. I climbed the attic stairs, and with the dim light of the whale-oil lantern, found my way to the narrow cot in the small attic bedroom that was to be mine. I looked out the garret window at the bright moonlight and despite my exhaustion reflected positively on the day. I thought briefly on what my fate would have been had I waved goodbye to Marion Randolph and returned to the Prince George and then to my Brock Street bedroom. I would not have spent the night alone. Which of Kingston's fine gentleman would have given me my initiation into womanhood?

"I lay in the dark with only a thought or two of the possibility of bats sharing my space and contemplated my current position. I would be expected to work hard, but I had been given four changes of clothing—surely castoffs of Cordelia's, but they were considerably more fashionable than my Prince George uniform or the Sisters of Providence charity garments. I was able to eat my fill at both of the meals, even though I took my portion in the kitchen and not until after I had served the family. I already felt affection for Charlie, had a kindle of interest in Clifton, and despite her snobbishness, felt a slight fondness for Cordelia. I knew what to expect from Mrs. Randolph and was not in the least put off by her bossiness. Mr. Randolph had been kind and considerate. Before dropping off to sleep, I recited a quick prayer of thankfulness for whatever fates had landed me on Randolph Island, where I felt I had found paradise."

I stopped my reminiscing for the day. Clara seemed content to leave it there, too.

It didn't leave my mind, however, and as I prepared for bed I went over the events and choices I had been presented with that summer. The *what ifs* crept in again, although a life in a Kingston brothel couldn't have been better. Either way, though, I had been required to put myself on the auction block to the highest bidder. At least the deal I made with the Randolphs gave me some control of my life.

Marion
1891

Dorothy's thirteenth birthday preparations were on my mind as I began mixing the cake for her sixteenth. Only fourteen years old, I had taken over most of Mrs. McCready's head housekeeper duties. She was still there, but a stroke had left her unable to do much. She could still bark out the orders, but since arriving in the Simmses' mansion in the North End of Saint John, I had gotten used to that. I had come in October, leaving school and becoming a full-time winter employee. I had been disappointed to leave school, but leaving Winifred was a dream come true. I had even been able to visit my brothers and sister several times in the months I'd spent in the city.

We were back to the summer house now, and I quite enjoyed my status as part of the year-round staff. Winifred hadn't been hired but was working at a neighbouring summer residence. I hoped I wouldn't lay eyes on her.

"Are the salads finished?"

"Yes."

"Have they been put in the icebox? Have you packed ice around them?"

"Yes, Mrs. McCready."

"We don't want to poison the Americans."

I continued mixing the cake, somewhat annoyed that the family of Americans coming on the *David Weston* this afternoon were getting as much attention as Queen Victoria would warrant. Apparently the Randolphs from Chicago were special. I would have wagered it was the son Dorothy was looking forward to receiving. I expected her parents were hoping the visit would result in a suitable and lucrative marriage offer for Dorothy. It wouldn't hurt business for Mr. Simms, either.

But I didn't need reminding how to attend to salads and cold cuts. I was every bit as capable as old Mrs. McCready, who sat in the corner stewing over the running of this household. Could she not see that I was as efficient as she'd ever been, even in her prime?

Lillianne
1917

I woke early and began my second day on the island. I was to use the privy, which was a considerable distance from the house, not the indoor water closet. I was to attend to all my personal grooming in the tin washtub. I filled the washtub and scooped cold water into my hands, washing my face, shoulders, and armpits before pulling my dress over my head. I twisted my long hair into a tight bun. I shivered as I watched the sun rise.

An hour later, I began setting the large mahogany table in the dining room with the second-best china for the large breakfast to be served promptly at eight, as laid out the night before in Mrs. Randolph's monologue.

"Charles and his father will rise with the sun, but Clifton and Cordelia needn't think they can sleep the morning away just because we are on holiday. We will begin our day with a good breakfast, and afterwards they will busy themselves with the day's tasks. Cordelia must spend most of her day practising the cello. She has a recital at the Colonial Theatre in Chicago in September. Clifton will no doubt spend his days sketching the flora, fauna, rocks, and water. His obsession with nature is harmless, and he may as well get his fill before going off to Princeton in the fall. Mr. Randolph will be with us for two months and is very much looking forward to his leisure time before returning to the demands of business. Vacation, however, is no excuse for abandoning civilized habits. Meals will be served promptly at eight, noon, and six."

Clifton was the first to enter the dining room. He was sporting a crisp white shirt, the rolled sleeves exposing his pale, thin arms. His light-brown trouser legs were tucked into a pair of leather boots that made a singsong sound as he walked across the hardwood floor toward the table. He sat down and with an exaggerated flourish tucked his linen napkin into the collar of his shirt.

"Good morning, Miss McDonough. I trust you slept well. It is a glorious day."

"Good morning, sir," I replied.

"Oh, please, there is no need for such formality. My friends call me Cliff. Would you prefer Lillianne or Lily? Lily is a beautiful name and a beautiful flower. Did you know there are one hundred species in the lily family? The *Lilium bulbiferum*, or the fire lily, and the *Lilium candidum*, commonly called the madonna lily, are two of the most impressive."

"Are you talking Latin gibberish again about some silly plant? It makes you sound like a dandy, big brother," Cordelia said as she entered the dining room swishing the full taffeta skirt of her apricot dress. She seated herself across the table from her brother. "Would it be too much to expect a cup of hot coffee? I certainly hope it has been brewed properly. I cannot abide it too strong or as weak as dishwater."

I filled Cordelia's cup and proceeded to fill Clifton's as he passed it to me. I didn't think it was the right time to inform him that I would be pleased if he would call me Lily.

Charlie bounded into the room, hugged his brother, and bowed to his sister in an exaggerated manner.

"How was your beauty sleep, big sister? By the sounds of your snoring, you should be especially beautiful this morning."

"The way you say *big sister* makes it sound like a statement on my girth, not my birth order. And what would you know about beauty?"

Mrs. Randolph walked through the doorway.

"Have you seen your father, children? I believe he took the rowboat out earlier, but I trust he is back. Are the griddle-cakes ready, Lillianne? I would like an egg sunny side up. Mr. Randolph will want them scrambled, and the children all prefer a well-cooked boiled egg."

Mr. Randolph walked into the room, his relaxed attire a sharp contrast to the formality of his previous day's wardrobe.

"The water was like glass this morning, Marion. I wish you had come with me. There is nothing like seeing the sun rise over the wide expanse of the calm, early-morning water."

"I have no time for such foolishness, Clifton. I have a house-hold to run, and today I must begin the preparations for the weekend. Entertaining the Donaldsons, the Emersons, and the Windsors requires much forethought, and I can't attend to that sitting in a rowboat, paddling aimlessly in the water with you. We do have a reputation to uphold. I will not have Geraldine Windsor finding fault with the offerings at my table."

"You know, they are not the royal Windsors, Mother," Clifton said. "He is merely a ball-bearing manufacturer from Philadelphia."

"Don't tease me. You will learn soon enough the importance of making the proper contacts and maintaining an exemplary reputation in society."

"If I want to be as pompous and self-absorbed as the rest of them, I suppose you're right."

"Drink your coffee, son, and don't get your mother all riled up. She takes her social responsibilities very seriously. What adventures will you embark upon today, young Charles, and what do you have planned for this lovely day, my darling daughter?"

"I might get on with my day if I ever get my egg. She seems to be just standing there minding our business and not attending to her duties."

I quickly left the dining room, Cordelia's glare bringing a crimson flush to my face.

*

The rest of breakfast was uneventful, and I was just finishing with the cleanup when Mrs. Randolph walked into the large kitchen. I looked up from my task without stopping. I'd learned at the Prince George she did not take kindly to idleness. I'd also learned that as demanding as she was, she had a kindness I had not seen at the Higgins mansion and rarely saw at the Prince George. Her demeanour reflected her social status and wealth, but her tone even at its bossiest still held a certain understanding and compassion.

She began at once. "I want no waste in my kitchen, but I don't want obvious re-use of food. There are inventive ways to present leftovers, and I will school you on these tricks as the summer goes along. The provisions we have brought along are pretty much all we have to work with except for whatever Mr. Tibbetts brings to the island once a week. He will deliver fresh eggs, meat, milk, and some vegetables. I will have a menu plan drawn up shortly and you will not waver from it. I hope you saved the bacon fat from the cast-iron pan. I have no tolerance for wastefulness."

"Her tolerance for me sometimes seems in short supply, too," Clifton Randolph called out as he crossed the room and wrapped his arms around his wife from behind, forcefully kissing her on the cheek.

"Clifton, such actions in front of the staff. Whatever would your mother think if she were still with us?"

"Oh, darling, do we have to let her rule us from the grave? I see no shame in showing my wife the affection I feel for her. Lillianne will be like family by the end of the summer, and she may as well learn right away that I can barely keep my hands off my beautiful wife."

"You are without morals, Clifton Randolph."

"Isn't that what drew you to me, Maisy, my love?"

"The naive girl you gave that moniker to no longer exists."

"She still lurks in there somewhere, my love, and sometimes you actually let me see her. Lillianne, has she told you she was about your age when she turned my head?"

I did not answer. Mrs. Randolph's reddening face and stern look were evidence enough that it was not in my best interest to encourage her husband to tell me more.

He spun her around and kissed her squarely on her mouth. She broke away, picking up the stack of china plates from the sideboard.

"Clifton, if I am to properly instruct Lillianne, you will have to remove yourself from this kitchen. It is not decent to have the man of the house hanging about the scullery."

"Now you sound just like Mother. It wasn't my intention to interrupt, but I was hoping you would join me for a stroll. I missed you in the weeks you were away. I was hoping we could play the part of young lovers and drink in this beautiful day, enjoying the time we finally have together."

"Oh, you are such a romantic. Young lovers, indeed. I'm not feeling young, I can tell you, after the ordeal I've been through. Give me an hour or so, then I'll take a silly walk with you."

He kissed her one more time and left the room.

"It is my belief you will not find a more efficient kitchen in any of the surrounding summer residences," Mrs. Randolph began again. "I was diligent with its design. Clifton needed some convincing when I argued the need of the modern ice box and large gas range. I know how difficult tending to a wood fire in the heat of the summer can be."

I looked at this woman sporting a navy-and-cream shirt-waist dress with a crisp lace collar, silk inset, and row of pearl buttons. I could not picture her ever having laboured over a hot cooking surface or feeding coal or wood into a gluttonous range. Cooking with gas was foreign to me, but even after only one use, I agreed with her assessment of it.

"I expect the dishcloth and towels to be laundered immedi-ately. I'll not have them souring in the sink. The butcher block needs a good scrubbing as well. Careful attention to this after every meal will ensure the cleanliness of all your prep surfaces. The mistress of the house should be able to enter at any time and find things in order."

I continued working as Mrs. Randolph explained her expec-tations of food preparation, storage, and cleanup. She moved about the large kitchen giving instructions with precision and expertise. She was obviously no stranger to the smooth running and feeding of a household. She finished with exact directions for how I was to prepare the noon meal. She moved quickly around the room taking out the required pots and utensils, her last gesture being to open the large window above the sink.

"I want you to stop for a moment and go get a crystal vase from the china cabinet. Go outside and pick a bouquet of lilacs and set them on this windowsill. There is no reason you cannot enjoy some beauty while you labour. This afternoon

I'll instruct you on the proper cleaning of the ceiling fixtures and the lamps."

＊

I spent most of the afternoon absorbed in the careful cleaning of the light fixtures and lamps on the main floor. Each globe had to be removed and washed in hot soapy water. The prisms needed dusting and the brass polished. I checked the oil in each fixture and replaced the wicks. I was putting the last chandelier back together when Mrs. Randolph entered the drawing room.

"Take a half-hour break before you begin the preparation of the evening meal."

I briefly gazed at the large oval mirror, taking my hair from the clip before pulling it up and redoing the bun. I removed my apron, slung it over my arm, and stepped out onto the wide front veranda. I took in the beauty of the scene in front of me: the long slope to the sandy beach and the wide expanse of jet-blue water in contrast to the clear blue, almost cloudless sky. I could see Cordelia lying on a wooden lounge chair.

I walked around back to the well house, drawing up a pail and then reached for the tin cup hanging inside the door to dip out some water. I took a long sip, letting some of the water drip down my chin. The afternoon sun was hot, and upon stopping my work I realized how warm and stifled I felt. I decided to walk to the water's edge and possibly remove my Oxfords and stockings to dip my bare feet in the lake. I had no timepiece, so I would keep my break very short.

I walked down the steep stairs leading to the shore with no intention of disturbing Cordelia, who appeared to be sleeping under the cover of a large straw hat. Her colourful dress was pulled up, exposing her long legs to the sunshine. My mind quickly went to the baking-soda paste I knew could remedy sunburn.

Cordelia sat up as I approached. "Mother let you out, did she? Quite a slave driver, she is."

"She is very precise in her expectations."

"Well, that is a generous assessment."

I began to walk away. I knew discussing my employer with her daughter was not wise, and I did not consider myself Cordelia's social equal. I would take the few minutes of respite to enjoy the beauty of the day.

"Do you swim?"

I turned to see Cordelia had risen from her lounge chair and was following me down the sandy beach.

"No."

"I don't know about Canada, but public bath houses and swimming pools are cropping up all over Chicago, although I suppose a life in domestic service does not give you an opportunity to learn a skill like swimming. Not that Mother would ever allow us to partake in such activities."

I did not respond, but Cordelia kept talking as she fell into step with me.

"I learned to swim several summers ago, but Mother does not know. Father was careful to take us clear around to the other side of the island before beginning our lessons. Mother will not permit us to even enter the water, although she does allow Father and the boys to take the rowboat out. It seems to me she should see the value of us knowing how to swim. Father will teach Charlie this year, I expect. I think Clifton and I were about Charlie's age the first time Father prompted us to put our heads under water."

We walked a distance before stopping by a large rock. I could no longer see the house and was mindful of getting back in time, but I sat to remove my shoes and socks. I was anxious to put my feet in the cool water, but couldn't imagine allowing my head to be immersed.

"I will teach you if you like."

"I will not likely have much time for that. Do you swim often? Does Clifton?"

"I suppose you are picturing my brother in a swimming costume."

I blushed.

"I have an extra suit you could wear. We will have to figure out just how to find enough time and how we would get you out of the house without Mother seeing you in my suit. I wear mine under my flowing dress, and she has no idea. She seldom comes to the shore, so doesn't notice when my hair is wet."

Cordelia pulled the dress up over her head and dropped it onto the sand. She ran straight into the water and after a few steps threw herself into the rippling waves. Seconds later, her head surfaced and she swam several strokes into the deeper water. I stood, letting the cool water reach my ankles. I stared at Cordelia's quick movements and the splashing water. I had never seen anyone swim before and I was awed by the beauty and freedom of it.

*

Days later, she brought her suit to my attic bedroom, and I now stood in the dark trying it on, imagining actually entering the water and dipping below the surface of the lake. Cordelia hadn't mentioned swimming again to me, hadn't actually spoken to me except to ask for something or put me in my place. I was beginning to think I had imagined the interaction we'd had on the beach on the far side of the island.

But the swimsuit reminded me of Cordelia's promise and of my desire to learn to swim. I was even determined to put my head under water if given the chance.

*

I was reaching in front of Cordelia to remove her grapefruit dish the next day when she whispered, "Mother is leaving with Father to row to the Windsors' summer home right after breakfast. They will be gone until late afternoon."

I looked quickly at Mrs. Randolph, but she was deep in a conversation with her husband.

"Put the suit on and join me on the beach when they are out of sight," Cordelia whispered, then increased her volume. "I certainly hope my egg is not the runny, miserable mess it was yesterday. Is there no egg timer in that fancy kitchen of ours, Mother?"

I set the egg cup down in front of Cordelia, muttering my apologies and assuring her that her egg was well-boiled.

"Perhaps you should prepare your own food, sister dear," Clifton said. "You do know there are homes in this world where people are not served and catered to. Did you know there are people suffering right now in the grips of war who do not even have enough to eat? Perhaps if you thought of others, you would not be so nasty and self-centred."

"Mother, tell Clifton I am not interested in his lectures this morning. I thought coming back from New York, he would be less rebellious and not as high and mighty."

"Cordelia, I do not want you to speak like that again. Your brother has suffered enough, and it certainly does not hurt you to be reminded of your advantages. Charles, take that spoon off the end of your nose. Can we not have a civilized breakfast?"

                        ✿

I was taken aback when I saw from the top of the stairs that Clifton was sitting on the beach beside Cordelia. Charlie was standing throwing stones into the water.

"There you are. I was just saying to Cliff that maybe you would chicken out. But you're not going to get a better day than this one. There is hardly a ripple in the water, and Mother and Father are well out of the way."

"Let her at least get down to the beach, Cor. You go on about how bossy Mother is, but you're cut from the same cloth."

"Are you going to teach me, too, Corey?" Charlie hollered, spinning around to face me.

"No time like the present, little brother. But you can't breathe a word of it. You can tell Father, but Mother would take a fit if she knew we got wet past our knees. We could take to the water where we are, but let's go to our regular spot. We know the bottom, and I've never seen an eel there."

I was nervous about the swimming but hadn't even considered fish, eels, or other dangers.

Clifton rose and walked toward me. He took my arm in a gentlemanly way and I stepped off the bottom step. We all began walking around the island.

Mrs. Randolph had left a long list of tasks and clear details for both meals, even though she didn't expect to get back before dark.

"We had a good big breakfast, Lillianne," Clifton said when we got to the spot. "Let's just enjoy ourselves and we can all go up to the kitchen later and grab some bread and cheese. We'll tell mother we ate in the civilized style she holds in such esteem. Heaven forbid she would sanction a lakeside picnic."

"Can we have a picnic later? Can you pack us a picnic, Lillianne?" Charlie pleaded.

"Leave Lily alone, Charlie. We're going to swim a bit and work up an appetite and then we'll figure out our lunch."

Part of me was tempted to go back up to the house and pack an impressive picnic. I knew the ins and outs of kitchen work, but fraternizing with my employer's children and incautiously entering the lake was another thing entirely. What was I thinking, donning a stylish bathing suit and coming down to the beach the minute my employers were out of sight?

Cordelia laid a blanket out flat on the sand. The water was rippling a bit more than it had been, but the breeze was warm and the sun was beaming down. Beads of sweat were gathering on my forehead and I was looking forward to the cool water. Would I have the courage to actually put my face in? Would I let myself drop into the water as I had seen Cordelia do? I would not likely be able to move my arms in the way she had.

"The first step is to get comfortable in the water, Lily," Clifton instructed. "No one will push you to do anything. Walk out to your waist and get used to the water. Charlie, do you think you could start by dunking your head?"

Charlie ran right past me, and with a huge splash plunged into the water. He resurfaced with an exaggerated flourish and then dipped again. He was not letting fear hold him back.

"Now show me how to kick my arms and legs," Charlie hollered.

"Slow down, little brother. You'll not be swimming across the lake just yet. First you need to swim underwater. This will come naturally, and when you have your buoyancy you can tackle swimming above the water."

Clifton turned to me and extended his hand. "What about you, Lily? If you drop into the water, I'll be right here. There is nothing to fear."

Standing this close to Clifton was directing my fear elsewhere. He did, indeed, look dashing in his suit, but the kindness in his eyes and the curve of his chiselled chin were equally captivating. A dip below the water seemed necessary to quiet my stirrings. I had never felt the way this young man was making me feel.

"Just let yourself fall," Cordelia hollered from the shore.

*

As I climbed the attic stairs after midnight, my thoughts retraced my day. I had actually felt my body float. Over and over I had let myself fall into the waist-deep water. Even after the trip to the house to fill a picnic basket, I'd entered the water again. I hadn't wanted the afternoon to end. I, of course, returned to my duties and served a proper supper in the dining room to Cordelia, Clifton, and Charlie. It was awkward, but I made sure that the familiarity that had been fostered as we spent the afternoon on the beach was not present in the dining room.

Cordelia returned to her role even without her parents in attendance. Charlie and Cliff, however, were much the same as they had been all afternoon.

"Sit with us, Lily," Cliff said when I entered the room with the soup course.

"Don't be ridiculous, Clifton. Lillianne is not a houseguest."

"Mother wouldn't know," Charlie offered. "She could sit with us."

I set Charlie's soup down, not responding to the discussion. I knew better than to allow myself that luxury.

*

Mrs. Higgins had been alone that day. I had set a large platter of steaming-hot corn on the cob down on the grand mahogany table, doing as the kitchen staff had instructed regardless of the fact that the frail matriarch of the house could not possibly eat a fraction of the bounty.

"Sit with me, dear, and have a cob of corn. It is scandalous that it should go to waste. No common sense, apparently, in the planning of our meals. Come sit beside me and keep me company."

I had tasted nothing quite like the explosion of kernels and I let the juicy, buttery drips fall from my chin, so absorbed in the pleasure I hadn't even heard Mr. Higgins enter the room. The back of his large hand broke my trance.

"What is she doing? How dare she sit her sorry arse at my dining table? Have you completely taken leave of your senses, woman, allowing a servant to do so? Is this the chaos that ensues when I leave the house?"

I stood, quickly gathering up my plate and scurrying from the room, the pain of the blow still pulsing. I blinked my eyes, struggling to keep the tears from falling. I would not show this man the fear beating in my chest.

"If I see you eat at my table again, you will feel more than the back of my hand," Mr. Higgins barked as I retreated.

For the next hour I was delivered a proper and lengthy tongue lashing, making my few seconds of blissful eating seem as diabolical as if I'd murdered the master of the house in his bed—a thought I considered often in the next few months.

*

The morning heat blended with a gentle breeze in the small clearing where three lengths of clothesline were strung across bars fastened on two poles. I was pinning the load of table linens I had scrubbed in the large tub in the back porch and laboriously wrung out by hand—they were too fine to be fed through the hand-crank wringer.

My mind was on the activities of the afternoon before, remembering the way it felt to sink below the cool water. I had actually put aside my fear and dropped into the glorious water. I screamed as Charlie ran into the clearing, nearly knocking me off my feet.

"You scared the life out of me," I exclaimed.

"Sorry, Lily. I didn't know you were back here. I'm hiding from Cliff. He probably heard your scream."

"Get right down in this wicker basket. I'll cover you with linens and he'll never know you're here."

I returned to pinning the lace tablecloth, pretending nothing was out of the ordinary as Clifton came through the hedge.

"Have you seen that little scamp? He's got me trudging all over the island with his game. I heard you holler and figured he was back here."

"A wasp startled me. I've not seen him."

"Would you like my help?" Clifton asked, reaching to take the top item from the basket.

"No, thank you. I just have a couple more to hang."

"You did wonderfully yesterday, Lily. You seem a natural in the water."

"Thank you. I quite enjoyed it, which was a surprise."

"I wish you had the freedom to swim as often as you like. I'm sure after the heat of your labours this morning a dip would be welcome. It's wrong for Mother to work you so hard. Why can *you* not enjoy the pleasures of youth? Why do status and expectation limit your freedom? It seems to me this life of supposed privilege restricts us all from being who we most desire to be."

There was a weight and an emotion in Clifton's voice that brought me up short. I did not have a proper response, but I felt his sadness and pain.

"Oh, I'm sure I'll get to swim again. I have the whole summer ahead of me."

I felt the need to assure Clifton that I was fine with my condition. I considered my words but was interrupted by Charlie's loud and sudden escape from his hiding place.

"I am smothering in here!"

I took another tablecloth from the basket Charlie had just bounded from and turned to hang it on the line. I felt the tension even though Charlie was chattering incessantly. I wanted to offer Clifton some assurance that my status was all right with me. I wanted to quickly tell him I was the daughter of Frederick and Claire McDonough and I knew my worth even though it seemed I was only a housemaid in his parents' grand summer home. The freedom long days on the beach afforded him and his siblings was a freedom I felt in the very core of my being. I was not a mere housemaid; I was a beloved daughter. The words even as I tried to form them seemed hollow and silly, but the deep feeling of value I kept within was not.

Clifton came closer and reached to hold up the end of the lace tablecloth, speaking in a whisper. "You are very beautiful, Lily McDonough, and quite captivating. It is possible that you are the breath of fresh air that will get me through this summer."

With a shaking hand I pinned the last corner, quickly snatched up the wicker basket, and hurried through the hedge and back into the house.

*

"Take this lemonade to the gazebo for Cordelia. She has been practising for an hour and will be parched. On your way back in, please see if Mr. Randolph is still in the drawing room."

I took the silver tray holding the large tumbler of lemonade from Mrs. Randolph. She hadn't said anything, but I felt from her tone that she thought I had taken too long hanging out the linens. She could have taken the refreshment to her daughter, but her manner gave me a hint that possibly just the pouring of it was an imposition caused by my slothfulness. Mrs. Randolph wasn't cruel and intolerant like Mr. Higgins, but my status was still very clear. I also knew that what I was beginning to feel for the Randolphs' oldest son could never have a positive outcome.

As I got closer to the gazebo I could hear the strains of Cordelia's cello. The music seemed to be finding its way out the open windows, across the wide lawn, dispersing in the open air and sweeping across the lake. The beauty of sound and sight brought tears to my eyes, delivering me away from this place and into the drawing room of my memory—my mother sitting at the piano while Father stood behind her, his violin bow complementing her playing while I looked up from my spot on the rich oriental rug.

Cordelia's voice broke through. "I thought I would die of thirst. I asked Mother an hour ago to send you out with lemonade. Did you have to swim to the mainland to purchase the lemons, for God's sake?"

"Is there anything else I can get for you, Miss Cordelia?"

"No." She answered curtly, taking a large swig from the tumbler. "I suppose bringing the pitcher would have been too much to ask."

*

Mr. Randolph looked up from the papers on his desk.

"Good morning, Lily. Is it not the most glorious day? I am just about done with this drudgery. I would like to have left all the trappings of business behind me for the month, but it seems I have some responsibilities. Mr. Tibbetts will be here later today, and I must send this correspondence back with him to be posted."

I stood awkwardly, not wanting to interrupt and not knowing what response was expected from me. Mr. Higgins had never spoken to me directly unless it was a reprimand, and I was definitely never expected to respond.

"I am glad you got to have a bit of fun yesterday, Lily. Marion can be somewhat of a tyrant. I'm not sure why she can't let our summers here be less formal. I would be happy to eat picnics and live as if we were not dictated by social constraints. Clifton told me you had a swimming lesson. I'm sure you were told this is a pastime we do not talk about with my wife. She has a fear that everyone she loves will be swept away in deep water as her poor mother was. There is no point in arguing with that irrational thinking, so we just make sure any swimming we do is well out of her sight."

"Mrs. Randolph asked me to see if you were still in the drawing room. Is there anything I can get you, sir?"

"Oh, please don't bother with that *sir* business. Something else I wish we could let go while we are on the island. I like to forget sometimes that I am now the head of the Randolph empire. My mother would be so disappointed in my lack of self-importance and arrogance. Tell Marion I'm in here. She is probably anxious to discuss a social function for the weekend. So much for my desire to rest and relax. Marion won't let an opportunity to flaunt our social status go by, even while we are here on this beautiful, peaceful island refuge. Send her in and I'll see what she has planned to impress our guests."

"Father, can we have a bonfire tonight?" Charlie asked, bounding into the room. "Cliff said he would help me get a great pile of wood ready. Can we, Father?"

"I don't see why not. Set about and get it ready and I'll make sure we all come."

"Will you come, Lily?"

"Of course she will."

"Mother doesn't like the beach."

"You leave Mother to me. You and Cliff gather the wood and I'll look after the rest."

As soon as Mrs. Randolph instructed me to take my afternoon break, I made my way quickly to the shore. I was anxious to see how big a fire the boys had laid. I'd heard their activity on the beach as I tended to my tasks.

"Well, haven't you two been busy beavers," I said as I walked up to the large pile of brush.

Cordelia was unwrapping the towel from around her head shaking out her wet hair. "You'd think they were preparing an elephant's funeral pyre. They wouldn't even swim with me. And they think Mother will come down. When was the last time she ventured down to the water's edge?"

"Father said he'd get her to," Charlie said. "He said everyone was coming. That means you too, Lily."

"Of course Lily will come," Cliff said. "There's a full moon tonight. It is going to be a perfect evening for the season's first bonfire."

"Help me drag these logs over," Charlie hollered. "Corey, grab the end of this one, and Cliff and Lily get that crooked one. We need to circle them around the campfire. It's going to be a grand night. Maybe Mother will let us sleep on the shore."

"Now you're really dreaming," Cordelia snapped. "If Mother sits her fancy self down on a log and stays for more than five minutes, I'll be surprised. She might let the rest of us stay longer, but there's no way she'd allow such debauchery as sleeping out under the stars. Especially by the water's edge. She'd have us all swallowed up in a tsunami."

*

I was just putting away the last of the supper dishes when Mrs. Randolph walked into the kitchen.

"I suppose you've heard that Charles and Cliff have prepared a bonfire for us all to attend this evening. They want to wait until dark, which means, of course, that Charles will have to stay up past his bedtime. Clifton has convinced me to let some of the rules loosen so the boy can have his heart's desire, which apparently is catching fire to a pile of sticks and watching the flames shoot embers into the night sky. A campfire, for heaven's sake. If they had to live in the wilderness and cook over an open fire, they would soon thank me for the luxury they scoff at. These children know nothing of poverty or hardship. You can come down as well, Lillianne. Charles, Cliff, and Cordelia all pleaded your case for a night off. Apparently, I am a slave driver. There again, they have no idea how cruel and thoughtless mistresses of fine homes can be. Especially when they see the girl in their employ has caught the prize their own privileged daughter could not."

I quickly wiped the sink after rinsing and wringing out the washing cloths. I lingered, allowing Mrs. Randolph to continue speaking. Leaving to go hang the wet cloths on the clothesline did not seem an option when she was still very much caught up in her dialogue.

"Dorothy Simms made a marriage eventually, but it came to a bad end. Not all the sons of the rich and powerful are as generous and loving as Clifton Randolph. In many a well-bred son hides a cruel and miserable man who finds release in the abuse he measures out to his weak and powerless wife. But I am nattering on. I will let you finish up your work while I go and change out of this dress. I don't need this orange taffeta dotted with ember burns. I'll scour my closet for an outfit more suitable for sitting on a stump and singing silly campfire songs with my children. The sacrifices a mother must make."

*

The flames of the bonfire rose high into the night sky. The stars were bright and the moon was full. Cordelia had come to my attic bedroom earlier and given me the pair of cotton trousers and the light jacket I was wearing.

"The night air will be cool, and the wretched mosquitoes will descend upon us. Wear these trousers, socks, and shoes and you'll not be chewed alive."

She was partway down the stairs before she turned to speak again. "I know I act like a spoiled brat and a stuffy priss, but it's a part I play. I'm glad you're with us for the summer, Lily. I've not had many friends in the last few years. Mother feels friends and fun are a complete waste of time, and all my attention should be given to becoming a young woman who will be a desirable commodity on the marriage market."

I looked across the fire at Cordelia laughing at something Charlie had just said. Her face showed a happiness I'd only seen right before and after she swam. It was as if the constraints she held so tightly were loosened by the magic of the lake. Looking at the dark expanse of water sparkling in the moonlight, I wished for the release I'd felt in the water the day before.

Even Mrs. Randolph seemed more relaxed. She had found an outfit very different from her usual attire. She was wearing a similar outfit to what Cordelia and I were wearing: pants and loose jackets that freed us from the corsets and expected clothing of our places in society. I was not naive enough to believe that a simple costume change altered my place, but I was going to allow myself to enjoy the evening. Having Cliff sitting on the log beside me certainly helped with that.

Mrs. Randolph rose from her seat. "Enough of this," she said. "I suppose you all want to stay until the last coal burns out, but I'm going up to bed. Clifton, can I count on you to make sure these children go up to the house at a civilized hour? Don't let Charlie fall asleep in the sand like a vagabond."

An hour later Charlie was wrapped up tightly in a woollen blanket, lying near the fire. Cordelia and her father had gone for a swim in the dark water. I wanted to join them, but couldn't muster the courage or the abandon, and I had not, like Cordelia, worn my suit under my clothing, waiting for the opportunity to enjoy the late-night swim. I could hear Charlie's gentle breathing and the swimmers' revelry. I wanted this night to last forever.

"Down in the valley, valley so low..." Cliff began singing and slipped his arm around me. Charlie stretched and turned away from the fire, seemingly getting ready to do exactly what his mother had warned against. I closed my eyes, listening to the words of the ballad Cliff was singing, embracing the night air and the sound of his beautiful, clear voice.

"Roses love sunshine, violets love dew; Angels in heaven know I love you... Let me start that verse again," Cliff said. "Lilies love sunshine, lilies love dew; Angels in heaven know I love you. Know I love you, dear, know I love you; Angels in heaven know I love you."

Cordelia and Mr. Randolph ran toward the fire, shivering and shaking, grabbing nearby towels and huddling near the fire. I was grateful for their timing and for the dark night that hid my blushing face.

*

Mr. Tibbetts arrived Wednesday morning, proudly bringing his new Rival garden tiller. After he laboriously turned the sod by the shovelful in a patch beside the well house, he fixed the blade to the metal piece that wrapped itself behind the single wheel of the contraption and began pushing the tiller to prepare the ground for the vegetable garden he and I were to plant.

"Victory Gardens are being planted all over the United Kingdom and in much of the USA," Mr. Tibbetts said. "Parks, school grounds, churchyards, and backyards everywhere are being planted to provide food for those at home and for the troops. I mentioned this to Mr. Randolph, and he thought it would be a good idea to plant what we could here. I've mentioned a vegetable garden other years, but he never saw the purpose of it."

"Can I try? It looks like the blade moves pretty easily through the soil."

"This is the best tiller you can buy, my girl. The handles adjust for man or boy—and for a young lady, I suppose, if you've a mind to try it."

I took hold of the handles and walked behind the tiller, finding that it wasn't as easy as it looked.

"You are quite a worker, Lily. Mrs. Randolph should be paying you the wages of at least three for all you are doing here this summer. Other years she has had a staff of four or five and worn them to a frazzle. But I wouldn't have seen any of them put their hand to the plough. I'll stay and help you get the seeds in the ground. As good an idea as Mr. Randolph might think having a garden is, I don't expect he'll drop a seed or tend to any of the hoeing or weeding needed to ensure a good harvest. Sorry to say, my dear, this garden will just make more work for you, and I know you have no shortage of work to do to keep this family satisfied."

I continued tilling, thinking about what Mr. Tibbetts had just said. I knew it would do me no good to complain about the work I was given to do day after day. But something about the thoughts of planting seeds and watching them grow seemed like pleasure more than an added burden. I would far rather be outside in a garden than cooped up in the house, caught up in the drudgery of cleaning and cooking.

"Has the rationing gotten any worse? Before I left, the Prince George was having trouble getting all the sugar they needed."

"There are shortages of everything. Even potatoes are scarce. They always are this time of year, but it's worse than I ever remember. Even getting seed potato was difficult. And butcher's meat is hard to buy. Nothing but the best cuts are available, and the common folk can't afford them. I was able to get some good cuts for the Randolphs this time, but I expect that is going to get harder and harder. This garden and fresh fish might be the fare as the summer goes on. There's lots of liquor moving, though. Not that I would know anything about that. Why don't you hoe up a row of tilled ground? Just take the blade and move the soil as you go, trying to make a straight row, and then mound it up from the other side. When you've made a row, take the end of the hoe and make a furrow along the top and drop the corn seeds along the furrow, about a foot apart. I'll finish tilling the patch. And then I'll cut up our seed potato."

I was dropping the last corn seed when Charlie and Cliff came through the opening in the hedge that bordered the garden patch.

"Show us what to do, and Charlie and I will help you," Cliff called.

"Can you believe a cob of corn comes from this little seed?" Charlie exclaimed as he bent and picked up a corn seed.

"That's all Lily needs, is for you to come along and pick up the seeds she just dropped."

"You can cover those corn seeds, Charlie. Just push the dirt from both sides of the furrow covering the seed. By the time you're done I'll have the peas planted and you can cover them. Cliff, if you like you can take the hoe and make the rows for the potatoes. I'll show you how. Mr. Tibbetts just went to cut up the seed."

With Charlie and Cliff's help, Mr. Tibbetts and I finished the planting just in time for me to get supper ready. By the look of the dark clouds, our garden was going to get a shower, which Mr. Tibbetts said would be good to help germinate the seeds. I had no experience in gardening, but I was looking forward to seeing the first sprouts appear.

Maybe being a good gardener is hereditary, and I will take to it like my mother did. As a little girl I would close my eyes when I stepped outside and let the plethora of colour thrill me when I squinted my eyes open. The hollyhocks grew high above the roses, foxglove, and peonies. Lavender grew low to the ground, and poppies poked their red heads in among the other flowers. Mother always filled the house with bouquets from the first blossoms until the latest frost in the fall. I wondered if any of those flowers still bloomed around what was once my red-brick home.

✳

Friday morning began with sheets of rain hitting the kitchen window, adding to Mrs. Randolph's anxiety, which had been rising rapidly since the day before.

"God willing, the rain will let up by the time the boat arrives. If it continues, my guests will be drenched to the bone coming in to shore. I want the smell of the delicious food to permeate the house, not the odour of houseguests smelling like wet hound dogs. Geraldine Windsor is a big woman, and if her undergarments get wet it will take days to dry them out. Surely the sun will break through and present Randolph Island in its splendour. Did you get the windows in the parlour washed yesterday? If the sun does come out, I don't want the first thing Evelyn Donaldson sees to be streaky, dirty windows in the Randolphs' parlour. And Mabel Emerson will inspect every corner of her room. You did beat the rug yesterday? She found mouse droppings between the floorboards while visiting the Conrads' summer home and never returned. Elizabeth Conrad was mortified."

I recalled the dead mouse I'd removed from the bottom shelf of the pantry on the day we arrived. Charlie had seen me throw it out the back door, and I hoped he wouldn't tell the story in his dramatic manner when the guests gathered. No doubt Mrs. Randolph would keep Charlie at a distance from her dignified guests. He certainly could liven things up, but his style of entertaining was not what Mrs. Randolph was striving for.

Yesterday Cliff and Cordelia were well briefed on their entertaining duties when their mother spoke to them at length around the breakfast table.

"Clifton, I expect that you will spend some time conversing with the men. You may even partake in a cigar or two after the evening meal. These men will be important contacts when you enter the business world. You should especially solidify your place with Walter Donaldson. It is common knowledge that he is ripe to take over the entire lumber industry in the state of Michigan, and his mother's people have holdings in much of the construction trade. Stanley Emerson is more convinced of his own importance than anyone else, but nevertheless he has considerable influence in Chicago. And we know what the war effort has done for Robert Windsor's coffers. You can learn a lot from these men, and I expect you to stay around and not take off after each meal to engage in your frivolous drawing hobby. Show them that Clifton Randolph the Fourth has grown into a man and will be a force to reckon with when he enters business circles. Cordelia, you will no doubt impress the guests with how much you have grown as well. You are a striking young lady, and any of their sons would do well to pursue you. I would like you to entertain after tomorrow evening's meal. That piece you are preparing for the recital will be very impressive. Not one of those families has a daughter with your talent and beauty. I know Mabel Emerson will be green with envy, as she had such hopes for Victoria, but even after five years with a renowned pianist, she can barely play a note. She played for us at Mabel's Easter luncheon and it sounded like a scalded cat."

*

As if Mrs. Randolph really had influence, the sun came out shortly after lunch. The heat quickly dried the floorboards of the front veranda, and I set out the furniture I had hurriedly put in the shed earlier this morning. Most of the preparations for the evening meal were complete, and I was to perform a quick but thorough last look at each of the rooms in the house and the sun porch. Mrs. Randolph had already changed into a gown to greet her guests. Miss Cordelia was decked out as well, and even Charlie had been cleaned up and dressed as a young gentleman. He pulled at his high collar as he tripped along behind me, telling me a completely made-up story of a whale he had just seen swimming to shore.

"I wanted Clifton to take me around the island for a swim, but mother made me get dressed and said that I was to stay away from the beach. I have to be on my best behaviour, she said. Father says all I have to do is speak politely to the ladies and then I can make my escape, like Harry Houdini. I am going to eat in the kitchen with you. Mother doesn't want her company exposed to my table manners, she said. I don't know what is so bad about my table manners. Even Cordelia laughed at me the other night when I made my milk come out my nose. Do you know that Harry Houdini escaped from an oversized milk can filled with water in just three minutes? He stayed behind the curtain for up to thirty minutes and the crowd was sure he was dead. I can almost hold my breath for one minute but Cliff says I can't keep quiet that long."

"I'm not far off the truth, am I?" Cliff interjected as he walked up the veranda steps. "Mother is calling for you, Lily. Charlie, help me finish putting these chairs in place."

*

"This beef is delicious, Marion. The soup was very flavourful as well. Who did you engage to be your cook this summer? I was able to hire a woman who took her training in France."

"That's what she told us, anyway," Stanley Emerson added. "I would be surprised if she has seen anything more French than a kitchen in Montreal. Just the same, I certainly have been well fed so far." He patted his vest, which seemed to be almost bursting the three buttons that ran down over his substantial midriff.

Well fed and well lubricated, I thought as I poured a third tumbler of brandy and set it in front of Mr. Emerson. Everyone seemed to be enjoying both food and beverage, and there was no more mention of the cook's credentials. I was sure Mrs. Randolph would prefer her guests to think there was an experienced cook in the kitchen, not the slip of a girl serving them.

"You would not believe the rumblings in Kingston when we arrived," commented Walter Donaldson. "Everyone from the premier to the busboy at the Prince George made disparaging remarks about our war effort. They've been brainwashed by Lloyd George and Borden."

"They don't balk at the munitions and other supplies we provide," Robert Windsor added. "What would the war effort be without the commerce of the United States? With their economy, they should be thankful this war is providing employment for their young men."

"Must we talk of such troubling things, Robert?" Geraldine Windsor asked. "We come to the islands to escape such concerns. Is it not enough that I must listen to Mrs. Thomas go on about her son being on the frontlines? She has been my summer housekeeper for the last five years, but I have a mind to terminate her employment if she continues to prattle on about her problems."

It seemed like forever before everyone moved into the parlour and I was able to begin clearing off the table. I could hear the strains of the "Moonlight Sonata" coming from Cordelia's cello as Charlie and I sat at the butcher block in the kitchen to eat our share of the evening's repast. The beef was indeed tasty and the soup divine, if I do say so myself. The entire meal was nothing for Mrs. Randolph to be ashamed of, and as I finished my piece of German chocolate cake, I couldn't help but feel a bit of pride in having pulled off the first and probably most elaborate meal of the weekend. Training in the best orphanage in Ontario was my claim to culinary fame, and apparently it had met the standards of the well-bred group of Americans now being serenaded by the proper Miss Cordelia Randolph of Chicago, Illinois.

*

Saturday's luncheon was to be a picnic and required my hauling the china, cutlery, and linens down to the improvised dining table set up on the beach. Apparently, the Windsors had put on a lovely picnic, and despite her aversion to eating outside, Mrs. Randolph was anxious to offer a similar experience. Mr. Tibbetts arrived earlier and helped me construct the table and bring down the supplies. Between trips I attended to the food preparation, and this picnic did not have a simple menu. I thought last evening's supper had been a challenge, but bringing the entire noon meal down to the shore and presenting it as if it were being served in the dining room was no small task.

The day's oppressive heat had taken the Randolphs and all their guests to the water's edge shortly after breakfast. All the ladies except Mrs. Randolph were dressed in their swimming attire and thought themselves quite striking. Mrs. Windsor was decked out in a suit that appeared to be about the same yardage as the sail her husband had hoisted up the mast on the sailboat the men were aboard. Mrs. Emerson and Mrs. Donaldson were sporting matching striped suits, making them look somewhat like a set of clowns. Mrs. Windsor's bathing cap looked like a large tea cozy sitting on her head. Cordelia looked much more fashionable in her snappy black-and-white suit with matching bathing cap as she waded tentatively into the water, admonishing Charlie for daring to splash her. This was, of course, an act much different than Cordelia's behaviour in the water when out of her mother's sight.

I set plates of cold tomato aspic down and headed up to get more, hoping the hot sun would not compromise the form of each molded creation. It would have been difficult enough to present this meal inside, but having to bring it the distance from the kitchen only guaranteed that something would not meet with Mrs. Randolph's approval.

On my return, the men were coming to shore and the ladies had already seated themselves. Cliff reached the table first. He took the loaded tray from me and placed it on the table.

"Sit down, son. Lillianne is quite capable of attending to things. You must be ravenous from your morning of sailing."

I picked up the pitcher of lemonade and started filling the ladies' glasses. I was capable of attending to things, all right. Why couldn't I make repeated trips back and forth to provide a meal that could have been more easily served inside the house? The trips up and down and several more to clean up and put everything back in order were nothing if the guests could enjoy the day on the beach. I could certainly attend to things and be just about finished in time to prepare the evening meal. And God forbid any of these fine ladies should lift a finger to help me. I brushed a strand of hair from my eyes and brought the end of my apron up to my forehead to wipe away the drops of sweat. I could see Charlie still playing in the rippling waves and for a moment thought how wonderful it would be to let the cool water cover and free me.

After the meal, the men sat back on the reclining beach chairs, leafing through sections of the copy of the *New York Times* that Mr. Tibbetts had brought with him to the island this morning. Charlie had been released to his imaginings near the water's edge. Cordelia and the ladies had taken to the shade of the gazebo, and with his mother out of sight, Cliff had perched himself away down the beach on a large rock, sketching something he was attentively viewing off in the distance.

"It is being called the Selective Service Act," Stanley Emerson read from the front page. "Congress passed it on May 18. General Crowder has claimed all along that he was displeased with it, but he assisted Captain Johnson in guiding it through Congress. Its enactment has given the federal government the authority to use the draft to raise an army. We are entering into this war full force, and Roosevelt is getting what he has wanted all along."

"Let me see that," said Mr. Randolph. He almost upset the tumbler of whiskey I was passing him in his haste to take the newspaper from his companion.

"It is requiring all men aged twenty-one to thirty to register for military service. June 5 is the date for the first draft."

"President Wilson has said all along that any American forces would be of a voluntary nature and has not supported a draft of any kind," Mr. Donaldson interjected.

Mr. Randolph's voice rose as he continued his comments. "Wilson was obviously swayed by the Secretary of War and the influence of the others who have been pushing for this bill to be passed."

"Does it have a substitute clause?" asked Mr. Emerson.

"No, but any registrants employed in industrial enterprises essential to the war effort are exempted. Robert, you'll certainly be called upon to employ sons of family and friends, my own son included if it comes to that. For now, I ask that there be no discussion of this whole nasty draft business when Cliff is around. I would like to avoid any thoughts of this until at least late August, when the family returns to the States. And for God's sake, let's not mention it to the ladies. They will get the vapours worrying about something I am sure will never come to pass for the young men of our circle."

"Take this newspaper, Lillianne, and make sure it is used to start tomorrow's fire."

*

My weary feet could barely carry me as Charlie took my hand and led me to the water's edge. The cool evening air felt wonderful as it blew through my loose hair. Supper had been served, and the adults had retired to the parlour. Everything had been cleaned up and I was taking a short break.

"Cliff is going to take me out for a moonlight paddle."

I turned and saw Cliff coming down the wooden steps.

"You can be the captain, Charlie, and I'll be your first mate. Lily, I don't suppose we could convince you to be the fair damsel in distress we have rescued."

"No, I'll keep my feet on solid ground, thank you."

Charlie took a paper pirate hat from his brother, set it atop his head, and grabbed a wooden paddle. Cliff quickly took off his shoes and socks and pushed the boat out into the shallow water.

"Come on, Captain. Let's set sail. We'll leave this land lover behind and she will miss out on our adventure. The wind will carry us out to sea and to points beyond."

*

"I'm going to Chicago with you when you go at the end of July, Father," Cliff stated as soon as his father sat down at the table for breakfast on Monday morning.

"Don't be ridiculous, Clifton," said Mrs. Randolph. "Why would you go with your father? He'll only be gone a week or two. What would you possibly want to go back to the city for in August?"

Cliff stood and pulled a folded newspaper page from his pants pocket. "I am going so that I can register for the draft, Mother. As I'm sure Father knows but did not see fit to tell me, our country is finally going to enter the war in a meaningful way. I will be twenty-one in August, and it is my obligation both legally and morally to step up and do my part. I will not hide on this island. I will do what my country requires of me."

"What is he talking about, Clifton? His entrance to Princeton in September has been arranged. After all we've been through, I cannot believe any other plan would even be considered. And he must be mistaken about there being a draft. Did not President Wilson base his whole re-election platform on the claim that he had kept us out of the war? Surely someone with Cliff's promising future will not be required to march off to this terrible campaign."

"Cliff is right, Marion. Congress has passed a bill requiring all men from age twenty-one to thirty to register for military service. I was hoping we wouldn't have to deal with it until the end of August, but somehow the boy has gotten wind of it."

Mr. Randolph looked at me accusingly. I had realized when starting the fire yesterday morning that the section the men had been reading concerning the war was not in the wood box, and I knew that those pages must had been folded to make the pirate hat Charlie had so proudly set upon his head for Saturday evening's paddle. I could only have stopped Cliff from seeing the news if I'd burned the paper as soon as I returned to the kitchen on Saturday afternoon.

"Cliff, you may feel the need to register as the law requires, but you will not be called up," Mr. Randolph began, speaking to his son but looking directly at his wife. "We will postpone your entry to Princeton, and you will immediately take up employment in one of Robert Windsor's factories. Your employment in an industry essential to the war effort will exempt you from military service."

"Oh, thank God." Mrs. Randolph rose from her seat and embraced her son. "You have worried me for nothing. I don't approve of postponing your entrance to Princeton, but if working for Robert Windsor for a year keeps you from the battlefields of Europe, I will certainly agree to that plan."

Cliff released himself from his mother's embrace and headed for the doorway of the dining room, then turned and spoke, his voice and demeanour showing both anger and determination. "I *will* register and I will *not* shirk my duty. I will do whatever my country requires of me. You may think that you can orchestrate every detail of my life, but not this time. I will not let your money and influence keep me from joining the allied troops who so desperately need our help. I *will* return to the States, Father, with you or without you, even if I have to take the rowboat all the way to Gananoque."

Cliff left his parents in stunned silence. I wanted to run

out after him, offering him some comfort, but of course I just walked around the table and poured coffee into Mr. Randolph's already half-full cup, hoping he would not direct a tirade of blame on me for not having successfully kept his son from reading the newspaper.

✻

"Mother has been crying all morning," Charlie announced as he bounded out the back door and came up to where I was dumping the wash water from the metal tub. "I don't know where Cliff has gotten to, and Father just hollered at me when I asked him if he knew where he was. I walked down along the shore as far as the big rock but I didn't see Cliff anywhere."

Charlie had missed the breakfast conversation, having come late to the table. Charlie was puzzled by his mother's emotion and his father's irritation. Cordelia had shown no reaction and had gone to the sun porch, where she had been practising her cello all morning.

"Let me finish what I'm doing and I'll walk down along the shore again with you. I didn't hear Cliff come back into the house, so he has to be outside somewhere. Was the rowboat still tied up? Maybe he went for a row."

✻

When we headed down the steps to the beach, we could see Cliff out in the water in the rowboat. We got all the way to the water's edge before he noticed us.

"Why don't you sit here and wait for Cliff to row in? Maybe he'll take you out for a row before lunch."

"You should come with us, Lily. Yesterday Cliff rowed me all around the island. There is an eagle's nest in a tall tree on the other side. Cliff said if I could stay quiet long enough, I might be able to see the eagle flying back to its nest or maybe swooping down to catch a fish. Cliff told me an eagle can see a surfacing fish from a mile away."

"I have to get back up to the house to make lunch. You go with Cliff and try to keep quiet and maybe you'll be able to tell me all about the eagle or some other amazing thing you saw. I'm sure Cliff will be happy to have your company."

"Do you know what has Mother so upset? Cliff probably knows. He tells me stuff. Nobody else does. Cordelia acts like I am some sort of bug and shoos me away. Mother barely notices me and father is usually busy. You always listen to me, but Cliff tells me not to bother you so much."

"Remember the being quiet part, Charlie? Cliff is getting closer to shore. Wade out and meet him, but let him get in close enough so you don't capsize the rowboat."

*

Neither Cliff nor Charlie came to the table at noon. Mrs. Randolph was extremely upset and kept going back and forth from the dining room to the sun-porch window, from which she had a clear view of the water and the rowboat in the distance.

"They keep rowing out farther and don't seem to have any intention of coming in to eat. Go out and call to them, Clifton. Maybe they don't know what time it is."

"It won't hurt them to miss a meal, Marion. If Cliff is hell-bent on going off to war, he may as well get used to missing a meal or two. He has no idea what fighting in a war entails. He has some romantic idea about serving his country and being a hero. He won't think it's such an adventure when he finds himself wading through waist-deep mud in the trenches."

"Surely he will come to his senses. You don't go back to the States until the end of July. That is plenty of time for him to think this through. Maybe he'll come to the right decision on his own. He must see we only want what is best for him. He has trusted us in the past. Please go call them in. We'll pretend none of that nasty war talk even happened. He will come around and accept the best plan for his future. I just know he will."

Cordelia looked up from her lunch. "We should have a party and take Cliff's mind off this war foolishness. We could invite some of the young people from the neighbouring islands for a dance. We could string lanterns on the gazebo and have a summer cotillion."

"Maybe you have something there, Cordelia. I will invite some of the young ladies, and maybe I can divert Clifton's attentions. If he were to become smitten, perhaps he would think differently about rushing off to Europe."

"I think you're being overly optimistic on that front," Mr. Randolph muttered, pulling himself away from the table. "But go ahead and try."

Two hours later I was beating the parlour rug on the front veranda and noticed Cliff sitting at the edge of the grass bent over his sketchpad. I left my job and went into the kitchen, quickly setting a lunch out on the bamboo tray. I headed out the back door.

"I brought you something to eat."

Cliff set his sketchpad down on the grass and took the tray from me. "That is very kind of you, Lily. I am getting a bit peckish, but not hungry enough to go back to the house. I have no desire to see either of my parents. I thought seriously about rowing away from the island and never coming back."

"I wouldn't want you to do that." Embarrassed by my words,

I turned my head, picking up the sketchpad from the grass. "Your drawing is amazing."

"Thank you. I was sketching a blue heron. He was perched on that outcropping, but he flew away as you approached."

"I'm sorry. How did you get such detail when the bird was so far away?"

"I take the basic outline from what I see and fill in the rest from what I know. I studied art with an emphasis in ornithology. I find birds beautiful and magnificent. When I am patient, I am always rewarded with impressive sightings in this area."

"Were you studying art in New York?"

"No. I was studying at a small art college in Springfield, an indulgence before the serious business of attending Princeton. My parents do not value my interest in art. They don't value the very essence of their son, for that matter. They are determined to squelch any real passion I have for anything."

I heard my name being called from the front veranda. "Your mother has probably come upon the discarded parlour rug." I reached out and touched Cliff's arm before standing and rushing back to the house.

*

For the rest of the week, Cordelia and her mother were caught up in the planning of a gathering of about thirty young people. Mr. Tibbetts had been recruited to provide a shuttle to bring the partygoers to the island Friday evening and transport them back to their residences at midnight.

"It is just like Cinderella's ball," Charlie said. "Are you one of the ugly stepsisters, Corey, and Lily the poor kitchen maid who will wear the glass slipper?"

"Mother. Tell Charlie to leave me alone. And please assure me you won't allow him to be anywhere near the party."

"Charles. Stop teasing your sister. You boys have no idea the work and the stress that goes into planning a social event. Go out back with Lillianne and leave your sister alone."

*

"I want to be a circus clown when I grow up, and a train engineer and maybe a horse trader."

Charlie was following me back and forth along the path that led from the well house to the water cistern. I was on my fifth trip, and the cistern was only about a quarter full. Charlie's chatter was making the task easier, and since he didn't require much response, my energy could be given to carrying the two large pails without slopping much of the precious water.

"Mother says I will be a businessman like father, but I would rather be a scientist, a bull fighter, or a vagabond. I don't really know what a vagabond is, but it sounds like fun. What do you want to be when you grow up?"

"I pretty much am grown up, and I don't expect I'll be much more than I already am."

"You could be a princess. You could be a nurse like Florence Nightingale or write poetry like Emily Dickinson. Mother reads me her poems, but I like it better when Cliff reads me the poetry of Tennyson.

"Half a league, half a league
Half a league onward
All in the valley of Death
Rode the six hundred.'"

Charlie picked up a stick and charged ahead, ready to join the legions of soldiers riding into the valley of death.

What *did* I want to be when I grew up? In the last few years I had not given much thought to that. Getting away from the Sisters of Providence had perhaps been one of the things I dreamed about, but, past that, what future did an orphan girl have? The best I could hope for was domestic employment, which would provide the necessities of life and a bit of dignity. Not a princess, a nurse, or a poet. A writer, maybe, if dreaming was something I had the luxury of doing. It had been a copy of *Anne of Green Gables* stolen from the Sisters' library shelves that had started me dreaming of putting words to paper. I, too, was an orphan, but there were no idyllic country settings or kind, elderly siblings in my story. If ever I could write, the story I would fashion would be much different.

On my return to the well house, I was met by Cliff carrying a bucket of water.

"Many hands make light work," he said.

Charlie ran up behind me, happy to see his brother.

"Cliff is going to be a famous painter. He will fill the walls of art galleries all over the world with paintings of exotic birds, plants, and animals. He and I will go on African safaris and I will capture wild animals for my zoo and he will paint them."

Cliff poured some water from his bucket into one of my empty ones. "How about for now you help Lily fill the water cistern? Surely even a runt like you can carry half a pail of water."

With determination, Charlie headed toward the back porch.

"Your little brother has been entertaining me with his dreams and aspirations. If I had half his energy and a bit of his imagination, my work would be done for the day and I could lounge on the beach."

Cliff and I entered the well house. In the closeness of the space I could feel the crispness of his white shirt and the warmth of his bare arm. Cliff set his pail down and leaned against the rough timber of the wall.

"No one has spoken of my choice to enlist. They think all this hoopla about a party will distract me. I think Mother even believes she'll find a wife for me Friday night and that will keep me home. I am going to enlist. The thought of the horror I will face frightens me to the core, but I will go. I cannot think of others doing their duty while I cowardly allow my father's money and influence to protect me. I am determined to be a man."

Tears filled his eyes. I reached out and gently kissed Cliff's cheek. He turned his head, returning my gesture with a kiss on my lips. I pulled away, grabbed the pail, dipped it into the well, then pulled it out awkwardly, sloshing water as I rushed from the well house.

*

I was under no illusion that I would be included in the party. It was one thing to allow the hired girl to come to a bonfire, but another thing altogether to have her mingle with the invited guests at a summer cotillion. As I put the finishing touches on the decorations festooning the gazebo, I let my mind wander back to my childhood home. What would the parties be like if my mother were organizing them for me? I finished sweeping the steps, looking back at the lanterns already illuminating the dance floor.

An hour later, looking out an upstairs window, I could see the guests arriving on the shore. Mr. Randolph and Cliff were at the water's edge receiving them, but Cordelia had been instructed earlier to make her entrance after the guests were gathered in the gazebo.

"This isn't my coming-out party, Mother."

"No, but you need to create an air of mystery. Many of these young men have not seen you for several summers. A young lady makes a proper entrance."

"Does Clifton have to wait and be announced, too? It is him you want on exhibit tonight, is it not?"

"Don't be so vulgar. Clifton can greet the guests as the master of the house would. I want his masculinity to be evident."

"Good luck with that one."

I missed Cordelia's entrance, as I was busy in the kitchen preparing the refreshments. By the time I made my first trip to the gazebo, she was already dancing and appeared to be enjoying the attention her mother predicted her form-fitting purple gown would elicit. Cliff, on the other hand, was sitting on the bench outside the gazebo and jumped up quickly to take the tray of drinks from me.

"Your mother would not want you to pass this tray for me, Cliff. She was very specific in her instructions, and one of them was the efficient and professional execution of my duties. She even found this cap and apron so there would be no confusion as to my position."

"She's just afraid the boys will think you more intriguing than the lovely Cordelia."

"Why aren't you dancing?"

"I'd rather be sitting out back with hopes of seeing that barred owl I got a glimpse of two nights ago. Do you think Mother would notice if I took my sketchpad and sat up in Charlie's tree house waiting for a sighting?"

Mrs. Randolph came up behind me, startling me and making it very clear that she would indeed notice if Cliff were not participating in this social gathering.

"Clifton. Victoria Emerson is asking for you. You remember

her, don't you? We sailed to their mansion a few years ago. She's turned into a lovely young woman and seems very anxious to reunite with you."

*

I wasn't sure what prompted me to look out the attic window when I finally went to bed. I had lost count of the trips I'd made from the kitchen to the gazebo. Apparently, dancing works up quite an appetite and thirst, and it was all I could do to keep the partygoers satiated. I was anxious to get to my bed and put the whole evening out of my mind. Normally I stuffed down any feelings of being of a lower status when I was serving and attending to others. I could usually keep their superior manner from making me feel inferior.

But serving a crowd of people of my own age was different. The young men and women I served tonight were downright rude and dismissive. I remembered Cordelia telling me her haughty behaviour was an act. Could all these young men and women be caught up in the same performances? Or did they truly believe they were far superior to the girl serving them? The whole night had left me angry and irritated. I welcomed sleep and a new day.

I could see lanterns on the shore. For some reason, Mr. Tibbits was not sailing away, and the Randolphs were not returning to the house, even though it was well after midnight. The lantern lights seemed to be zigzagging along the shore and up and down the steep lawns. I opened the attic window.

"Cordelia! Spencer! Cordelia! Spencer!" The two names were being called over and over. Was there any point in going to bed before the racket on the shore quieted?

I heard Mrs. Randolph's voice downstairs a few minutes

later. "I thought you had drowned."

"Your mother was frantic, Cordelia. What the hell were you thinking?"

"This lovely evening was completely ruined by your actions," Mrs. Randolph continued, her voice high-pitched and frenzied. "It won't be tonight's event, the food, or the hospitality of the Randolphs discussed in homes tomorrow, but the indiscretion of Cordelia Randolph and Spencer Hitchcock, discovered in such a compromising condition."

I could hear Cordelia's sobs mixing with her mother's heated words.

"At least it was your brother's lantern that illuminated your dalliance. But that won't keep all the partygoers from imagining what you two were doing clear around the other side of the island. And then to bring you around both looking like drowned rats. I am mortified."

Mr. Randolph's voice halted Cordelia's sobbing and her mother's hysterical ranting. "Best we all get up to bed and discuss this in the morning."

"I'll not sleep a wink," Mrs. Randolph replied.

*

Breakfast was quiet and strained, though Charlie was his usual chatty self, totally oblivious to the tension in the room.

"Mother, Cordelia is not eating her waffle. Can I have it? She hasn't eaten her grapefruit, either."

"Lily can get you another waffle. Leave your sister alone," Mr. Randolph said.

"I wished you'd let me stay up last night," Charlie continued. "I wanted to see Mr. Tibbetts's boat leave. He said if I was still up he'd take me out on the scow. He let me help pull it up on shore when he arrived. I kept watching to see when he was leaving, but I must have fallen asleep."

"Thank God for that," Mrs. Randolph muttered, her first words of the meal.

"He said he'd be back next week and take you out," Cliff added.

"Oh, he'll have heard lots from his passengers, I expect. He'll have a good story to tell about the goings-on at Randolph Island."

"Marion, I don't think Mr. Tibbetts cares about the silly goings-on of our family. Three of his sons are serving overseas. He has worries far greater than our daughter having a bit of romance on a summer's night."

"Oh, Clifton. You make it sound so innocent. A well-bred girl does not go off into the dark with a young man."

"What do you mean, Mother?" Charlie asked. "What young man?"

Cordelia stood up abruptly, almost knocking her chair over.

"Sit right back down, young lady," Mrs. Randolph barked, almost causing me to spill the coffee I was pouring into Mr. Randolph's cup. "You'll not get off that easy. Charles, take your plate into the kitchen. We have something to discuss with your sister, and it is not for your ears."

I followed Charlie into the kitchen with the empty coffee carafe. I could see before leaving that tears were streaming down Cordelia's cheeks.

"Why is Mother so mad?"

"Dogs are mad, Charlie."

"Why is Cordelia in trouble? Usually Mother is upset with Cliff or me, not Corey. What did she do?"

"It is not my place to talk about it. Here, have another waffle. We'll sit for a minute and leave the others alone."

"Last year Mother was always hollering at Cliff after she went to Springfield and brought him home. She cried every day, and then she and Cliff went on the train to New York. Will she make Corey go to New York?"

"I don't think so. Just eat the rest of your breakfast. I have to take more coffee into the dining room."

"Let up a bit on her, Marion. Don't you remember the headiness of being attracted to a young man?"

"How dare you say such a thing? Cordelia has had a fine upbringing, unlike what I was offered. I did not know any better, but Cordelia has prospects and a reputation to protect. What do you suppose every young man who left this island last night is now thinking of her?"

"I know what one of them is thinking," Cliff said. "Spencer Hitchcock seemed quite smitten with my little sister."

"Spencer Hitchcock is a naive young whelp with only his stirrings to lead him. He obviously has no common sense or judgement or he wouldn't find himself in the mess he did last night. And I'm sure in the light of day he'll see the carelessness of his actions and probably be quick to judge the morals of the girl who last night seemed so desirable. I know his mother will bring him up smartly and talk some sense into him, and it won't be in Cordelia's favour."

"Did my mother's judgement of you sway *my* desire?"

"Clifton. I'll have no more comparisons. We have a responsibility to protect our daughter's virtue, and even if you do not take that seriously, I do. We need a plan to undo the damage last night did to our daughter's reputation. Cordelia, if all you can do is sit there and snivel, leave the room and go to your practising."

*

Mrs. Randolph's anger and frustration caused her to focus on the cleaning of the entire house, and it was late afternoon before I was given a break—with instructions it be no more than ten minutes. I quickly escaped to the beach. I could see Cordelia sitting on the large rock and I was drawn to her. We were not friends, but I felt sorry for her and was anxious to offer some comfort. I thought of the contrast of today's misery compared to the glow she had had on the dance floor last night.

Spencer Hitchcock and Cordelia had made a striking pair. Spencer was a few inches shorter than Cordelia but had a handsomeness that caught my eye. Before I'd seen him with Cordelia, I had heard his flirtatious chatter with several other young ladies. He had even at one point made a comment to me that brought colour to my cheeks. I was used to men commenting on my endowment and was glad my apron had covered me appropriately. Men's comments were part of the condescension I felt every day. I was thankful neither Mr. Randolph nor Cliff had taken such liberty with me.

I remembered seeing Cordelia and Spencer walking away from the gazebo on one of my trips but hadn't really thought anything of it. There had been some other pairings throughout the evening, but not the match Mrs. Randolph had hoped her son might foster.

"Are you all right, Miss Cordelia?"

"I'm humiliated and embarrassed and wish we'd not been caught, but I cannot honestly say I wish it hadn't happened. I just wish we'd kept our wits about us and gotten back before the others started down to the shore. If we'd slipped back into the crowd in time, I would just be enjoying the memory of the night, not living down the shame."

Cordelia started to cry, and I reached out and put my arms around her.

"He is a dreamboat," Cordelia began after composing herself. "I know you'll think me silly, but I think Spencer looks like the pictures of Douglas Fairbanks I've seen on covers of motion-picture magazines. He was such a gentleman. Mother has said such nasty things about him, but he was lovely. Have you ever been in love?"

"No, of course not," I answered, hoping if Cordelia looked my way she would think the heat of the sun was causing the flush on my cheeks.

"We walked in the moonlight and he said the sweetest things to me. He was such a gentleman. It was my idea to go swimming. Thank goodness Mother doesn't know that part, even though my hair was wet and, as she put it, we looked like drowned rats."

There were a few seconds of silence before Cordelia proceeded. "I've never felt anything like it, Lily. The water on my bare flesh... I can't begin to explain it."

I did not say anything in response, trying not to show my shock at Cordelia's words. I kept listening, although part of me was quite sure I didn't want Cordelia to confide in me in this manner.

"I couldn't swim in my gown, and once I was down to my undergarments I couldn't see the harm in going further. It was dark and I rushed right into the water. Spencer stripped as well, and at first I thought we'd keep our distance. You will think the worst of me, but I'm not sorry. I felt more alive than I'd thought possible. What followed, if I am to be honest, was uncomfortable and not the least enjoyable, but those few minutes as we caressed in the water were worth the rest of it, even Mother's condemnation. She lets on like she's known no similar euphoria, but I know that to be false. You'll not breathe a word of this, will you?"

"Of course not."

"Mother is in a rage. She says I have ruined the summer's holiday. She says we now have to all go back with Father at the end of July. She has to get my reputation back intact, she says. We have to throw a huge Chicago society event, apparently, to solidify my good name. She assures me the small crowd of young people who were witness to my indiscretion can be quieted by a proper event broadcast on the society pages of the *Chicago Tribune*."

Cordelia
1934

If nothing else, I felt a huge relief that tomorrow we would sail into Southampton and disembark. My discomfort would be much greater if I'd sighted Spencer Hitchcock and his insufferable wife during the first days of our voyage. It perplexed me how I hadn't run into him earlier. And to think it was Clara's insistence we attend the captain's ball, which brought about our chance encounter.

He spoke to her first; her resemblance to me may have caught his eye. Perhaps assuming Spencer Hitchcock even remembered his brief foray with me is presumptuous. He did seem to show a glimmer of recognition when I approached, but looked quite confused when the gentleman on my arm introduced me as Dr. Kingston.

"I thought perhaps you were an acquaintance I once met from Chicago," Spencer said.

"And whereabouts are you from, Miss Kingston?" Veronica Hitchcock asked with a false sincerity and not a bit of genuine interest.

"I am from Saint John, New Brunswick, Canada."

"Is that John Murdoch I see at the table near the bar?" Veronica said, tugging at her husband's arm. "I did not know he and his wife were on board. Let's take a seat at their table, Spencer. Elmira was a Humphrey, you know."

Clara turned to me as they walked away. "Did you know that man, Aunt Cordelia?"

"No, not really," I answered. "I believe my parents did. Perhaps he was a chum of your dad's. Let's go find our own table, Clara."

Marion
1896

I picked up the newspaper and read the announcement again.

"It is with pleasure Clifton and Charlotte Randolph of Chicago, Illinois, announce the upcoming marriage of their only son, Clifton Randolph the Third, to Marion Elizabeth Kingston, daughter of the late Fernwood and Isabel Kingston of Saint John, New Brunswick, Canada. The nuptials will take place on April 30, 1896, at All Saints Episcopal Church, Hermitage Avenue, Chicago."

With pleasure, indeed. Charlotte Randolph was filled with many emotions these days, but pleasure was certainly not one of them. Since her son had come home from his last trip to Canada with his *fiancée*, Charlotte Randolph had done her best to alter the future her son was determined to inflict upon them. She'd hoped the stern talking to she gave her son shortly after Clifton met me on the family's first visit to the Simms's summer home on the Saint John River had been enough to set Clifton straight. When he talked of going back, Charlotte felt certain the ridiculous crush he'd developed on the Simms's housemaid had passed. She knew Dorothy Simms did not interest her son but felt confident he had come to his senses.

So it had been a shock when Clifton stepped off the train with me in tow. A greater shock when she realized my condition, even though I'd barely begun to show. Her first solution had been to declare I would be sent to a nearby home for unwed mothers, all my expenses covered, the baby would be adopted out, and I would be quickly returned to Canada as soon as I'd given birth.

Clifton vehemently refused such measures, and his mother finally relented. It was then, of course, that rapid arrangements were made for the upcoming wedding.

"It will be told that your family died in a tragic accident. You can decide what type of accident that may be, as I'm not familiar with what might befall a couple in New Brunswick. Is there a rail system? No; motorcars, I assume, perhaps a horse-and-buggy mishap. Both died, whatever cause you choose, leaving you a poor orphan. They were well-to-do and you come with an impressive dowry, however. Perhaps your mother could be a relative of J. Thomas Simms. There will be no mention that you were in their employ. We will generously be seen as offering to host this wedding and warmly welcoming our son's unfortunate betrothed."

After establishing my tragic story, I repeated it often enough to almost convince myself of its truth. I did not mind pretending I'd come from good breeding and old money. I had witnessed women with that status enough to play the part convincingly.

A rap on the ornate oak door roused me from my thoughts. I folded the newspaper and went to answer the knock.

"Miss Kingston, are you ready for the final fitting of your gown? Mrs. Randolph instructed me to bring it up to you."

"Yes, thank you, Mavis. Could you just hang it on the wardrobe door? I will call for assistance if I need it."

I gazed up at the gown. I had had no part in its choosing. Mrs. Randolph had gone to the dressmaker with my measurements a month ago and commissioned the creation of this ridiculous concoction of ruffles, taffeta, and lace.

"We'll attribute your thick-waistedness to your mother."

I wanted to mention that perhaps a design with a cinched waist was not the most practical in my condition, but of course my opinion was not wanted and would not have been tolerated had I opened my mouth to speak.

When the seamstress had brought the dress two weeks ago I had attempted to put it on, but there was no way the line of fifty pearl buttons at the back could be fastened. This should not have come as a surprise, but Mrs. Randolph carried on so, completely blaming the poor woman for failing to correctly measure and cut the fabric.

The seamstress assured Mrs. Randolph that alterations could be made.

I slipped off my dress and took the gown off the hanger. My whalebone corset had been fastened as tightly as possible when Mavis dressed me earlier. By myself I would not be able to fasten the buttons, but at least I could see if the dressmaker's alterations would allow me to fit into this hideous gown. I certainly didn't want Mrs. Randolph present for the revelation. Thank goodness the wedding was in three days. Surely if I was able to squeeze into this gown today, I would still be able to the day I became Mrs. Clifton Randolph the Third.

Lillianne
1993

"The postman is here for your package, Mother."

I had worked late into last evening finishing the foreword for my publisher. I still could not believe they were putting the energy and expense into a new release of *Beyond Wind and Whitecaps*. The first edition had been published seventy-one years ago. It had gone to several printings but had virtually disappeared except for an occasional surfacing in antique book circles. For some reason, my current publisher was keen to reissue my first novel. Apparently if an author lives long enough, it becomes fashionable to commercialize their early work.

What goes around comes around. Or everything old becomes new again. Clichéd and trite. Exactly what was wrong with that book, but if my publisher thought there would be interest, who was I to argue?

Mark Twain said history doesn't repeat itself but at best it sometimes rhymes. Karl Marx said it repeats itself first as tragedy, secondly as farce. And Joseph Conrad said some long wordy thing about history repeating itself, ending with something about a wild bird.

I looked up at the large painting on the wall. Cliff's obsession with birds never lessened, and this painting of the red-tailed hawk was one of several he'd painted during the short time he lived in this home. The highlight of those months for him was painting the large birds of prey native to Ontario. This painting was the only one he left behind when he moved out.

"Mother, did you hear me?" Clara said from the doorway of my study.

"Yes, I am just addressing the envelope and closing it up."

I walked out to the front foyer and passed the envelope to the young man standing there.

"Are you no longer required to wear a uniform?" I asked, not sure why I cared. I didn't think this young man was an imposter just waiting to flee with a few pages of my writing hoping to sell them on the black market for a tidy sum.

"I'm a private courier, ma'am. I don't actually work for Canada Post."

"I can't keep up with the modern ways. Clara, once you see this young man out, would you mind bringing me some tea?"

*

Clara set my cup and saucer down on the table beside my chair. "I thought you might nap."

"I don't think I'd sleep even if I were to lay down. My mind is racing, and I'd rather talk while you are here. Perhaps if I gab a while I'll be able to rest later. Do you know where your father's paintings were put when he and Martin moved from their big house?"

"Father has a studio space he still maintains. He doesn't paint there anymore, but I think he has his work stored and some displayed."

"All this thinking about my first novel coming out again is making me think someone should organize an exhibit of your father's early work."

"That sounds wonderful. He does have a young man, an agent, I suppose, who looks after selling for both him and Martin. They each have a name and reputation that sells their work. I will mention it to him when I go to Toronto next week. He will be pleased that you suggested it."

"Who would have thought your father, Cordelia, and I would be still living in our nineties? Poor Charles died so young. To think his fate was sealed simply by travelling in the wrong place at the wrong time. Polio wasn't understood in 1917. But really the die was cast and poor Charlie's fate sealed weeks before he travelled. To pinpoint the blame seems fruitless."

"You're talking in circles. I know Uncle Charles died at age nine from polio, but what do you mean by the blame? He caught a disease. Who could be blamed for that?"

"The family was not scheduled to leave the island until the end of August. Mr. Randolph had planned to travel to Chicago by himself at the end of July, but factors worked to change that. It has always been my belief that if Charlie had not been on the train travelling close to the young boy from Montpelier, Vermont, he might never have contracted polio. And, of course, blame could be given to the young boy's parents, who ignored their city's quarantine and snuck him out in the middle of the night to travel by train to some pressing affair in Chicago. But the parents of Walter Morrison suffered enough with the loss of their own son, and Marion Randolph, even in her grief, could see no value in pursuing legal compensation.

"I am weary now. Any thought of that dear boy fills me with sorrow. There was no point in laying blame, but so many lives were altered during those few short weeks on the island."

Lillianne
1957

I took hold of Leah's hand and walked from the cab to the door of the gallery. It had been a busy day of meetings with my publisher, and for a while I feared I might not get away in time to fetch Leah from the hotel and make it across the city to the Parkside Gallery opening. I hadn't even told Leah on the way where it was we were going. I wanted her to be surprised when she saw her grandfather and Martin.

Leah spotted the name on the banner in the lobby. "That's Granddad's name, Gram. Is he here?

"Yes, Granddad and Martin both. Your granddad's paintings and Martin's sculptures are on exhibit. Your mother and I wanted to surprise you."

"Will he recognize me? I was a little girl the last time he saw me. Can I go in alone and see if he knows me?"

"Of course he'll know you, sweetie. I send him photographs. But go ahead and enter the gallery and I'll hold back out of sight. It might be me he doesn't recognize, though—I am getting so ancient."

"You are not ancient. You are my beautiful Gram."

"Go ahead. Go surprise your granddad. He will be thrilled."

From my hiding spot I quickly scanned the walls laden with artwork of an exhibit entitled Natural Stirrings. One painting in particular caught my eye. The tiger looked so lifelike it seemed you could see its heart beating and fur undulating. The magnificent creature stood, its head turned slightly toward its prey, every blade of grass, each rock, adding to the beauty and wonder.

"Cliff is going to be a famous painter. He will fill the walls of art galleries all over the world with paintings of exotic birds, plants, and animals. He and I will go on African safaris and I will capture wild animals for my zoo and he will paint them."

A tear came to my eye, remembering Charlie's words from so long ago. Cliff's outburst interrupted my thoughts.

"Leah? Martin, it's Leah! Where have you come from, my sweet girl? Let me hug you and make sure you are real."

"Of course I'm real, Granddad. Gram brought me."

I walked toward the lovely sight of Cliff with his arms around Leah, her legs dangling in the air as he twirled her in delight.

"Hello, Lily! Thank you for coming and bringing our precious granddaughter. My night is complete."

Lillianne
1917

Rows of beautiful flowers covered the page, and each one, whether in the foreground or fading into the background, appeared unique. You could almost feel the wind as it moved each stem. I could see several of the orange-headed weeds I called devil's paintbrushes growing in the grass a few feet away from where Cliff was sitting, and he had taken the detail of those few and created the effect of hundreds of them undulating in the wind.

"This is beautiful." I didn't allow my words to convey the emotion the sketch was causing me to feel. Staring at the page, I felt an overwhelming sadness.

"Devil's paintbrushes," he said. "In Latin, *pilosella aurantiaca*, sometimes called fox and cubs, orange or tawny hawksweed, or grim-the-collier."

Cliff picked up the orange pastel and continued to give each blossom its colour.

"The Maxim machine gun was dubbed the devil's paintbrush. The name came from the way the gun could mow down men as if they were shafts of wheat blowing in the wind. How can something so beautiful be compared to an act so barbaric?"

Cliff dropped the pad and put his face in his hands. I moved closer, and heedless of the consequences if anyone were to see us, I put my arms around him and rested my head on his stooped shoulders.

"Cordelia's midnight romp has completely upstaged my

announcement. It is as if Mother thinks it a whim or practical joke. I see no point in pressing the issue, but I have not changed my mind. I will register as soon as we get to Chicago. Mother can go about planning the biggest party of the season, but I will prepare for military deployment. I wonder if she'll even notice."

Mrs. Randolph came into the kitchen later to offer last-minute instructions as to how I was to present the fillets of fish. She had earlier voiced her disappointment in the lack of red meat and the constant diet of fish we'd been forced to endure.

"At least some fresh vegetables and some artful arrangement on this silver tray can make it palatable," Mrs. Randolph grumbled. "I told Mr. Tibbetts in no uncertain terms that I expect him to have a better selection for us when we return. Clifton has paid him generously, and I am beginning to wonder if he is pocketing some of our money and using this ridiculous rationing business for his own profit."

I did not respond.

"I am considering leaving Charles behind when we go to Chicago. At first Clifton said we should bring you along as well, but I hate the idea of the dust and grime accumulating while we are gone. I expect we'll be at least three weeks. I would rather have you here keeping the house in order so we don't have to start from scratch when we return for the last two weeks of our holiday. Clifton has even suggested we simply close up the place for the season and stay in Chicago, but I reminded him how ghastly those last days of August can be in the city. We get so little time here as it is, I can't think of leaving for the season so early. I also reminded him that the Labour Day galas on the neighbouring islands are by far the grandest of the seasonal events. It is imperative we get Cordelia to at least one of them to completely erase the blemish the cotillion left on her reputation."

My first thought as she spoke was the frightening prospect of being alone on this island. Having Charlie for company seemed a good thing. But my thoughts quickly went to the luxury of being here with absolutely no one demanding anything of me. I could enjoy the solitude and push the fear aside. What dangers would I face? Being alone with all the comforts the house offered would be no hardship.

"I am somewhat on the fence with regards to Charles. Perhaps we will give him the choice. You, however, will be paid well to stay and tend to things while we are gone."

"It is up to you, Mrs. Randolph. I will gladly do whatever you require of me."

*

The carefree holiday feeling of our first weeks was gone. I had been invited to no more bonfires or other such activities. I hadn't noticed revelry of any kind. Even Cordelia seemed not to be spending much time on the beach. I heard no further discussion of the travelling plans and simply set about attending to my tasks for several days before the topic was brought up again.

"I want to go with you all," Charlie exclaimed. "I need to be in Chicago to say goodbye to Cliff. If I stay here, I will miss seeing him in his uniform. I want to stand at attention and salute him as he sails away to fight the Hun."

"Don't be ridiculous," Cordelia said. "You can't sail to Europe out of Chicago. He'll take the train to New York."

"He'll be going nowhere," Mrs. Randolph said, her voice clipped and forceful.

"I will not argue with you," Cliff replied. "Charlie, I think you should come with us. I need my little brother, if for nothing else than to shine my boots. I can't go off to war without spit-shined boots."

"We will figure all that out once we get home," Mr. Randolph stated. "Let's just enjoy the week we have left before we travel home for a spell. It will all work out, I am sure."

The next morning, Mr. Tibbetts came into the kitchen carrying a fishing pole. "Mr. Randolph tells me they will all be leaving in a week. He says you're staying behind. I told him I'd check in on you as often as I can. How do you feel about being here all by yourself?"

"I'll be fine. To be honest, I'm rather looking forward to the solitude."

"I got this out of the shed and I'm going to show you how to use it. You can catch walleye or trout this time of the year fishing from the shore. The best plan is to wade out as far as you can and cast out into the deeper water. Or you could walk on the rocks that jut out on the far side of the island and cast from the furthest rock. I am going to show you which lures to use and how to cast. Just in case you run out of provisions, you'll know how to catch yourself a fish. I know a slip of a thing like you won't eat a lot, but the taste of a fresh trout might be a welcome treat."

*

"I saw Mr. Tibbitts teaching you to cast a line earlier," Cliff said as I joined him on the shore during my afternoon break. "I hope you are fine with staying behind, Lily. I'm sure if you voiced any concern, Mother would reconsider."

"I am fine with staying, even though I have never been completely alone in my whole life. I was an only child, but my parents were always nearby. Until, of course, they left by train to visit my grandmother. I had a nanny, though. Afterwards, I was one of many orphan girls, and during those years I certainly was never alone."

"You've not talked of your past before."

"I try not to dwell on it. I would have you know, though, that I was not always a poor orphan. My parents died in the San Francisco earthquake. I don't speak of it. I was taught very quickly that trying to claim my lineage only got me harsh punishment. I am not telling you this for your pity."

Cliff reached out and touched my hair. "You may think I have no scope to understand your suffering, but I know, too, what it is to be forced to hide the truth of your identity. Sounds silly, I'm sure, with a moniker like Clifton Randolph the Fourth. No question as to who I am, I suppose—but, oh, the sad truth of that false identity. I am not who they wish me to be." He paused. "Let's go for a swim. Mother, Father, and Charlie have rowed to visit the next island. Cordelia has barely left her room, she's in such a state. It has been weeks since your first lesson, but I believe you will remember your learning. Run now and get your suit on."

I did as Cliff suggested, and as I hurried to my attic room, I tried to process the excitement and tension of the strong emotions I was feeling.

I was falling in love.

He held a mystery and a sadness I could not pinpoint, but every fibre of my body wanted to help quiet that pain. I sensed a sorrow so similar to my own.

*

Lying on the sand beside Cliff, the hot sun beaming down on our glistening bodies, I felt as if there were no one else in the wide world. I looked up at the clear blue sky, a few snowy white clouds lingering, and allowed myself the fantasy of this moment. I was Lillianne Elizabeth McDonough lying with my beau. I was his equal and his chosen one and our love was sanctioned by our families. I was Frederick and Clara McDonough's lovely daughter and a worthy partner for the Randolphs' oldest son. My future was wide open and filled with vast potential. I was worthy, loved, and valued. I could be exactly who I was born to be.

*

I looked out at the starry sky through my attic window. The afternoon had been like a dream. I told Cliff things I barely knew I still remembered and shared my deepest desires. He had held me in his arms. I had done most of the talking. It seemed once I opened the dam of my deepest emotions, there was no stopping. Even as I spoke I felt selfish not allowing him the same release. He kept encouraging me and did not offer any of his own secrets. There would be time enough for that. We would have our whole lives to get to know each other. He had not said those words exactly, but I was not wrong in the closeness I felt and the feeling that our afternoon together had created. The bond between us was so great it could not be broken. I would wait for him if he was to go to this awful war. We would face any opposition his family gave us and we would be together. I would never again be the beloved daughter of Frederick and Clara McDonough, but I would someday be the beloved wife of Clifton Randolph the Fourth.

*

The morning the Randolphs were to leave was a frenzy of activity. I cooked a substantial meal to prepare them for the late-afternoon sail to Kingston, where they would stay the night before catching the train in the morning. The days before had been a blur. Clifton and I had barely spoken and had not even a moment alone together. I was in the garden when Cliff came through the hedge, carrying a leather case.

"I want you to keep this safe, Lily," he said. "When I am gone, open this case. I have left you something that I hope will make our time apart bearable." He embraced me, then leaned in for a kiss shorter and less passionate than I desired.

Our hurried goodbye was torturous. I set the basket of vegetables on the butcher block and hurried up to my room with Cliff's leather case. I so wanted to take to my attic room and hide until he was gone. Watching him leave without being able to properly send him off, pretending that assisting his leaving was nothing more than a chore like all the others, would take all of the acting ability I had perfected in the years I played the role of orphan and domestic servant with no value or identity of my own, never letting any of the pain surface.

When the family left, I finally ran up the back stairs, grabbed the case from its hiding place, and sat down on my bed, where I could see Mr. Tibbetts's boat disappearing from sight. I opened the case. A sketchpad sat on top, and folding back the spiral cover I saw a drawing of a beautiful ornate table set in a room with bay windows, a crystal vase filled with white lilies sitting on the gleaming wood. The veins on each white petal were a deep rose. On the table beside the vase, Cliff had drawn what looked like a leather-bound volume with my name etched in gold on the spine. Under the sketchpad I found a bundle of papers, several empty notepads, his charcoal, and pastels. I flipped through the stack of drawings. Gripping the stub of the orange pastel, I stared at the drawing I had watched Cliff sketching days before as tears streamed down my cheeks.

Lillianne
1993

"I have never shown you the sketch your father gave me when his family left for Chicago that July. I never framed it or displayed it in any way. It was so touching and personal that I always felt the need to keep it hidden. That seems so silly now."

"What was it? A nude of you?"

"No, I've never seen your father sketch the human body—and if he did, it would probably be male."

"You didn't know that then, though, did you? I've never asked you, but how long were you married before you knew Dad was a homosexual?"

"I'll go get the sketch from my room."

"I can go."

"No, I will. I may have other things hidden, you know."

"You? The woman who so freely writes and reveals every detail of our lives, even though some might think you artfully camouflage them?"

"Oh, you poor dear, having a writer for a mother. You have no idea the deep secrets my writing and my life have concealed."

When I returned to my study, I passed the sketch to Clara. It had faded some, the paper brittle and aged, but the drawing was still obviously a near replica of the room we were sitting in.

Clara was stunned. "How did Father draw such a likeness to this room when he had never been here?"

"That was the magic of it. Cliff had taken his pastels and fashioned this drawing just from the details I had shared with him. For the first time in my life, I had shown someone who I was and where I had come from, and they had completely absorbed it. I took that sketch as a deep, clear sign that Clifton Randolph completely saw me and loved me in a way I had been craving since the day my parents left this home. That connection fuelled my belief that my life was changing because of Clifton Randolph. With that ember of first love, I began the six weeks of solitude that only served to cement the fairy-tale love story I had conjured up in my head."

"You were alone for six weeks?"

"If I am to tell you the story of those weeks, I'll need to sit these old bones on a more comfortable seat. Perhaps I'll go to the living room and get myself settled in my armchair. And tea and a biscuit would be nice."

After we were settled, I began. "The first two days went quickly. I rose each morning about the same time as I normally would. I did my grooming in the water closet and enjoyed the luxury. I started the fire in the cook stove and filled the water tank in anticipation of filling a hot bath for myself, not for the pleasure of another. I cooked each meal and put two settings of the finest china at the mahogany dining table, letting myself imagine Cliff dining at the other end. I cut fresh flowers and filled vases in every downstairs room.

"I swept and dusted. I beat the carpets and conducted myself somewhat as I would have if I had been under the watchful eye of your grandmother, but with every task I allowed myself some flight of fancy. I danced through the main hall with the broom in my embrace as if it were my wedding waltz with the handsome Clifton Randolph.

"I knelt in the row of carrots, thinning the green tendrils of growth, wishing that Cliff would emerge from behind the hedge. I took to singing and speaking aloud to myself and at times to the imaginary Cliff I conjured up. Being completely alone on this island at first seemed oppressive, but as those first two days elapsed, I felt a joy I could barely contain. Nothing I did or said, no look or action on my part, was being judged or dictated in any way, and it was a freedom I didn't even know was possible.

"On the evening of the second day I lit the wicks in every lantern downstairs, going from room to room, enjoying the soft light. I sat in every corner of each room, allowing myself to feel as if it were a room in my home, not one I was employed to clean. I imagined being the mother in this home, having my children run to me and sit upon my lap, seeking the love I had been seeking since I was six. On that day, on that island all alone, I realized that I was prepared to take the next part of the journey, and the next part would be of my own making. I would join with Cliff and together we would create the life we wanted, not one that others and circumstances dictated.

"The morning of the third day I washed, dressed, and taking an empty notepad from Cliff's case, made my way to the shore. I found in my solitude a voice and determination I did not know I possessed. I was happy about the love I felt for Cliff and the dreams I had for our future, but beyond that I was thrilled with the love I felt for myself, a love my dear mother and father had made strong within me. In the stillness of that morning air, I put pen to paper. In that pad I began writing a story that had been bursting within me for as long as I could remember. I began to pen *Beyond Wind and Whitecaps*, believing the writing itself was the greatest witness to the beating of my heart."

Lillianne
1993

I stood and walked across the hall to my study. From a drawer in the desk I pulled out a tattered notebook. The ink was faded, the cursive old-fashioned and perhaps unreadable, but I knew every word as if I had written it yesterday. I returned to the living room and passed it to Clara.

August 8, 1917

One week has gone by, and as much as I am revelling in the freedom of being alone, there have been times I find myself craving the sound of another's voice, even Mrs. Randolph's demanding tone or Cordelia's condescension. I certainly would love Cliff or Charlie to be with me and would take pleasure in their company. But I do not miss the numerous chores that Mrs. Randolph would have for me, and I am enjoying the hours I am able to sit, filling pages of this notebook. I've also begun working on a story in another notebook.

The garden is growing wonderfully, and I have been picking fresh vegetables for my small meals. I could not possibly use all the produce I pick daily. I have used mason jars to preserve some of the pickings, as wastefulness was certainly not something impressed upon me by the Sisters of Providence.

Last night I took the liberty, after I extinguished each flame downstairs, of carrying the lantern upstairs to the second floor to the room and the bed where Cliff last slept. I took my night's rest under the cover of a red-and-white nine-patch quilt on that bed, feeling the connection to Cliff I am so badly missing. Two more weeks, I assured myself. Two more weeks and he will return. I will leave this island and begin a life that will tie me to Clifton Randolph the Fourth and I will never again be completely alone.

August 15, 1917

Another week has gone by. I have diligently kept every room in this spacious house clean. I have even swept the attic every day, even though I have not slept there since the night I lay my head on Cliff's pillow. I have the sketch he left me propped up on the parlour table and look at it several times a day as I go about my duties. I have been writing daily and have about twenty pages of my story written.

It is my hope that by the time I fill that notebook I will have relocated and possibly even be Mrs. Clifton Randolph the Fourth. My anticipation is high, as is my nervousness about what will come to pass in a few days when the Randolphs return. I sincerely hope that the arrangements include our immediate departure from the island, as I am sure his mother and sister will be very hostile toward me. His father no doubt will disapprove as well but may approach it more kindly. I will have my things packed in case Cliff and I leave on the same boat that brings them back this week.

I was frying the last of the salt pork at noon when it dawned on me: I have not seen Mr. Tibbetts since the day the Randolphs left. It has been raining hard for the last two days, so that is probably the reason he has not come to the island. Something must have come up to keep him away.

August 19, 1917

This morning I pulled a sizeable trout from the water. It was not giving up without a fight and it took all my strength to reel it in. I have had a few bites before, but this was my first time catching a fish. Cutting the head off and gutting it was not pleasant, but the thought of frying it in a pan of butter and serving it with new potatoes, carrots, and greens was enough to put my squeamishness aside. After four more days looking to the shore and beyond, there has been no visit from Mr. Tibbetts, and several meals with no meat or eggs led me to the shore this morning.

I did an overall inventory of the larder last night, calculating to the expected day of the Randolphs' return. I must sparingly use the flour, sugar, and butter. I hope the Randolphs will have the presence of mind to bring supplies back with them. At least there is a good supply of fresh vegetables available. And now I know that catching a fish is possible.

August 22, 1917

Yesterday started out calm. The sky was cloudy and it felt like it might rain, but I spent the morning in the garden hoeing the corn rows and picking peas and beans. Thinking today might be the day of the Randolphs' return, I worked diligently without letting my anxiety get the best of me. After lunch I took the lounge chair and story notebook to the shore, but very soon the wind picked up and made sitting there difficult. The waves crashed into shore and the swells created frothy whitecaps. I stood at the water's edge and looked across the wide expanse, hoping that if the Randolphs were sailing today, they were close by and within minutes of arriving.

After two hours preparing the house for the worsening storm, I watched the sky darken from the front veranda, quite sure that there would be no boat take anchor at Randolph Island on this day.

Last night was long and very frightening. I did not light any lanterns but went upstairs when the black sky brought an early close to the day. The wind howled and I wrapped myself in the red-and-white quilt, listening to and feeling the bones of the house fighting against the gale to keep standing. The windowpanes vibrated and every creak and moan seemed like it could be its last, like the very ceiling could come down at any moment. I must have finally fallen asleep, because I realized I had survived the terrifying night when the sun's rays streamed through the window and woke me.

I am so grateful that the Randolphs were not travelling on the water yesterday. I cannot imagine the horror of finding oneself on a ship in such a gale. I am disappointed that Cliff has not returned yet, but am hoping that today is the day he will come back to me. I have packed my bag in anticipation.

August 29, 1917

I have been alone for four weeks. I cannot imagine what has kept the Randolphs from returning. Mr. Tibbetts has not come either, though he probably thinks that the Randolphs have been back for a week. But he must wonder why they did not engage him to sail them back to the island. He must be ill or something for him not to stop by to check on me or resume his work for the Randolphs. Cliff must have been held up, or perhaps he was sent overseas as soon as he signed up. But even if he has gone, surely the rest are anxious to get back to the island.

I have enough whale oil for about another week and should probably use it sparingly. As each day goes by I find myself wondering what I'll do if they don't come back. I know that is ridiculous. I thought briefly yesterday that maybe I had been wrong about Cliff's feelings for me. Maybe he led me on for his own entertainment and had no intention of returning and taking me with him. I spoke sharply to myself and tried to put that idea out of my mind.

No one else on earth but the Randolphs and Mr. Tibbetts even knows that I am on this island. Rosemary probably concluded that I left with Mrs. Randolph when I didn't return to the Prince George, and she would have no reason to question my whereabouts now.

I will continue keeping house, tending to the garden, writing and carefully watching the provisions available to me. Any day now the family will return and the worry of being stranded here alone and all my doubts will fade from my memory.

September 12, 1917

My heart is broken and my spirit nearly broken as well. They have been gone forty-three days. I have tried to convince myself that all is well, but Cordelia has her recital in Chicago tomorrow and Charlie will have returned to school. The Labour Day festivities are over, and most of the residents on the neighbouring islands have likely left. Something terrible must have happened to delay their return, as coming back to the island now would be pointless. But surely they would not heartlessly leave me stranded.

I can feel a change in the air, especially in the early morning. The days are getting shorter and even the water looks different than it did in midsummer. It seems a deeper blue and is rarely without the white-caps the rippling waves create. I have been thinking for the last day or so that I will need to leave this island before the weather gets much colder, and of course the only way of leaving is by water. It is not that I think I could get in the water and swim to another island, but at least now I can swim a bit so I would not be as terrified to get in the rowboat and row to the closest island.

Thankfully I have the garden and have been enjoying its bounty. I have been eating my fill of corn on the cob and all the other vegetables. I have caught several fish since I landed the first trout. There are blueberries near the shore on the far side of the island. I have picked the bushes quite clean and enjoy their sweet taste. The sugar is gone and only about a cup of flour remains. The butter has been gone for two weeks, but I still have lard.

After filling my basket with the vegetables I will cook for my noon and evening meal, I change into the bathing suit Cordelia gave me and make my way to the shore. Each time I stand here on the sand I search the expanse of water, hoping to see an approaching vessel. I have stood in this same spot so many times in the last weeks, sometimes letting the heartbreak I feel pour down my cheeks. I can sometimes hear Cliff's voice calling to me from across the waves. He calls my name but offers no explanations.

I wade into the water, watching it rise past my waist. I drop myself in. I sputter as I go under and quickly stand back up. I go to shallower water so that when I drop I can put my hands on the bottom and pull myself along, kicking my feet a bit. I do that back and forth, eventually letting my face go under and raising my arms, moving them a bit. I am so much more confident than when I first began and am even able to keep myself afloat for short times. In the deeper water, I also find I can stay upright, lifting my feet and moving in such a way that I am buoyant for a few seconds. I will keep practising this, hoping that each day will give me a bit more courage.

It will certainly take courage to leave this island alone. Staying here much longer would be foolish. As the cold weather sets in, it will be riskier to travel the waters in the small rowboat. If I were to find myself stranded by bitter autumn weather or an early onset of winter, I am not even sure the wood in the woodshed would last. The whale oil is gone and I light candles at night but often go to bed before I need them. Even the matches I have will need to be carefully guarded, for if I were to find myself without fire, my meal choices would be quite different, and I do enjoy the warmth of the cook stove on these cool mornings. I have resorted to cooking on the cook stove in the summer kitchen, since I have long been out of gas. I have salt but do not know how to prepare fish to preserve it.

It is hard to think about the Randolphs not return-ing, but I must prepare myself for leaving if they do not come back soon. I will watch the weather and choose a fine day within the next week and take the rowboat to the nearest island, the one I can see from the jutting rocks on the other side. I pray that there are people in the building I can see. I hope the residents are still there and that I can arrange to leave with them when they depart for Kingston or Gananoque. And I hope when arriving in either of those ports I can find out something about the whereabouts of Cliff and his family.

Perhaps I am worrying and planning this all for nothing, and they will arrive soon with a valid reason for having been away so long. I hope to find myself feeling quite silly to have built their delay up in my mind to be such a disaster.

September 14, 1917

I have found myself unable to concentrate on my writing but will attempt a short diary entry, possibly my last. In the last two days, I have spent most of my free time swimming. I am actually able to call it swimming now, as I can advance from the shallow to deeper water and back without standing. I have also taken the rowboat out and rowed back and forth close to shore, moving the oars in a way that moves me along. I am leery about heading into the deep, rougher water but will attempt that after a bit more practice.

When I leave I must take anything that I would not consider leaving behind, because if I find people on that island and they tell me they are leaving immediately, I will not have time to row back to get any possessions. I will dress in a couple of layers so that I will have two changes of clothes when I get to the mainland. I will, of course, pack Cliff's leather case with his sketches, my notebooks, and my treasured photograph of my parents. I will wrap the case in the slicker that hangs in the back porch and bind it securely with twine in case the rowboat capsizes or is swamped by high waves. I will take a basket of produce to offer to the people. Much more than that is not required, and I will not overload the rowboat.

I will close the house up as best I can, but surely the Randolphs do not expect me to fasten storm windows, drain the cistern, or store all the seasonal furniture. Perhaps they have arranged for Mr. Tibbetts to come later to do that work. I can't imagine that they have just totally disregarded my situation here.

I had nodded off, and Clara's words jolted me awake.

"What was it that delayed them?"

"Oh, many things happened in the weeks they were in Chicago. Poor Charlie had been stricken with polio, although, when they returned, your grandmother was refusing to believe his poor health was due to that dreaded disease. She had left Charlie behind in Chicago to convalesce, but it wasn't until months later, when he became gravely ill, that she accepted the diagnosis. She blamed herself after his death, believing if she'd stayed in Chicago and gotten him the proper treatment, he would have survived. I don't know the truth of that but can only imagine her guilt for having been so preoccupied with Clifton and Cordelia that she'd downplayed Charlie's condition."

"So Granddad, Grandma, Aunt Cordelia, and Dad came back to the island and left Charlie in Chicago?"

"Yes, that's right. No mention was made of Cordelia's cello recital or Clifton's plan to enlist, but it didn't take long before I realized Marion Randolph's attention was totally directed toward her two older children. The hardest lesson in Charlie's death for your grandmother was probably the realization she could not manage and be in complete control of things. She certainly hadn't realized that during the days spent on the island right after the family returned."

"And what about Mr. Tibbetts? Why had he not checked in on you?"

"Poor Bert met a violent end. I was heartbroken when I heard what took place just days after the Randolphs left. Times were very hard, he had a large family, and rum running was a lucrative business—but it was also nasty and dangerous, with uncertain waters, arrests, and the bitter conflict between American and Canadian rum runners. Bert and his crew got themselves tangled up with the US Coast Guard, then found themselves in a bar in Alexandria. Wrong place at the wrong time. A bar fight started and Bert took the worst of it. Terrible end for such a gentle, kind man. The Randolphs helped his widow out for many years. And we always hired his son Tom until we lost the island."

Marion
1917

I spent the last week in a terrible state. Since returning to Chicago, all my attention went to planning the banquet. I quickly employed Wilkins Printing to produce some lovely embossed invitations. I had them hand-delivered and was so pleased when the replies came in steadily. I was thrilled with the response, as Chicago is next to empty during holiday time. August is a ghastly month, so I guess a social event is welcomed by those who have to be in town.

I was in the kitchen putting the finishing touches on the banquet-menu planning when Cliff burst into the room waving that wretched piece of paper. I nearly fainted when he passed it to me.

"Look at this, Mother. I have officially been recruited into the United States Army. Clifton Oliver Randolph the Fourth is now an enlisted officer. You should be pleased at least that our last name got me a higher rank than private."

Mrs. Roberts, sensing my distress, led me to a chair and put a cold cloth on my forehead.

"I report on the day of your big shindig, so I'll not be in attendance. I will instead be in uniform and en route to my basic training posting."

Clifton had been alarmed with the news as well but surprised me with his response.

"He is a grown man, Marion. I know you thought you could prevent this, but some things are out of your control. Other families must make the sacrifice, so why should ours be exempt? And I know you don't see it, but maybe military service is what he needs. If it makes you feel any better, maybe he won't pass his basic training, or maybe he won't be sent overseas. He is, after all, not the most masculine man."

I hadn't slept a wink all night and now found myself wrestling with the plan I'd come up with in the early morning hours. I was not going to discuss it with Clifton, knowing he would be dead set against anything I might do to interfere with Cliff's recruitment. But as unpleasant as it would be, I couldn't just let the day go idly by knowing that at four o'clock, while flower arrangements were being set out in the grand dining hall, my beloved son would be reporting at the Queen Street recruiting office, being fit for a uniform and a future that could see him shot down on a battlefield in Europe.

What mother could allow that to happen when she had in her possession documents that would extinguish all possibility of military service for her only son? I quickly went to the front foyer, looking through the sidelight to see the door just closing on the car that daily delivered Clifton to his office. I would wait for the driver to return and have him drive me to the Queen Street recruitment office.

I rushed upstairs and opened the small wall safe. The documents from the Rochester Psychiatric Hospital held a detailed and lengthy diagnosis that, when presented to the recruiting office, would unquestionably make Clifton Oliver Randolph ineligible for military service. And surely a sizable donation would ensure the discretion of the authorities.

Lillianne
1917

Midafternoon on September 14, I spotted the boat. I left the house and went to the front veranda to see if the vessel I'd noticed from an upstairs window was getting closer. I felt a rush of excitement but also a degree of panic, thinking that if the boat passed by, it would force my decision to row away from the island. I waited until I was sure it was approaching before running down to the shore.

I realized as I got to the shore how happy I would be to see another human being, even if the passengers were not the Randolphs. I did not consider myself in danger, and if it were strangers on board, I would explain my situation and ask for transportation back to the mainland. Whatever that would involve would be a great improvement from my current isolation and helplessness.

Cordelia's voice came across the waves to greet me.

"Hello, Lillianne."

I then heard Mr. Randolph's directions to the boat's captain, warning of the shallow and rocky waters ahead. I saw the boat put down anchor and watched as the family got in the rowboat and began to paddle to shore. I was overcome with excitement to see Clifton and waded out a bit to get a better look.

Clifton sat stooped on the seat directly behind his father. I was shocked by his appearance. He was thinner and paler than when he'd left. When he reached the shore, he lifted his head and his face was vacant and expressionless. What had happened to extinguish the life from the young man I'd fallen in love with?

The next few minutes were a frenzy of disembarking, helping the crew unload the luggage and supplies, and getting the family situated. Mrs. Randolph's commands were reminiscent of our May arrival, even though I had diligently kept the house clean and orderly. I had already begun preparation for the evening meal but would, of course, have to increase the amount of food.

As I rushed to the garden to pick additional vegetables, I hoped Cliff would come find me so we could reunite in private. He had not so much as given me a nod, and I had heard him say nothing as the business of getting settled was conducted.

It was Cordelia instead who found me in the garden.

"How have you been, Lily? Nobody but me seemed to worry about you when we stayed away longer than planned. I was anxious to see you. Things are in a turmoil. I was desperate to get back here and at least get away from some of the mess. If only for one more swim, which may be difficult, as Mother seems to be making it her mission to suffocate Clifton and me. She's been a shrew. Father is very upset with her. It's just a mess all round."

I paused before replying. Cordelia's words had come fast and furious but had not given me any concrete details as to what the mess had been or what had kept them away so long.

"I was relieved to see you arrive. The first while was enjoyable and I had enough supplies and provisions. But I was running out of everything and was beginning to worry. I've not even seen Mr. Tibbetts in your absence."

"I suppose you've not heard. He's been murdered."

"What?"

"A bar fight, we were told. Father inquired about him when we got to Kingston for our charter. It was not easy to find out much, but Father was told of his death. Word is, he was rum running. A treacherous trade."

The tears streaming down my cheeks were for Mr. Tibbetts and for his wife and family, but as I stood there crying I realized just how worried and afraid I'd been. I was relieved the Randolphs had returned, but the tension Cordelia was describing and the terrible news of Mr. Tibbetts's violent death were hitting me, and I was unsure I could collect my composure. I wanted to sit down and sob and give in to my sense of hopelessness that had been building and now seemed to have overtaken me. I did not, quickly finishing my task instead. Cordelia retreated to her role as well and left the clearing without acknowledging my weakness or offering to help.

*

As I finished serving the second supper course, I took careful notice of Clifton. I had removed a full bowl of soup from his place and noticed he hadn't yet lifted a fork to the plate of food I'd put in front of him.

"You must eat, Clifton," Mrs. Randolph pleaded. "Lillianne has prepared this lovely meal. If for no other reason, show her the courtesy of eating a bit of it."

I lingered, waiting for Cliff's reaction to his mother's words, hoping to see a glimpse of our former intimacy. He did not raise his head.

"He will eat sooner or later, Marion," Mr. Randolph said in a clipped tone I'd never heard from him. "He won't starve himself to death."

When I took Cliff's plate away, nothing had been touched. I was not confident even the dessert I was bringing would tempt him. The remainder of the meal was silent, and the tension mounted. Cliff did not raise his hand to his mouth or raise his eyes from the downcast position. It was as if as he was a mannequin placed in the sitting position at someone else's bidding.

I touched Cliff's shoulder and leaned toward him with the coffee carafe.

"Would you like some coffee, sir?" I asked.

"Leave Clifton alone, Lillianne. This is a family matter and not your concern. You have done enough." Mrs. Randolph's last words hung in the air before she added, "Take your break before cleaning up."

"Marion, don't snap at Lillianne. Surely even you cannot find a way to blame her for this."

Mr. Randolph got up abruptly and left the room.

*

I sat down on the big rock, trying hard to choke back my tears. Had the *mess* been Cliff's announcement that he had fallen in love with me? Had Marion Randolph made such a fuss that she'd put Cliff into a catatonic state? Why had she dragged him back to this island to watch him wallow in such misery if it was her judgement of our union that so deeply wounded him? Was it simply to further enforce her complete control of him and his choices?

The sun had just about set when Cordelia joined me on the shore. I welcomed her company.

"I have never seen Father so short with Mother. He is usually quite tolerant of her, but even though he did not intervene in any way, he is angrier with her than I've seen, even with her past meddlings."

I wanted to simply ask if the whole mess was caused by Cliff's declaration of love for me. But even as I tried to form the words, I doubted such upheaval could be caused by that. I did not believe Cliff would react to his mother's disapproval so profoundly. I kept silent, hoping Cordelia would keep talking and tell me more.

"Cliff is in a bad way. Worse than the last time. His rum-fuelled bravado that caused such a devastating scene at Mother's banquet fizzled by morning, and as days went by, every spark of Cliff's fury faded, leaving him this sad and sorry shell."

"Your Mother's banquet?"

"Oh, yes. As soon as we got back to Chicago, Mother set about organizing a huge banquet. She even rescheduled my recital, planning it for the evening of the banquet. The recital gave her the excuse for such excess. She didn't want anyone to see it as a desperate attempt to select a suitable prospect for me to heal my damaged reputation. She carefully selected the most influential of families to invite, covering all the bases: lucrative business contacts for Father, families with suitable young ladies for Cliff, and marriage prospects for me. This was no small feat, as many of Chicago's elite were still summering out of the city, but Mother pulled it off. By the day of the event, nearly one hundred of Chicago's finest had RSVP'd their acceptance. After the firestorm, Mother was wishing fewer people had attended."

I was burning to ask what Cliff's rum-fuelled outburst had been about, but part of me was reluctant to hear that it had had nothing to do with me. A man furious about his family's disapproval of the woman he'd fallen in love with would be unlikely to ignore that woman once back in her presence. But what had Mrs. Randolph meant when she said I'd done enough?

"The whole mess about Cliff's enlistment certainly took the attention off of me. Mother barely came out of her room for a full week, then announced we were all going back to Randolph Island, even saying at one point we might stay for the winter. Father quickly put that idea to rest. But, nevertheless, here we all are, with enough provisions to last until Thanksgiving at least. I guess the length of our stay will depend on how quickly Mother gets over her humiliation."

"Did Charlie stay behind because of school?"

"Charles is poorly. He took a fever about a week after we got home and did not improve during our stay. Mother hired a nurse to care for him while we're gone. That is another contentious issue. Father thinks a mother should not leave her sick child. But Mother is too concerned with her own embarrassment right now. And keeping her thumb firmly on Cliff."

Lillianne
1993

"Clara, you asked me when I first knew your father was a homosexual. In 1917, I would not even have known that word or understood its meaning. I just knew that your father held a deep and debilitating sorrow. When he returned to the island in September, he was broken, and a part of me knew the affection he'd shown me on the shore that moonlit night was not what I'd thought. He had been kind and caring, but the connection I had taken as love had been in my imagination. I was a long time coming to the truth of that. I was told that truth finally in the very place the lie had been fabricated."

"Did Father ever really lie about who he was?"

"No. I mean the story I told myself about our love and our future together. I was not the only one who manufactured that fantasy, but I was probably the one most desperate to believe it."

"Mother, you are talking in circles again. And you seem so troubled when you talk about those years. It is all water under the bridge. Maybe you should just let the past go."

"I wish that were possible. If I could, I would sink into the comfort of senility and let my guilt and anguish go, but apparently I am not being given that luxury. Your poor grandmother was allowed that escape. By the time your grandfather died and your father and Martin moved into the Chicago house, Marion Randolph didn't know her own name. She signed 'Maisie Kingston' until the day she died. I would like to tell you more about the summer we returned to the island with you. It was possibly the happiest time of my life, and certainly a time when your father finally felt some peace.

"We returned to Randolph Island the summer just after you'd turned two. Your father played with you from the time we left Kingston Harbour until we anchored off the island, keeping your seasickness at bay and keeping you both distracted. I was in quite a state. I was filled with such emotion as I sailed closer to the grand house we had left two summers before. I envisioned the closed-up rooms of the house left empty for more than a year and thought of the work involved to clean them and prepare them for the season. Marion had sent Mavis and Betsy along with us for the summer, and I knew they would attend to those tasks when we arrived. I didn't think I would be as demanding as the previous mistress of the house. I was anxious to transform the island into a restful summer getaway, encouraging Cliff to bask in the beauty and peaceful qualities he'd always enjoyed there. We would claim the gifts this place had to offer and move on from mourning Charlie and the difficult days that had passed. The absence of our dear, sweet Charlie would be the sorrow most difficult to overcome, but our pleasurable days here would be the best tribute we could give him, knowing he had loved the island so deeply and with such joy.

"I was grateful that we were having our summer on the island alone. Your grandparents were staying in Chicago, and Cordelia had already moved to Saint John to take her nurse's training.

"I brought seeds with me and planted a garden right away. The Rival tiller was in the shed, and as I pushed it through the fallow earth I wept for Bert Tibbetts, remembering his kindness. His oldest son was our handyman that year, and the resemblance to his father was unnerving. More than once

I caught myself thinking it was Bert coming to shore when I looked down from the house.

"The weather was splendid in our first few weeks. The house welcomed us and seemed to quickly transform itself into the sanctuary I had envisioned. Cliff spent many of his daylight hours sketching the wide variety of natural life the island offered. You played nearby, never letting your beloved father from your sight.

"Your father relished the small joys of being on the island. He built a fire on the beach every night, he took the rowboat out often, swam regularly, and had a good appetite for the delicious meals Mavis prepared for us. He helped me in the garden and instructed Tom Tibbetts in the groundskeeping. He took great pleasure in the season's beauty.

"He freely and generously showered you with affection, but even as we slept side by side in the room that had been his parents', nothing more than a kiss on the cheek transpired between us. He was kind and caring toward me but did not show any physical affection. I blamed his lack of interest in sex on his grief. I adjusted my expectations, telling myself to just be grateful for the closeness we had and his devotion to you.

"At the beginning of August, after three days of steady rain, the sun came out and Cliff and I headed to the beach. You were napping. Tom and Betsy had left in the morning, sailing into Kingston to purchase supplies. Mavis would never leave the house while you were sleeping, so being on the beach with Cliff felt private.

"Cliff looked very handsome in his one-piece swimsuit. His body had already become firmer and more muscular than it had been in May, and the sun had bronzed his pale skin. I waded out in the deeper water to where he was swimming.

"'*You've come a long way from the skittish girl who wouldn't even put a toe in the water,*' he cajoled.

"I fell into the water and let my body float back up to the surface. I moved my arms and legs, gliding closer to Cliff. Standing beside where he stood, the water reached just below my breasts. I felt a twinge of desire and I reached out to embrace my husband. My touch seemed to startle him, and I saw the expression on his face instantly change. Something about his demeanour shook me to the core.

"Cliff took my hand, and without saying a word led me toward the shallow water. Tears were streaming down his face and I silently followed.

"We continued walking along the shore until we were out of sight of the house. Cliff sat me down on a large rock and began a deluge of words he seemed unable to contain. I remember his exact words.

"'*I cannot keep what I dread to say any longer. Each day that passes without speaking a truth I have buried so deep within seems like a day closer to my destruction. I mean you no harm, but must speak this truth to save myself.*'

"I briefly considered standing and shutting this discussion down abruptly with the excuse of returning to the house to see if you were awake. Part of me felt a strong compulsion to avoid the next part of his explanation and to convince myself that his words were coming from a state of confusion or perhaps severe sunstroke. I did not move, however, and he continued.

"'*My story begins months before I met you, years before, perhaps, but I will start three weeks before the day we met each other on the dock in Kingston. Mother had come on the train to Kingston and I had accompanied her part of the way. I had been deposited in an asylum in New York City, where I spent three weeks being treated. It is what I was being treated for that I must finally divulge to you. Please bear with me. This is very difficult. I have spent so much time concealing it from myself, it is no wonder it is nearly impossible to tell you, but I can deceive you no longer.*

"'In the fall of 1916, after much pleading, Mother and Father finally allowed me to enrol in the Art Institute in Springfield. They had tolerated my obsession with drawing and my interest in nature. They did not believe sketching birds and flowers could ever be considered a vocation, but they felt if they indulged me I would come to that realization on my own. They agreed to allow me one year at the Art Institute, and then I was to transfer to Princeton. I took the opportunity and decided I would fight the battle to stay longer after I completed the year. I took lodging in the residence there and completely immersed myself in the life it afforded. I was euphoric and devoured the freedom and satisfaction of my new surroundings and my artwork. It opened up a whole new world for me.'

"I could see Mavis in the distance as she came across the beach with you in her arms. I rose and called out to her to please take you back to the house and that I would be up shortly. I tried to steady my voice as I shouted to her, not wanting to alarm her in any way. I felt that if I approached her, I would give in to the emotion I was feeling. I somehow knew your father's next words would be monumental.

"'In that place I found something out about myself that I had always suppressed. It is something I did not even know had a name or was real. To this day, I struggle with the thought of whether it is real or if it is that I am just damaged. Damaged and demonic, as the doctor who provided my treatment told me daily, delivering the jolts of electricity designed to cure me. That fall, I found a part of me that had lain dormant. In my drawing and in my relationships with other artists, I found myself. I met a man named Edmund, and in my relationship with Edmund I found my passion.'

"Your father's words hit me as if he had doubled up his fist and laid the blow. I gasped and looked away. Had I known this all along?

"*I loved Edmund, and our months together brought me more joy than I'd ever imagined I could have. It was a Saturday afternoon, and we had spent a lazy morning together. I was sketching him and we were oblivious to the sounds around us. The door opened and Mother entered the room with neither of us hearing her. She stood before our nakedness and my world came crashing down. The solution to my illness, as Mother called it, was admittance to an asylum for immediate treatment that would remove such urges and fix me.*'

"I did my best at that point to offer comfort to your father. He was trembling violently and I thought he would make himself ill. I had no idea where we would go from the honesty of his confession, but I had no desire to punish him. I gently kissed his cheek and walked away."

Marion
1918

I walked by Charles's room and saw his door had been left open. Clifton refused to allow me to instruct Peggy to pack up his possessions and give the room a thorough cleaning. But he was right that we didn't need the bedroom, and apparently he found some comfort in sitting amongst his dead son's books and toys.

I instructed Peggy to prepare the bedrooms on the third floor for Cliff and Lillianne to move into, and the adjoining bedroom for baby Clara. My attention to the decorating of the nursery and purchasing of the layette served to take my attention from the dark despair of sorrow. Clifton angered at any diversion I employed.

I also became interested in our business dealings, as my husband completely retreated from his responsibilities. I attempted to be patient with this but could not see how failing financially would lessen our grief in any way.

One of our major holdings was a company called Michigan Linen Supply. All the linens provided to the many hospitals in the city came from this company, and the revenue was substantial. We had several companies in the garment industry. We owned Cook County Lumber Company and several contracting businesses. We had shares in three of Chicago's best hotels and we owned a uniform company. We also had holdings in several wholesale food companies.

With our fingers in many of the economic pies of Chicago, we were affected by the hotbed of social and economic unrest. The war and the Spanish flu epidemic had shifted our foundations, and I feared any inattention to our interests could bring our fortunes crashing down. I was not willing to take that risk.

My first order of business was to conduct a proper assessment of our real-estate holdings. We couldn't afford to allow these buildings to deteriorate due to the squalor of poverty and illness. We had to balance rent increases and upkeep to keep those properties viable. My meeting that morning was with George Whitehouse, the manager of our Maxwell Street holdings. I expected resistance, but Mr. Whitehouse would soon see that dealing with Marion Randolph was much different from dealing with my husband, especially with the melancholy of his current state.

I sat across the desk from George Whitehouse after brief courtesies and refusing the offered tea and biscuits.

"I am not here on a social visit, Mr. Whitehouse. My husband is not well, and it has fallen to me to attend to some pressing matters, so I will get right to it. I want money directed to repairs and renovations of the properties we own on Maxwell Street. I intend to have some modern fixtures installed, the aging windows replaced, as well as painting and other upgrades done. I will be approaching the residents to inquire what the most immediate needs are."

"Mrs. Randolph, we have a rentals man who looks after all the maintenance on those properties, and you do not need to trouble yourself with such details. If you are interested in making a social impact, you could do so through the good works of the Daughters of the American Revolution, the Women's Temperance Union, or the newly formed Delta Sigma sorority group at the University of Chicago. They are making packages to send to our fighting men in Europe."

"Do not insult me with your advice, Mr. Whitehouse. I have been a member in good standing of every woman's group of any influence in this city since you suckled at your mother's breast. Please keep in mind that I am your employer, and any further condescension will result in your immediate dismissal. During my husband's absence, I will be making all the business decisions, and I would advise you to take them very seriously."

"My apologies, Mrs. Randolph. I must, however, advise against you going to the Maxwell Street holdings. The rentals man can inform you on their condition. It would be unwise to visit that area, and it is unlikely you would be welcome. The lower class is prone to anger and blame when much of their condition has been brought about by their own slovenly behaviour and lack of ambition. Many of the residents are not even American and some barely speak English."

"I will take my chances, Mr. Whitehouse. Make the arrangements for the rentals man to accompany me to Maxwell Street this afternoon and I will assess the situation firsthand. I will meet with you again tomorrow and instruct you further on the renovations to be made on the Maxwell Street properties. Have I made myself clear?"

Mavis
1920

To say I'd reached my lowest point the day I opened the door to Marion Randolph might seem a bit dramatic, but both my physical and mental state were dire. The state of my flat was deplorable as well, and I almost didn't answer the loud rapping on the door. I'd had the flat fumigated, as was the practice after any deaths from influenza, and I hadn't even bothered to rehang the curtains or put anything back in place. What once had been an apartment I took pride in, and a home I'd faithfully kept for my husband and daughter, was now an empty shell of peeling paint and clutter. I was indifferent to its squalor and my own unkempt appearance.

But open the door I did, and in a matter of seconds, two friends fell into each other's arms. We quickly shared the stories of our losses and pain. We wept, and after unloading our deepest pain, we talked and laughed as if we were again the two young girls of years ago. And before Marion left, arrangements had been made for me to return to the Randolph mansion and take up employment as her granddaughter's nanny.

I fully embraced life under their roof, and my love for sweet Clara is nearly as strong as the love I held for my own precious Catherine. I have put the memory of the love I shared with Delbert in a place I keep locked in my heart and feel blessed to have had the years I had as his wife. To watch Clara leave and not go with her was more than I could face, so I made the decision to accompany Lily and Cliff to Randolph Island. I would go wherever that sweet child went for as long as I was able.

Lillianne
1928

I was returning to the Royal York after a speaking engagement at the University of Toronto when Mavis met me in the lobby, and I could tell by the panic on her face something was wrong.

"Clara is gone," she exclaimed.

"What do you mean, gone?"

"I thought she was asleep in the other room. I must have dozed off for a few minutes. I went in to check on her and she wasn't there. Her nightdress was lying on the bed, the closet open, and her dresses and two travel bags were gone."

"Oh, surely she hasn't. When we got to Union Station yesterday, she begged me to buy a ticket so she could go to Chicago. It is my guess she has packed her bags and headed for the train station, sure she can somehow get on a train and make her way to Chicago."

"A ten-year-old girl on the street by herself at night!" Mavis gasped. "Why did I fall asleep? I will never forgive myself if something happens to that darling girl."

"Mavis, she will be fine. You stay here in case she comes back. I will walk to Union Station and see if that's where she has gone. Hopefully no train has left for Chicago in the last ten minutes, since God knows she could probably charm her way aboard."

Walking the blocks down Front Street to the station, I thought of the last few weeks since returning from our summer on

Randolph Island. This had been the worst year yet for the goodbyes when Cliff left to go back to Chicago. Clara was so upset she couldn't go back with him. She had paid special attention to photographs of the family mansion and had become obsessed with moving there.

The weeks since getting back to Odessa had been very busy, as the publication of my third novel brought with it several signings and speaking engagements. I had been too busy to give Clara the attention she seemed to be craving. I'd hoped this trip with me to Toronto would take her mind off her newfound determination to live with her father. And before leaving tonight, I thought she seemed to be in better humour after the full day we'd spent at the Sunnyside Amusement Park.

I found Clara sitting on a long wooden bench, her two bags propped up beside her. Her hat was slightly askew, and I looked at her with amusement before approaching.

"Are you waiting for a train, miss?" I asked.

She looked up, startled, and then quickly turned her head away as if I were a stranger or an annoyance to be dismissed. I sat down beside her, not saying anything for a moment or two.

"What time does the train for Chicago leave?"

"I don't know."

"Do you have money for a ticket?"

"No."

"I would miss you an awful lot, you know, if you went to live in Chicago."

"So?"

"Mavis was really worried when she couldn't find you. She is in quite a state."

"I don't know why I can't live in a mansion, Mother. I hate our house. Papa says there is a library in the Chicago house.

If you love books so much, why can't we move there and have a library?"

"Clara, Papa did not show you the pictures of the house to make you unhappy or discontent with your own house."

"He said that Aunt Cordelia had a closet as big as the gazebo and that when she was my age she had it filled with pretty dresses. Why can't I have a closet that big?"

"I don't think you need a closet that big, but how about we go to Eaton's tomorrow and buy a couple of new dresses before we leave the city?"

"Could I get a red velvet one?"

"Probably. But right now I think we should go back to the hotel so Mavis can see that you are all right. She was very upset. She loves you very much, you know—almost as much as I do. We would not be happy at all if you moved to Chicago."

"Oh, Mother, you know I wouldn't go to Chicago all by myself. If I could travel by myself, I would get on an ocean liner and go see Aunt Cordelia in London."

"Oh, I expect you will travel, my darling girl, but you have to get a bit older before I will just let you pack up and go off on your own. Give me one of those bags and let's get back before Mavis has the entire Toronto police force searching for you."

Mavis
1928

Keeping a grasp on this child's hand was a challenge at the best of times. Add to that my fear of losing her in this crowded train station, her natural energy and flair for the dramatic, and her enthusiasm about finally travelling to her father's home in Chicago. Having left the Chicago mansion before she turned two, Clara built it up in her imagination, and she could barely contain her excitement.

Clara always put me in mind of Cordelia. Her personality and her attention to fashion and flair certainly mirror her aunt's. Today Clara's long ringlets were topped off with a royal blue felt helmet adorned with a snow-white ostrich feather. She was wearing a fashionable coat trimmed with a Coney fur collar and cuffs and large brass buttons. After much persuasion, she slipped her winter overshoes on over her patent leather Mary Janes.

It was the birth of Cordelia that brought me back into the employ of the Randolphs the second time in 1901. As a young girl, my first period of employment in the Randolph household was as Clifton's young bride's lady-in-waiting. Marion and I used to laugh at the title, which Charlotte Randolph borrowed from British aristocracy. During the time I assisted Marion Randolph with all her personal needs, we developed a strong and lasting friendship, and she sought me out when her daughter was born.

I stayed in her employ until Cordelia went off to private school and I met and became quite smitten with Delbert Ryder, a handsome, hard-working carpenter. We married in 1910 and my own beautiful daughter was born the next year. Marion and I were worlds apart and definitely not in the same social circles, causing us to lose contact.

"They are calling for us to board, Mavis. Step quickly."

Clara breaks from my hold and runs ahead, almost knocking down an elderly gentleman in her exuberance. Our goodbyes had already been said, so Clara had no reason to look back at her mother. Lillianne would join us in a few days and we would spend Christmas in Chicago. This was a visit I was dreading and anticipating at the same time. I was anxious to see Marion but knew Clifton's poor health was another burden taking its toll on my friend. Charles's death nearly killed her, and I feared losing Clifton might be her final undoing. I knew how difficult it was to find your way back to the light when the darkness of loss consumed you.

Marion and I walked that path together in 1918, and this dear child I was struggling to keep up with was the joy we both clung to. Perhaps Clara could work her magic again. She certainly worked that magic on me every day.

Lillianne
1993

"You are exhausted, Mother. We've covered enough for one day. You should probably go up to bed soon."

"Yes. I think I will."

"Funny how you say you somehow knew all along, Mother. Do you remember when I was so determined to go to Chicago and live with Father? That summer on the island, I sensed he was keeping a secret from me. He probably didn't even know how many times he'd mentioned Martin's name, but I was determined to go to Chicago and see who this Martin was. At first I thought it was some other child taking my father's attention. I was sure it was Martin keeping my father from living in our house."

"The part you don't know is just how hard your father tried to live here and stay content with the life and the marriage we pretended to have. He held on for five years, and leaving you was one of his biggest heartbreaks. That is why we always made sure we had our summers on the island. And of course we had that visit with your father and Martin the Christmas before your grandfather's death, which brought the heartbreak of losing Randolph Island."

Lillianne
1928

I had been so tempted to stay in Odessa and spend Christmas all alone. Not alone, of course. Having fourteen glorious days with Will was in my grasp if I had just stayed home. I could have concocted a snowstorm or some other catastrophe to avoid travelling to Chicago. Clara was having such a wonderful time, finally dropped into the mansion of her dreams and in the company of her beloved father. She would hardly have noticed my absence.

I had almost given in to Will's pleas and my own desires when Marion's letter arrived. Except for birthday cards, it was unusual to receive correspondence from Marion. I opened the letter with some trepidation. The first page seemed harmless. Accounts of Chicago's early winter weather, a few staffing concerns, and a list of home improvements and purchases filled the first page, and I wondered why she had felt the need to write.

But the second page seethed with tension and the underlying control Marion Randolph had never shied away from exerting. Clifton was in grave health. The doctors attending to him gave him days, possibly weeks, to live, and the cancer was taking its toll rapidly.

> *My darling husband is just a former shell of the man you met ten years ago. If I were to be honest, that man disappeared*

when we buried Charles; maybe even weeks before, when my good intentions shattered our family. Even though his words claimed forgiveness, his eyes never did. And not seeing his darling daughter since he saw her embark on the ferry to the exile I sent her into was another factor in his undoing. A glimmer of light crossed his face when sweet Clara arrived, but in his delirium he called her Cordelia.

I was tempted to write to Cordelia and beg her to join us and allow her father one more Christmas, but my pride prevents me. She has failed to reply to any of my other correspondences. I believe my sister Victoria has turned her against me.

Many things must be discussed when you arrive. Cliff is completely absorbed in his ridiculous painting and has distanced himself from the business. I have had to rely on Stanley Emerson to assist, and some of our enterprises have been amalgamated. Trying to carry all our business interests has been too much with my attention to Clifton's health, running our household, and dealing with so many issues.

One of those issues is the blatant disregard Clifton has for decency and the preservation of our good name. He has been seen in public with a sculptor named Martin Forsythe and has even had the man stay under our roof. I need you to make an appearance in Chicago and attend some events on Clifton's arm with your daughter in tow to quiet some of the scandalous rumours cropping up.

Remember that any diversion from our arrangement will nullify the claim you have to Randolph money. I would never completely shut off my granddaughter's allowance, but I am sure even with your success an author's income would hardly sustain your lifestyle.

You may think me a tyrant and a heartless shrew, but my

*number one concern is keeping this family afloat, and it seems
not too much to ask that my son's wife show up occasionally
and take part in that endeavour.*

I looked out the train window, a light snow falling over the rural
landscape transforming to the spreading Chicago cityscape.

Lillianne
1917

September was nearly over and there'd been no mention of the Randolphs leaving the island. The man they hired came twice a week, and, so far, none of his tasks seemed to have anything to do with closing the house up for the season. Cliff tended to stay out of sight, only surfacing at mealtime. He was still barely eating and appeared very sickly. I hadn't even seen him outside once and assumed he was doing no sketching. That perhaps was the most troubling.

Cordelia spent much of her time outside, but I didn't see her swimming at all. That was probably because of the cool morning air, even though the days were staying warm. Cordelia and I had spoken since she told me of Cliff's outburst at the banquet, but I was no clearer on exactly what had caused such turmoil. I concluded that it had more to do with Cliff signing up for the army than any announcement of his intention to marry me. I had accepted our intimacy meant more to me than to Cliff.

The evenings were very pleasant, and that night I took my break on the front veranda. I thought it was unlikely any of the family would join me, even though the full moon was stunning. From my place on the porch swing I could see the lawn sloping to the water and the wide expanse of the lake illuminated by the bright sky. If I had had the courage or a partner to share it with, a nighttime row would have been most romantic.

"This is where you are, Lily?" Cordelia declared. "I'm terribly bored, but I can't get anyone to even play a game of Parcheesi.

They are all in such a funk. I thought Cliff would rally. Normally a night like this would have him outside drawing. Mother is as cantankerous as she was the day we arrived, and Father is a bear. I hope we aren't holed up here much longer."

"It is a beautiful evening. I was thinking the same thing about Cliff. It seems he hasn't been drawing at all."

"No one has mentioned going back to Chicago. I knew it would take Mother a while to get over the trauma of having Cliff make such abhorrent statements. I knew she was mortified, but she will eventually have to return to Chicago. I can't see Father relocating. I wonder if they are even considering that. Reputation means much more to Mother, but Father normally does her bidding. Perhaps they are at a stalemate and that is why we are exiled here."

"Is Cliff not legally obligated to enter the army if he returns to the States?"

"Oh, Mother took care of that. She kept pleading it was for his own good, but Cliff didn't see it that way. Even Father did not approve of Mother's tactics. The whole ugly thing may be the family's undoing. That and my scandalous behaviour, of course. There's been no mention of it, but I know Mother has not forgiven me my trespasses." She paused. "Let's take the rowboat out, Lily."

*

As I stepped into the rowboat, I thought briefly of the possibility of ending up in the lake. I'd slipped off my shoes and stockings, but my clothes would weigh me down if I found myself in the water. I pulled my jumper over my head, throwing it on to the shore, leaving just my blouse and undergarments. Cordelia had already stripped down to her corset.

"I would take this ghastly thing off, too, but I don't suppose you want to row next to a naked person. I have a secret you might guess if I took off this contraption. I believe my abdomen, which once was so flat, would reveal my condition. My tender breasts certainly are. I have missed two menses, and I fear my secret cannot be contained much longer."

"Oh my, Cordelia."

"Yes, that news is not going to help the situation. Mother will be devastated, and on top of all that's happened will think twice about arriving back in Chicago with her daughter carrying a bastard child, even if that child is an heir to the Hitchcock fortune. I'm in a pickle. You'd think I'd be happy to stay put here, but I can't even imagine spending a winter isolated on this island. As they say, I am between a rock and a hard place."

We rowed a few minutes in silence, Cordelia's words hanging in the air. The beautiful full moon illuminated the water and the island that appeared to have the Randolph family hostage. I, too, of course was caught up in that imprisonment, and I shuddered to think what the next few days and possibly weeks would bring. I had no advice to give Cordelia. I had believed my freedom would come through Cliff's love, but that had fizzled—or perhaps had been imagined in the first place. Whatever the case, it appeared Cliff was not going to rescue me from my servitude.

I looked up at the grand house while searching for words to comfort Cordelia. I glanced over and saw her demeanour had changed from the unflappable manner with which she had told me she was carrying Spencer Hitchcock's illegitimate child. Tears were streaming down her cheeks and she had begun to shiver.

"It seems to me," I began, not knowing exactly if I had the courage to present the solution that had just come to me, "that your mother's biggest concerns are appearances, perception, and reputation. I do not know what transpired at the banquet, but I know she retreated, because, as you have told me, she was humiliated. You are right in thinking your situation will make things worse. Perhaps a plan could be thought out that might remedy the damage of both situations."

"We do need a plan," Cordelia replied. "I cannot imagine one, though. Unless you have skills of an alchemist and can concoct a potion to rid me of this problem."

"Your mother needs a distraction, a mission. You have said how ambitiously she tries to control the family, especially Cliff. She also gets caught up with a mission, a purpose, and a project to manage him. Maybe your problem could be solved if she were to be convinced of the value of adjusting or manipulating his future."

"What are you talking about? How could her attention to Clifton help my predicament?"

"What if she was to marry your brother off and send him and his wife somewhere with you during your gestation, and the happy couple were to raise your child as their own? If distance and time were provided, who would be the wiser when the Randolphs arrived back in Chicago, a daughter-in-law and a grandchild in tow?"

"Your calculating scares me a bit, but you have nailed Mother's deepest fear. Her utmost concern is that the Randolph family stay unsullied and retain their status in Chicago society. Perhaps if Cliff were to return with a beautiful young bride on his arm and I came home still looking the part of a chaste young lady, Mother could weather the storm Cliff's outburst caused. It would certainly counter the statements he made. Possibly his outburst could be blamed on a nervous condition or a breakdown of some kind. I am sure Mother could work it out to her advantage."

We had both brought our oars to rest, letting the water gently rock the boat. The calm water, the star-dotted sky, and the silence seemed to be building a coalition between Cordelia and me. Together we could create a future that would serve us both.

"But where are we to find a young lady to present to Mother as Clifton's bride?"

"It could be me," I replied, picking up my oar and letting my answer settle in the still night air.

*

For the next four days, Cordelia and I debated exactly when and how we would approach Marion Randolph with our proposal. Each day I dreaded Cordelia would announce the flowing of her menses, which would, of course, change everything. Without Cordelia's pregnancy, Mrs. Randolph would have no immediate motivation to marry her son off to her housemaid. This had not happened, but Cordelia's fear of her mother's wrath caused her to keep postponing the discussion. We needed to choose the right time to propose our plan. As I served Mr. and Mrs. Randolph their after-dinner coffee, I heard news that I believed would convince Cordelia today should be the day.

"I am going to instruct our man to begin closing up the house tomorrow, Marion. It would be folly to wait much longer before leaving the island. I know you think we can stay here forever, but this house will be uninhabitable as the season becomes colder. I must put my foot down. We will leave by the week's end. And when we leave, we will go back to Chicago. You have a young son in need of his mother and your oldest son is getting no better in this exile. Your pride must be cast aside."

Mr. Randolph did not wait for his wife's response before leaving the room.

Leah
1956

Gram dropped me off at the YMCA. We left home before day-break to make the drive to Kingston for my early-morning practice with the under-twelve swim team. The drive seemed endless. Gram hadn't even had a car until three months ago, so driving me into Kingston every day for the last six weeks was quite a big deal for her, and I shouldn't have complained about how long it took us.

"We have to get this little fish into the water," she said every morning when we said goodbye to Mother before heading into Kingston. A fish is what Gram had called me for as long as I could remember, so it came as no surprise to her when I became obsessed with joining the Kingston swim team. My obsession became even stronger when I heard that Winnie Roach-Leuszler was coming to help coach. Maybe with the right training and hard work, I could someday join the ranks of female swimmers like Marilyn Bell and Winnie Roach-Leuszler.

I remembered the first time I heard her name. She had just successfully swum the English Channel on August 16, 1951, and that feat certainly deserved my attention, but it was the strange sound of her last name that made my five-year-old ears perk up. I listened to the radio report of her achievement and then got Gram to show me the newspaper article. I clipped it out and stuck it to my bureau mirror.

Even that young, I was aware that my last name was unusual in our small town. I was learning to print, and Gram taught me to make the letters properly for my full name. When practising, I would prop up the large, hard-covered volume bearing my mother's name on the table in front of me and laboriously print the nine letters of the name only Mother and I possessed.

The title *Faces of Courage* was not what caught my eye when a hard-covered volume arrived in the mail wrapped in brown paper, but the letters spelling *Clara Randolph Pasternak* grabbed my attention. I didn't even open the book to turn the crisp, glossy pages until a long time afterwards. My initial response to the book was probably triggered by the response I saw my mother have after she unwrapped it.

She first hugged the book to her chest, and then, while rubbing her fingers along the embossed name at the bottom of the cover, she began weeping. Her weeping brought Gram from her study and Mother crumpled to a nearby chair, saying the name over and over again through her sobs. Her sobs startled me, because I was unfamiliar with seeing emotion of any kind from my mother. I seldom saw anything but a deadpan expression as she did some of the daily tasks that included me.

Mother did the same things every day for me. Gran told her every morning to take me for a walk after my breakfast. She never ate with us but would appear after Gram took the dishes away to get herself a cup of coffee. When Mother finished drinking her coffee, Gram would tell me to get ready to go outside, no matter what the weather, and then she would tell Mother to take me outdoors for a walk. Those walks were short and I did most of the talking, always hoping this might be the day my mother would smile at me and say more than a few words.

Later, Gram would tell her to sit at the table with us and eat something at our noon meal. Mother usually had a boiled egg and toast. After lunch, Gram would send her and me out to the mailbox at the end of our lane to retrieve the day's mail. At suppertime Gram would tell Mother to clear the dishes off the table and the three of us would play a game of dominoes. At bedtime Mother got me undressed, helped me put on my nightdress, and tucked me into bed. Gram would then come in and read me a story and kiss me goodnight.

"Maybe tomorrow," Gram would always say. "*Maybe tomorrow your mother will be better.*"

Faces of Courage would never have been published if Gram had not sent the rolls of film from Mother's leather camera case, which hung in the front hallway, to a man at the publishing house. After receiving them, he agreed to compile a collection of the photographs Mother had taken in the months before I was born. Mother showed no interest when she signed the contract that resulted in the finished book. She showed no interest in anything and would not even hold the camera when Gram would take it from the case on the hall tree and try to get Mother to use it.

"*You should take some pictures, Clara. The fall leaves are brilliant,*" or, "*The snow is sparkling like diamonds,*" or, "*It is Leah's fifth birthday.*" Nothing Gram said in those years could convince Mother to use the camera.

I was glad when Mother got better, but, to be honest, after having waited day after day, month after month, year after year, I had given up hoping the words Gram closed each day with would ever come true. As far as I was concerned, my mother was always just going to be someone who silently walked through the house. Someone who apparently had looked deeply into the eyes of the children she photographed, the eyes that hauntingly stared out from the pages of the big book in the parlour, and decided to give her love to them, not me. The love I needed came from Gram, and I had stopped trying long ago to get it from my mother.

✻

"I will be back by eleven, Leah. I hope to get my errands done and back in time to see you do your final laps."

I always loved to swim, and I didn't even know why. I had never seen Mother or Gram swim. Gram told me about how she learned to swim on Randolph Island. Mother had only lately begun talking about Randolph Island and her summers there. She had barely spoken to me until two years ago. A doctor Gram convinced her to see was able to help her, and after a few visits Mother began getting better. I didn't know the whole story, but I knew my father died before I was born and Mother got very sick afterwards. My father was Jewish, but I didn't know anything about that. I read *The Diary of Anne Frank*, so I knew some stuff about what happened to the Jews during the war.

Fairfield Park was a place we regularly went for picnics during the summer months, and the beach there had long been my favourite swimming place. The first time we went I was three years old, and Gram said I begged her to let me go in the water. She stripped me down to my underclothes and let me wade in. She said I waded out in the cold water and kept going until the water was right up to my neck. With the water past my shoulders, I let myself drop. Gram was at the water's edge, ready to run in for me, but I quickly got back to my feet and let myself drop again. She had to make me get out when my lips started turning blue. After just a couple more trips to the beach, I had taught myself to swim.

Mother showed me photographs of Randolph Island. I wished we still owned the island and went there every summer. I wished a lot of things. I wished Mother had been well right from the start. I wished my father had not died. I wished my grandfather still came to Canada every summer. I wished when I was little I could have just once seen the look of happiness I saw on my mother's face each time she greeted a little child who came to her studio to have a portrait taken.

Clara
1993

I sat down at Mother's desk to write a quick note to Leah. For some reason, I felt a deep exhaustion tonight, and a heaviness. Listening to Mother dredging up the past left me anxious and irritated. I knew part of me wanted to simply pack up the house and send Mother into the Briarlea as a way of getting rid of the memories I revisited every time I walked through the front door. Mother, on the other hand, acted like she would cease to exist if she were to leave this house.

Leah was miserable when I forced her to move from here at eleven. She was deeply attached to her grandmother, and the guilt I felt about that almost led me to leave her with Mom and move to Toronto by myself. Now Leah said Hilary dreamed of possibly buying her great-grandmother's house someday. It seemed I would never be rid of it.

Professionals had a name for what I suffered in those years. A broken heart, Mother used to call it, and, of course, it was, but the long years I spent under that roof barely existing while my mother raised my daughter filled me with shame and regret.

Lillianne
1993

I knew it was the long-held secret causing me such anguish. I could not begin to imagine how after all this time I could tell Clara the truth. Not only had I deceived her, I had allowed Leah and Hilary to believe a lie about their own genealogy. In thinking of the days Cordelia and I conspired to create the path we led three generations on, I realized I would only find peace in the complete truth.

For years I transferred the blame and the shame of what we did onto Marion, believing her manipulation and control were responsible. I took very little of the blame, and Cordelia, of course, suffered enough in the punishment she was forced to accept. Clifton, too, paid a price. I was the main beneficiary of the plan, but perhaps in the end I lost the most. Whether or not Clara, Leah, and Hilary would believe that, I couldn't say. I couldn't let the fear of their condemnation prevent me from telling them the truth. But did I not owe Cordelia a say?

When and how I would speak that truth seemed every bit as foreboding as it was for Cordelia and me to speak to Marion Randolph about our plan on that September day on Randolph Island in 1917.

*

We entered the drawing room together, which probably seemed strange to Marion. We had waited until we were sure Mr.

Randolph was busy outside with the hired man. Cordelia spoke first and dealt the blow quickly and without fanfare.

"I am with child."

"Pardon me?" Mrs. Randolph said, her face becoming drained of all colour.

"You heard me correctly, Mother. My night of shame has a consequence I can no longer keep secret. Before you say anything more, please listen to the plan Lily and I have come up with."

Surprisingly, Marion held her tongue, and I spoke next.

"It seems we are in need of a solution to your daughter's predicament. I propose Cliff and I wed right away and spend the months of Cordelia's maternity somewhere nearby but secluded. After Cordelia gives birth, Cliff and I will have the child registered as ours, and at that time travel to join the family in Chicago. No one will be the wiser."

The seconds of silence hung in the air. I stood fast, not daring to look at Cordelia.

"I will have to think this mess through," Marion said, not looking up from the needlepoint she was pretending to work on. "I am in such turmoil already, and Clifton is forcing me to go back to Chicago. I suppose my son could be made to go along with the scheme. He is not showing much resistance these days, unlike the night he completely eviscerated the Randolph name. I expect I have the upper hand for a little while. We will have to move quickly."

Cordelia and I left the drawing room knowing we had put in motion the unstoppable force of Marion Randolph. At that point I gave the blame over to her, allowing her to orchestrate and manipulate all of our futures. The negotiations came later, giving me what I had wanted all along.

Hilary
1993

Professor Dunfield held up the blue file folder that held the manuscript I had laboured over since entering his class in September. Being only a second-year student, I'd considered myself quite fortunate to have gotten into his class, but after a full year of exposure to his cutting humour and cruel, slashing criticism, I was not so sure of my good fortune. Reviews of my work by other critics had been kind, but Professor Dunfield's continuous negative commentary had severely undermined my confidence.

"It appears that Miss Jacobs thinks having a renowned author like Lillianne McDonough as a great-grandmother ensures that she doesn't need to attend to any tedious revising, invasive editing, or tiresome worry about plot structure. Her work certainly lacks the nuance her great-grandmother's writing is so well noted for. Perhaps it would be to her advantage to spend a year under Miss McDonough's tutelage, since it appears sitting under mine for the last ten months has been of no value."

I retrieved my file folder off the lectern, slipping back to my seat as Dunfield began berating another student. Perhaps the last two years at Queen's had been a complete waste of time and money. I could not see myself mustering the courage to get back to my novel in the busy summer months ahead. Maybe I would leave it with Gram and see if she could get me on track. Stepping away while Colin and I trudged through the wilds of

British Columbia, planting trees, might be just what I needed.

Colin had worked last summer for a different tree-planting company but convinced me this year to apply with him to Summit Reforestation for our summer employment. As the time got closer, I was beginning to doubt my decision for several reasons, the major one being the thought of working in the heat and batting bugs all day. Last year I had worked at the restaurant in the Parliament Hill hotel. The tips had been excellent and living at home saved me money. But Colin convinced me we should have some adventure this summer and take a bit of time travelling after our tree planting was over. The way I was feeling today, I wasn't even sure I wanted to go back to school in September. If I was ever going to be a writer, maybe I could do it without the nasty advice of professors like Robert Dunfield. Gram had done it on her own, so why couldn't I?

Lillianne
1924

The snow drifted partway up the window in my study. The wind whipped all night, and keeping the large brick house warm was a challenge. I could hear Clara stirring. The early-morning hours were my most productive, and as I was expected to have my manuscript in the post before the month's end, I would continue working until I heard her feet hit the floor in the room above my head.

Beyond Wind and Whitecaps had been accepted by a Toronto publishing house, and I was working on the final edits. I could hardly believe I would soon hold in my hands the book that had begun to take shape so long ago. I penned the first pages of the story during the days I spent alone on Randolph Island. In the small slip room in the house beside the blacksmith shop on Amherst Island, I added to those pages. During those nights as I wrote, I believed that the man who slept beside me might someday love me in a way that wasn't contrived. My identity as Mrs. Clifton Randolph was something we had shaped to meet the needs of Cordelia and the Randolph family. I was still naive enough then to believe my purpose would cease without him.

The story I began on Randolph Island was of Octavia Halliday, a young woman of colour with no status, no value, and no identity, orphaned at a young age and raised in an oppressive and cruel setting. Her story was of romance, with her hero saving her through his love. Coming back to the story later, I crafted it into a much different story that would soon find its voice through publication.

Four years ago, Mavis, Clara, and I had travelled by motorcar to Odessa, not even knowing where the house, which loomed so large in my memory, was located. My inquiries must have seemed odd to the residents I approached.

"Do you know where Claire and Frederick McDonough lived in 1906? Do you know where I can find a house of double red brick construction?"

Many of the people I spoke to did not recall the names and could not help. When I added the detail of the McDonoughs' deaths in the San Francisco earthquake, it tweaked a woman's memory and she directed us to her grandmother, who was a fount of information. She told us that the McDonough house stood empty on Millcreek Road, crumbling from neglect and some vandalism at the hands of local hooligans. The property had been abandoned, she explained, because no next of kin laid claim to it. The grounds had grown over and been left to the elements.

"My son could take you there if you would like to go," she said. "It is only a short drive out of town."

I immediately took her up on the offer and within minutes was standing on the walkway of my childhood home. The slate stones that frost and time had shifted were uneven, and weeds grew high around the house. The neat and perfect gardens I remembered were long overgrown, but I could see several blood-red roses clinging to a vine on a crumbling trellis. I approached the roses and stood near them, letting the tears fall.

I passed Clara to Mavis and made my way up the rotting steps, watching my footing as I walked onto the veranda and tried the knob on the heavy oak door. The knob turned and I walked into the front hall clearly remembering what lie beyond the archway. Most of the furnishings were gone, but the parlour organ still stood against the far wall in the parlour, and Father's large roll-top desk was in front of the bay windows in the study. No doubt both pieces were too heavy to have been stolen. Some pictures still hung on the wall.

I moved through the downstairs in a trance, conjuring up the essence of my beloved parents. Each room brought its own memory to the forefront. The pantry door held markings of my growth from the time I could stand till February 1906. I stopped before the Royal Jewel cook stove. The nickel plate was dull and the cast-iron surface covered in thick dust and grime. I thought back to the day it had been put in place and how proud Mother was of its shiny ornamentations and its modern functions. Each Saturday night she would bail hot water from its deep reservoir to fill the washtub for my bath.

After moving through every room on the first floor, I headed back outside, unwilling just yet to investigate upstairs. I paused and lifted the door knocker on the front door. The gargoyle-like face had scared me so as a child. Immediately I asked the man who had brought us to the property to please drive us back to our lodging.

Cliff and I had returned to Chicago in June 1918, swaddling a newborn baby girl. Cordelia had not accompanied us but instead headed to her mother's hometown of Saint John, New Brunswick. An elaborate story was concocted to explain Cordelia's absence. Marion Randolph greeted us with a large and impressive reception, gushing over her granddaughter and daughter-in-law with convincing enthusiasm. Mr. Randolph welcomed the diversion from the dark days of mourning following Charlie's death. Mavis attended to Clara's care and we all provided the distraction and hope so needed in that sad and hollow mansion.

After a year in Chicago providing Marion Randolph with the image she wanted so badly to establish for her son, who was now dutifully working with his father in the family business, I approached her with my request. I was not willing to continue this charade without the concession I had been waiting to demand almost from the beginning. I wanted the funds and the freedom to return to the place of my birth. If possible, I would purchase the home that consumed my thoughts, and some reason would be provided for Clifton Randolph the Fourth, his wife, and his daughter to move to Ontario. I presented my proposal, making it clear I would not hesitate to reveal the truth if my request was dismissed.

I did not know then my most powerful bargaining chip was Cliff's sexuality, not the secret of Clara's birth mother. After Cliff's confession during our summer on Randolph Island the following year, Marion's quick consent became more understandable. At the time, I was just happy to finally be getting the opportunity to return to my childhood home.

After some digging, I discovered that the property had been taken by the county for back taxes but had not been put up for tender. By paying the outstanding tax bill, I was given the deed and full ownership of the house and the ten acres on which it stood. It was not habitable in its state and we took a rental property while the restoration was carried out. I communicated this to Marion, requesting funds. I was sent a substantial amount of money and plans for Cliff to join us later were put in place.

Structural repairs were made, replacing some of the rotting carrying beams and crumbling sections of the stone foundation. Floors were refinished and walls replastered. Some windows were replaced and a new back porch constructed. The ginger-bread trim was completely rebuilt and painted. The grounds were cleared, grass replanted, some trees trimmed, and the walkway had new paving stones set down. I instructed the gardener to clean out the garden without disturbing the roses, incorporating a new trellis without completely removing the old one. I tried to find furniture close to what I remembered being in each room. I set up the bedroom that had been mine for Clara.

Almost fifteen months after we arrived in Odessa, Cliff, Clara, Mavis, and I moved in just in time to put up a Christmas tree in the parlour. I draped garland from the stair railing and over the mantelpiece. That night I sat in the candlelit room after Mavis had taken Clara up to bed and cried tears of sorrow for my lost parents and tears of joy for my homecoming. In this home, I knew I could give the same kind of love to Clara that my parents had so generously given me. I then placed the several gifts that had arrived for Clara from her grandparents and her Aunt Cordelia near the beautiful tree and said a prayer of thankfulness. Randolph money had brought this house back to its original splendour, but McDonough love would flourish here, and Clara Elizabeth Randolph would always know that love.

Lillianne
1917

We sailed away from Randolph Island early on the morning of October 1. The Randolphs were moving into the same suite in the Prince George that Mrs. Randolph had left in May, taking three adjoining rooms. Arrangements would be made for a civil marriage ceremony to be conducted before Mr. and Mrs. Randolph took the train back to Chicago at the end of the week. Cliff, Cordelia, and I would take residence on Amherst Island the day after the wedding.

A dwelling had been found that was to be our marital home and Cordelia's hideaway. An aunt and uncle of the desk clerk at the Prince George lived on the remote island a short distance from Kingston. They were willing to rent the small vacant house beside theirs to the Randolphs for as long as needed. Cordelia's delivery was expected sometime in April, and the aunt happened to be an experienced midwife. Apparently most of the babies born on Amherst Island in the last twenty years had been pulled into the world by Sarah Brown's hands.

Upon arrival in the hotel, I noticed Rosemary Donavan looking my way, but she did not seem to recognize her former employee among the guests the bellboy and maids were attending to. Marion had insisted I wear one of Cordelia's finest gowns and the same fashionable coat Cordelia had been wearing when I first saw her on the dock. I was wearing the hat as well, and held my head just so as I walked through the hotel lobby. Staff would not be rude enough to stare, trying to decide if the rich young lady in the party was indeed the girl who used to work by their side. My attire and the company I was keeping elevated me to a different status from the one I held the morning I walked out through this same lobby in May.

As I unpacked my travelling case, I could hardly believe I was doing so as a guest. The extensive wardrobe that had been Cordelia's was now mine, as only a few of her garments were fitting her properly. A dressmaker was to be hired in the next few days to discreetly prepare a maternity wardrobe for Cordelia.

Marion and I would go to the shops the next day to purchase suitable wedding attire. Cliff was to wear a suit of his father's, which I feared would hang comically on his thin frame. Cordelia and Cliff showed no interest in any of those plans.

In fact, I'd not spoken to either of them or even heard them say anything since we sailed that morning. Cordelia and I hadn't talked since we'd stood before her mother with our plan. Cliff and Cordelia were both silent, as if they were indeed just pawns in Marion Randolph's game. They were both playing silent parts in the production their mother was directing. Mr. Randolph seemed compliant as well.

*

As we left the bridal shop on Queen Street, I found the courage to direct Mrs. Randolph's attention to the art shop we had passed when walking from the hotel.

"I would like to purchase some supplies for Cliff. Perhaps if I take them to the island with us, he will find the desire to draw again."

"You go ahead. I have some business to attend to at the hotel. Tell the proprietor of the shop to send the bill to Clifton Randolph the Third at the Prince George. I'd have no idea what to buy, but you can pick up a few things. I suppose it will be a long winter on that godforsaken island, and it wouldn't hurt if Clifton were to dabble in that frivolous hobby of his."

Marion
1917

Am I the monster Charlotte Randolph was? As I ran around the last two days putting things in place for Clifton's marriage, I couldn't help but make the comparison. Even though Clifton's mother was not pleased with the union, she saw the quick marriage of her son and the defiled housemaid he'd brought home to be the most favourable solution. Adjustments were made to present his lowly choice in a presentable light. Names and ancestry were changed and no one was the wiser. Some tutelage could turn a sow's ear into a fine silk purse. At least Lillianne seemed to have a certain culture to her. She did not come off as a scullery maid.

Some of my first forays into society life still mortified me. I had knowledge from observing the goings-on in the Simms mansion, but Chicago society was even more rigid and unforgiving. Poor Charlotte Randolph on more than one occasion had to take me aside and instruct me as to how I was to present myself. At least after marrying Clifton and Lillianne off on Friday I would gain a reprieve, as their months on Amherst Island would be without the trappings and expectations of high society.

And as for Cordelia, by the time she returned to Chicago, there would be no trace of her indiscretion. She would still be young enough to fit back into debutante society, and with any luck at all would turn some eligible suitor's head. Any scarring or traces of childbirth would remain respectfully hidden away until the marriage vows were recited. Surely Cordelia had learned the folly of so carelessly taking her clothes off. Both ghastly situations would be dealt with in the next few days, and Clifton and I could return to Chicago and attend to Charles. I would accept the consequence of feeling as manipulative and conniving as my mother-in-law. And having Randolph money to pay the officiant enough to overlook the absence of any proof of identity for the bride and forgoing the required reading of the banns came in handy as well.

From the first day I set eyes on Clifton Randolph, I flourished from his adoration and his complete loyalty. Even facing the wrath his mother unleashed toward him when we arrived in Chicago, he never faltered in his love for me. His anger and disgust were the most difficult part of this terrible mess. Even when I pleaded that my intervention was for our son's own good, he looked at me with such hatred. Without his love, I feared I could not go on.

My only leverage was his desire to get back to Charles. Clifton's worry and concern increased every day. *Am I a monster to not be as burdened with thoughts of Charles's health?* Children ran fevers and caught illnesses and they got better with rest and care. I employed the best possible childhood nurse before leaving. I could do no more for him. I believed Clifton's worry was more his way of not facing the awful truth Cliff so thoughtlessly broadcast to Chicago's most influential.

My only hope was that after Cliff's marriage, Clifton could begin to forgive me as we headed back to Chicago. Whether he admitted it or not, he was just as anxious as I to disprove the claim our son made. Marriage would do that, and eventually this terrible blight would be behind us. And he was receptive to a plan that would save his beloved daughter's honour.

Lillianne
1917

The ceremony was a blur to me. In fact, the entire day from the moment I began dressing was somewhat like a bad dream. Cordelia assisted me, and her demeanour did nothing to lighten the mood. She began crying from the moment she entered my bedroom.

"It is just hitting me," she sobbed. "I am allowing myself to be spirited away onto some godforsaken island where I will continue to get fat and disgusting. Then I will be put through, from what I hear, the most excruciating misery possible to get this baby out, and with not even the option of offering it up for a fraction of its rightful inheritance. The Hitchcock estate is far greater than the Randolphs can boast, and I'll not be able to claim a cent of it."

"I know this all seems daunting right now, Cordelia, but you must pull yourself together. And there is no need for you to worry about the pain just yet. Let's just act like we are embarking on a great adventure."

I spent the next hour encouraging and cajoling Cordelia, which gave me no time to wallow in my own self-pity. That hit me with full force when I entered the room on Mr. Randolph's arm and walked toward my groom. Cliff gave absolutely no response, let alone one a bride would hope from her intended.

He stood there, propped up against the archway as if he were a man of straw brought in to impersonate the groom. Even his expected responses as the magistrate conducted the ceremony were only muttered with his mother's constant coaxing.

My instinct was to put a stop to the charade, but instead I recited my vows dutifully and with contrived enthusiasm. What possible good would come from my refusal to participate? I would be faced with an even bleaker future than I'd been presented months ago, for possibly the hotel and Rosemary Donavan would even reject me if I were to put a stop to this union. I had made my bed, so to speak.

*

I watched the last of our luggage being unloaded from the back of a truck bearing the name William Brown and Sons Blacksmith. Cliff and Cordelia were still seated in the cab of Mr. Brown's truck. Amherst Island was to be our home for several months. Every possible comfort had been provided and adequate funds left to ensure we would be well taken care of until the time came to travel to Chicago in the spring.

Looking at my travelling companions sitting morosely as if they had been delivered to a torture chamber, I realized I would have to be the one to make the best of what stretched ahead of us. It was not a permanent imprisonment, just a place to wait until we could resume our places in the Randolph family. I had faced worse prospects and was determined to make the best of whatever the next few months would bring. I would be the mistress of a comfortable house and no longer anyone's maid. I would take the time to continue working on the fiction I'd started crafting during my solitude. I would also do my best to bring Cliff and Cordelia out of their funk. Perhaps without their mother's dour influence I could bring out some of the carefree, contented state they'd both displayed when the summer began. I started walking toward the house that was to be my first marital home, with the resolve to make these next few months enjoyable.

Lillianne
1919

Will Carlson was a jack of all trades. Stumbling upon him in my quest for a tradesman to do the work to bring my childhood home back to its splendour was a lucky turn of events. His work was of top quality, and from the beginning I felt I was definitely getting my money's worth. Randolph money's worth, I suppose, but a woman alone hiring a stranger to work might be in danger of being taken advantage of. I was never disappointed, though, when I travelled out to Millcreek Road to see Mr. Carlson's progress.

Today Will was busy stripping the upstairs ceilings of the old plaster. I stood quietly in the doorway of the master bedroom, trying not to interrupt his progress. Will had been nothing but a gentleman, but when he turned and saw me I felt something I'd been trying to dismiss for the last few weeks. My imagination quickly conjured a relationship between us, a husband and wife perhaps, working to fix up a home together. I felt a sudden urge to embrace the man who stood before me, his hair and beard covered with the fine white dust of the task.

"This is the last ceiling up here, Mrs. Randolph. Once I get it all down I'll clean up the rubble and start the strapping."

"I'd rather you called me Lily."

"I could do that, but only if you call me Will. Every time I hear you say Mr. Carlson I turn to see if my father has shown up. Did you bring the little one with you today?"

"No, I left her back with Mavis. You didn't need her toddling through your mess. I'll get the broom and dustpan and start cleaning up."

"Now, Mrs.—I mean, Lily, you're paying me good money, and I don't expect you to be pitching in."

"I don't mind at all, Will. The way I see it, if I help with the cleanup, you'll be able to get at the important work, which will get me into the house faster."

"When do you expect Mr. Randolph to come up from the States?"

"My husband is not well, and it may be a while before he is actually able to move here with us."

I thought back to the letter I'd received from Marion the day before. She wanted to make arrangements to have Cliff admitted to a facility called Maplewood Farm in New Hampshire. She sent along a brochure outlining Maplewood's impressive reputation in treating melancholy. She suggested I travel to New York to meet her and Cliff and then accompany Cliff to New Hampshire. She believed he would be more receptive to going if I were the one who proposed it to him.

I was overwhelmed with guilt at having left Cliff in Chicago in the first place, with plans of staying months while the house was put to rights. Even though Cliff's health was not perfect when we left Amherst Island, I deceived myself into thinking he would get no worse in our absence. Possibly the best thing would be to bring him here even before the house was ready; being with Clara seemed to be good medicine for him. But if the claims of Maplewood's brochure were to be believed, a stay there would be beneficial and could in the long run better prepare him for coming to live with us.

"I will be away for a few weeks. I have to travel to the States and seek treatment for my husband. I plan to leave Clara behind with Mavis. I will make sure to leave you enough funds to continue with the work. Perhaps before I leave you can give me an idea where you think six weeks will get you. I am hoping to move in by summer's end."

"That should be possible, Mrs. Randolph."

Lillianne
1993

"Did I ever tell you about the months your father spent in Maplewood?"

"Maplewood? I don't recall. What is Maplewood?"

I watched as Clara scurried around trying to complete some chores she considered necessary before leaving for Toronto. She had hired a lady to stop by every day during the three weeks she would be away visiting Leah. I had assured her that was not necessary, but she had arranged it anyway. Now as she fussed about I was determined to share some secrets from the past that might make the whole mess easier for her to understand.

"When I travelled to reclaim this house, Cliff stayed behind in Chicago. I brought you with me, but at the time it seemed better for your father to stay behind. He was grieving terribly for Charles and did not seem ready to leave his home and his parents. But in the weeks that followed, your father became very melancholic—depressed, they call it now. Whatever the term, he was low, lethargic, and what your grandmother feared the most, had given up the will to live.

"Thank God your grandmother had realized that the New York asylum she sent Cliff to previously was not the answer. I knew Cliff's experience there had been devastating. Your grandmother found a facility in New Hampshire that came highly recommended for the treatment of patients showing the degree of illness your father was exhibiting. She contacted me and asked me to take Cliff to Maplewood Farms, and I did so.

"I did not see an alternative. The house was not ready. You, Mavis, and I were living in two rented rooms, and I did not think our circumstances were what Cliff needed. In November of 1919 we travelled on the train to New Hampshire, and your father was admitted to Maplewood and remained there for seven months."

Clara continued tidying up, sweeping and rearranging things, listening but not showing much response.

"The staff insisted that Cliff write daily letters to us as part of his therapy. At first his letters were nearly incomprehensible. It was almost as if he was dictated random facts and instructed to put them on the notepaper. It was probably at least four months before I saw a glimpse of your father in the lines he wrote. And then sketches began to come with his correspondence. More than the words he wrote, the drawings gave me the hope that Maplewood was somehow helping your father to live again.

"At the end of May, a large envelope arrived, crammed with sketches. The message I saw in those drawings was a pleading from your father for me to come and bring him home. Contrary to your grandmother's wishes, I travelled immediately to New Hampshire and brought your father home, and we made arrangements to spend the summer on Randolph Island—the summer I told you about yesterday.

"I had known it when I first met your father, I knew it on Amherst Island, and I knew it without any doubt when I received those sketches: art was what would save your father. His love of nature has always given him the peace he so desired. He was able to keep his well-being for six years here in this home with us, but then realized he needed more. I am thankful every day that he was able to find that refuge with Martin.

"Of all the mistakes I've made, loving Cliff was not one of them. And you need to know that you played a huge part in your father's well-being. Your father loved you dearly and did not regret the choices he made along the way that gave you to us."

Clara
1946

I lined up the noisy, excited, rambunctious gaggle, each one decked out in their finest rags and holding some pitiful possession that sadly spoke of the dreary existence this camp provided. One little girl held a soiled china doll whose unclothed body was missing an arm and one foot. A tall boy of about ten held a bicycle tire, half the spokes missing and barely any rubber gripping the metal.

Across the yard I could see the same man I'd noticed several times since arriving in Feldafing a week ago. Layers of axel grease could not hide his good looks, and for some reason I'd often found myself scanning crowds of young men as I moved through the camp, looking for this particular one.

I raised my voice above the children's chatter, trying to concentrate on my task rather than look over to see if the man working on the fender of a large truck was noticing me. As I focussed my camera, the man's voice startled me.

"An American with a camera. Do you think we are just waiting for you to come along and take our pictures, that our lives mean nothing until we are put in your glossy magazines?"

"For your information, I am a Canadian, sir, and I have not asked to take your picture. And furthermore, if I wanted to use up all my film taking photos of dirty, scruffy, rude men, you would certainly not be my first choice."

"My apologies, a Canadian! I suppose calling you American might be as insulting to you as if you were to call me Hungarian. We Polish, dirty, scruffy, rude men have to hold on to our identity here in a camp made up mainly of Hungarians."

"Perhaps if I wasn't so busy right now, I could take the time for a European geography lesson from you and I could also teach you a few things about Canada. But as you can see, I have several children anxiously posed to have their photograph taken, so I must ask you to please get back to your business and stay out of mine."

"Gladly, Canadian with a camera. I wouldn't want to deprive your fellow countrymen of the sight of our raggedy European children lined up with treasures most Canadian children would long ago have thrown in the dustbin. And as for the lessons I could teach you—this yard, right now, in the view of children, would be neither the time nor the place for that kind of learning."

"My name is Clara, and I am sure even as bold and cocky a Pole as yourself must have a name so that I may address you if that time or place ever comes. Maybe our next conversation might be a bit more civil if you see fit to interrupt me again while I am here."

"I am Gabe Pasternak and I believe, Clara the Canadian, whether you photograph me or not, I may be one bold, cocky Pole you will not soon forget."

Lillianne
1920

Yesterday Clara and I checked into the Parker House Hotel in Boston, and tomorrow we would take the train to New Hampshire and bring Cliff home from Maplewood. Marion was not happy with my decision and did not share my opinion in the wisdom of this choice. My plan was to return to Chicago, have a short visit, and then travel to Kingston, where we'd arrange transportation to Randolph Island, where Cliff, Clara, and I would spend the summer. Mavis and Peggy would accompany us as well. We would use the summer to decide what our next plan would be.

I believed a summer on the island would be good for Cliff. He could relax and spend time sketching and continue his healing. I couldn't see him returning to Chicago afterwards, but I had to remain open to what Cliff wanted. I was hopeful that he would be able to participate in the decisions we made for our future. I was anxious for him to see Clara. She was so delightful, and I was confident her charm would cast a powerful spell on her father. She certainly had the rest of us in her grips. I had to believe we could move forward and build a life for Clara.

*

The pouring rain made the start of our journey by train from Boston to Portsmouth rather dismal. I tried to imagine us arriving and driving through the gates of Maplewood into a bower of cherry trees bursting with blossoms. Not being a botanist, I did not know the life cycle of the cherry blossom, its exact duration from blossom to the time when the final flowers fall from the tree replaced by the budding new growth, and did not know if the trees Cliff may have been looking at while creating that beautiful sketch he had sent would still hold their spring bounty. Somehow the hope of beholding that stand of trees is what I kept focusing on as our destination got closer and the sky brightened. Clara was nestled in my arms and I diverted my thoughts to her peaceful sleeping face, anticipating passing her to Cliff for him to hold for the first time in several months.

*

"I will have you and your party wait in this sitting room until Mr. Randolph has finished dining. We were somewhat surprised at your sudden decision to remove him, but legally we cannot stop you. The doctor is not able to meet with you, and unless you wait and come back tomorrow, there will be no consultation to provide an analysis of Mr. Randolph's psychological condition. You are taking a risk removing him from our facility, and we cannot be held responsible."

"I understand your concern, Nurse Perkins, and I certainly appreciate all this facility has offered my husband, but it is my belief that what he needs now is familiar and comforting surroundings, time with his daughter, and the love we can provide him. I was very encouraged to see that he is sketching again. I see this as a very heartening turn of events and enough to give me the assurance that I am doing the right thing."

"Mr. Randolph *has* become very preoccupied with his drawing, to the detriment of his therapy of late. I am sure this hobby of his gives him some comfort, but you may regret making a decision on such a frivolous observation. I hope you will not be disappointed when you take him, but we will certainly readmit him when you realize your mistake."

The sweet and condescending tone in which Miss Perkins delivered her speech did nothing to conceal her absolute disapproval in my being here and her strong view that my opinion was without merit. She did not appear to have any authority to push the matter further, and I was very anxious to get Cliff in the car and to get on our way to Portsmouth, where we would stay before leaving on the train for Ontario in the morning. I was determined to remove him tonight and did not intend to waste any more time defending my decision.

"I would like to be shown to Mr. Randolph's room so that I might pack his possessions. As soon as he returns from his evening meal we will get him, and I am quite willing to accept the consequences of my actions."

With a bit of a huff, the head nurse led us from the sitting room and down the corridor to Cliff's suite. Clara filled the silence with her delightful and uninhibited babbling, to which the indignant Miss Perkins paid no mind.

✳

Cliff was heavier. His face was clean-shaven, but his hair fell slightly below the collar of his white shirt. He did not look as vacant as he had when I left him, but his response upon seeing me in his bedroom was not exactly what I had hoped. He stopped just inside the doorway and spoke my name uncertainly.

"Lily."

"Cliff." I approached him slowly and led him to the settee, where Mavis was sitting with Clara on her lap. "It is so good to see you. I have missed you." I took Clara and gently set her in his arms, not withdrawing my hold until I saw that he was taking her from me.

He took her and propped her up, turning her smiling face toward his. He moved Clara onto his shoulder and held her close. Tears streamed down his cheeks. "I am so thankful you have come for me. I can be this beautiful child's father. I am so much better and I can be what you need me to be as well, Lily. You have been so wonderful through all this, and I owe you my life."

He passed Clara back to me and stood up. "I understand we are leaving right away. Perkins is in a bit of a lather about it."

"Yes. I hope you all right with leaving."

Cliff walked to a mahogany secretary at the far end of the room. He picked up a pile of papers and brought them over to me. I slowly leafed through at least twenty sketches, each one detailed and intricate.

"I am ready to go," he replied.

Lillianne
1917

In the short time we had been on Amherst Island, Cliff, Cordelia, and I had established a comfortable routine. I always rose first in the morning and got the kitchen and parlour fires going. After an hour or so I went upstairs to wake Cliff and Cordelia for breakfast. Cliff's appetite was still poor, but I felt he was at least getting enough sustenance, even though he showed no interest in his food—unlike Cordelia, who was insatiable. After breakfast Cliff and I would go out for a walk, venturing farther each day. When we returned I sat him in the parlour and gave him his sketchpad while I attended to my housekeeping. He drew a cow after our walk took us by McFaddens' farm. When he was sketching, he seemed at peace and the most content.

In the afternoon I would take Cliff out to see William working at the forge. He seemed to enjoy the sound of the hammer on the anvil. He smiled as William's son Samuel explained every step of the process, down to the sizzle of the hot metal being immersed in the cooling water. Cliff sketched each finished piece Samuel brought to him.

I then led him back to the house and upstairs, where he had a rest while I prepared supper. After the evening meal, I could usually convince Cliff to play a game of Dominoes with Cordelia and me.

At around nine o'clock I would take Cliff upstairs and get him ready for the night. After getting him into bed, I read from a volume of adventure stories I found in the parlour and he drifted off to sleep. I would pull the covers over his shoulders, kiss his lips gently, and extinguish the flame of the lantern. I stood a while watching him, silently praying for the next day to bring miracles, his clear mind, and the man I knew before—not this hollow shell sleeping quietly before me.

Cliff was docile and cooperative. He always spoke kindly to me and often apologized for being a burden. In our daily routine I bathed him and felt no embarrassment at seeing his naked body, but rather looked forward to a time when our intimacy will be as lovers, not as caregiver and patient.

In the small slip room off the parlour, I would take out my notebook and write. Just as the sketchpad offered Cliff some inner sanctum, putting words to paper gave me a release that nothing else provided.

Tonight, however, Cliff seemed irritated and went up to bed shortly after supper. In the dim light of the lantern, Cordelia and I sat in silence. Cliff's mood seemed to have permeated the house.

"Will this ever be a sweater one could actually put on an infant?" Cordelia asked, looking up from the tangle of yarn on her knee. "Sarah believes she can teach me to knit, but I fear I am a lost cause."

"You are doing a fine job, Cordelia. Did you expect you'd sit down and have a sweater knit just like that? Sarah can certainly make her needles move, but you are just learning."

"It's a wonder I can sit still to even try, the way this baby has been moving today. I had no idea it would be such a volcano in there."

I rested my hand on the mound that seemed to have gotten twice as big in the short time we'd been here. I was as naive as

Cordelia in this regard and was glad Sarah was right next door.

"Do you think Cliff will be like this for the rest of his life?" Cordelia asked. "I am beginning to forget the brother I knew. It is heartbreaking to watch this sad and vacant shell that must be fed and dressed and led about like a helpless child. He barely speaks."

"All we can do is keep trying. At least he enjoys spending time with Samuel. I think he puts him in mind of Charlie. I wonder how that dear boy is doing. For now, all we can do is be here for each other and make the best of things. I have to believe being with both of us right now is the best place for Cliff."

"I guess you're right. I know I feel a burden lifted, not having Mother's scrutiny and judgement heaped upon me every day. I will choose to see this island as an escape for now, not an exile. Are there any of those biscuits left? Thank goodness you are here to cook. Cliff and I would surely starve if we were relying on my culinary skills. You are a peach, Lily. There's no one I'd rather be cast away with."

I walked into the quiet slip room and gazed out at the dark field behind the house. A light snow had started to fall, and I was filled with the beauty of the still night. If I wanted to write in these night hours, I needed to quiet my nerves. I felt such pressure and responsibility to be the strength and anchor for Cliff and Cordelia over these next few months, and me only eighteen. I knew the Browns were right next door, but I was the one Cliff and Cordelia would look to through these next few months. A housemaid their mother had happened upon was now wife to a troubled young man and soon a mother to Cordelia's mistake, both glitches in the Randolphs' smooth running of things. Was this more than I was capable of? Had any of the training and discipline I'd received from the Sisters of Providence prepared me for the future I had stepped into? Did the love of my parents build a strong enough foundation to support this new life?

I fetched the lantern from the parlour and set it on my writing table. I reached for the notepad and fountain pen and began allowing the words of a story to distract me from the troubling thoughts tumbling around in my weary head.

Leah
1968

After two days of staying close to the toilet, I groggily made my way across the parking lot of the Cave and Basin Pool with the morning sun barely visible behind the mountain range. The choice of Banff for our pre-Olympic training location seemed like a good idea because of the high altitude of the mountains, but the small detail of there being no competitive-sized pool here had somehow gone unnoticed. So our training regime had had to be adapted to the small pool in the Parks Canada facility. As if that were not challenging enough, some error in food preparation made the entire team of swimmers and coaching staff come down with a severe case of food poisoning.

This was my second year on the coaching staff, and despite the occasional envious moments, I did enjoy working with Elaine, Marilyn, Angela, and Marion. Six years ago, I had to face the crushing disappointment of not qualifying for the women's relay or any of the individual events, which meant if I were to go to the 1964 Olympics in Tokyo I would be so far down the substitute rooster that a tsunami would have to take out most of the swimmers before I would get a chance to compete. Daddy got me through the crippling crisis of defeat I felt when my lifelong dream was shattered by a matter of seconds in my finishing times in Perth at the 1962 Commonwealth Games.

Daddy: this amazing man who had come into my life only

six months before that defeat but took on the role of father so completely that to call him anything but Daddy never entered my mind. God knew my mother had never been Mommy to me, and even more detailed stories of my father as she became able to share them never made him real enough to make me feel I had a father. But the first few times my mother brought Bud Alexander to meet Gram and me, I was quite sure if anyone could be a father to me, it was him.

Bud had been left with three young children to raise when his wife contracted a fatal infection right after the birth of their last baby. He immediately gave up his job as a train engineer, which often took him away from home, so that he could care for a newborn, two-year-old, and five-year-old. His expertise with large engines allowed him to make his living at home by fixing clocks and watches. After attending to the needs of his boys until their bedtime, he would labour long into the night making the miniscule parts of the timepieces customers left for him to repair, work again. Perhaps it was this vocation that gave Bud Alexander the patience and dedication needed to take on my mother and me.

Instantly having three older brothers was, for the most part, a perk as well. Even though two of them were married and the youngest lived in Sudbury by the time Mother and I moved into the Alexander household, my newly acquired brothers were a good part of the package. I felt too old to change my name from *Pasternak* to *Alexander*, but Bud and his sons, Gary, Thomas, and Kenneth, became the family I had wanted for as long as I could remember.

So it was Daddy who met me at the airport when I returned from Australia. Together we drove to Odessa, and he stayed there with me for almost a month. I couldn't help but think of the years my mother spent in the depths of her own misery as I struggled to come to terms with my disappointment. I knew that what I was facing was in no way as devastating as what my mother had gone through. I also realized that what Daddy had been through losing his wife and being left to raise his young boys was, in comparison to my situation, much more challenging. But never as Daddy listened and supported me did he chastise me for miring myself in self-pity; he just gently guided me to find my way out.

During those weeks, I got more of my mother and father's story from Daddy than I had from anyone else. I knew my father had died in Poland before I was born but had never been told the terrible details. I finally realized the extent of my mother's grief and shock, a widowed bride pregnant with me, coming back to Canada on the *Queen Mary*. I thought of the horror my father had survived and how he had somehow ended up in the same place as my mother, and together their love had created me. At sixteen, disillusioned by my situation but still a romantic, I held on to that fact, and suddenly I wanted to know everything I could about the Holocaust. I made daily trips to the Odessa library to immerse myself in everything I could find on the subject.

With every word Daddy told me, I could also see how much he loved my mother, and I felt shame for not being more understanding of her pain. He sensed this and assured me I had nothing to be ashamed of, as a young child has no capacity to see their parent beyond the immediacy of their own needs. His interpretation of my mother's struggle also served to put my grandmother's devotion toward me in perspective. By the end of those days I no longer believed Gram had been the only person who'd loved me. I finally accepted that my mother loved me all those years and had done the best she could.

With this newfound acceptance, I welcomed her when she came to Gram's and she and Daddy took me home to Toronto. In the next three years I forgot swimming, returned to school, and lived my final years of high school as a typical teenager revelling in the love of a mother and father. Then after graduation it was Mom's love and direction that pushed me back toward my passion and to the life I loved, returning to poolside not as a competitive swimmer but as a coach.

Clara
1993

"I will be back in three weeks, Mother. Bud and the boys are meeting me at Leah's and will stay for my exhibit. I didn't mean to give you the impression you weren't welcome. If you've changed your mind, we could get you packed fast enough. I have arranged for Mrs. Fillmore to come by every day to do a few chores and prepare your evening meal. And Hilary hopes to visit you for a few days before she and Colin leave for British Columbia, which gives you something to look forward to."

"I am perfectly content to stay put. I have made my last trip to Toronto as far as I can see. I'm happy for people to come see me, but I'm too old to be gallivanting around the country. If I were going to go anywhere, I'd get myself down to see Cordelia one more time. Her health is not good, and I don't expect she'll be travelling again."

"She's settled into a nice facility in Saint John, Mother."

"She was ready. She had no real attachment to her house anyway. It is the cottage she's attached to, and it can't be easy for her knowing she's unlikely to return to it. She has kept it, though, so perhaps she will." Mother paused. "I know you would have dragged me along to Toronto if I'd wanted to go, and I would love to see your exhibit, but only if I could come right back home afterwards. I'm very proud of you, you know. I don't say it nearly often enough. Now, you better get going.

You don't want to get into that crazy afternoon traffic on the 401."

I leaned over to kiss my mother. Her thin frame startled me as I hugged her. It was as if she were disappearing in front of my eyes. Would her body give out long before her mind and her fierce independence? The main focus of my exhibit was the black-and-white photographs I had taken of Mother last summer. If she attended Friday night's exhibit, it might not even be clear to patrons that the series of photographs were even of the same woman. Lillianne McDonough, the renowned and influential author, was now a frail shadow of the formidable woman she had once been.

"At least your father will be able to attend. He is very proud of you, too. How wise he was to give you that Leica so many years ago. He knew your art would come through the lens of a camera, not through words or painting. Please give Clifton and Martin my best. Now really you must get going. Maybe I'll have a couple of hours of rest before that insufferable Evelyn Fillmore gets here to boss me about."

"Oh, she's not that bad. You just hate anyone who doesn't bend to your wishes. Poor Hilary has no idea what she's in for. Don't scare her off."

"Am I really the shrew you make me out to be? Just because I like things a certain way and don't hesitate saying what's on my mind? The way I look at it, I've not got much time left to straighten things out."

Cordelia
1918

Sarah laid hot compresses across my engorged breasts. With each mewing noise coming from the other room I could feel the pulsing ache. Sarah assured me another day or two of this misery and the sensation would be gone. The agony seemed undeserved; I'd already withstood the unspeakable pain of bringing the infant into the world.

A girl. The poor wee thing, entering a world so determined to enslave her, to mold her and suppress any dreams or desires she might dare entertain. A world where she will likely someday have to labour in such anguish to rid herself of the seed so carelessly planted.

I had resigned myself to the choice I'd made. I had dutifully hidden myself away and for months played over the scenario, no longer wrestling with the idea of handing over my newborn to my brother and his wife. But during that last push, and as Sarah cradled the child and cut the cord, my heart lurched and it took all my strength not to call out and cancel this cruel plan we'd concocted.

In the end, strength and character were not traits the pampered Cordelia Randolph possessed. I was a coward and a puppet to the constraints my mother so carefully cultivated in me. I could not push against the proper and declare myself the mother of this bastard child. I could only retreat and whimper as if my pain were only physical.

I did not aspire to the theatre, but one might think me a natural actress watching the performances I delivered in the days following the birth. Firstly, I refused to hold the infant, stating I wanted no contact with the scrawny creature. I demanded she be taken to another room immediately and then delved deeply into the throes of self-pity.

The theatre. For some reason during labour, my muddled mind kept going to the photograph on the postcard Mother had received from her sister Victoria in August while we were in Chicago. The postcard was of the grand Imperial Theatre in Saint John, New Brunswick, and Mother had studied it at great lengths. Correspondence from Victoria was rare, but Mother seemed especially emotional about the short note her sister had written.

As I stifled the tears I felt rising in my chest, feeling as if my soul would explode, I concentrated instead on my plan, and Saint John loomed large. I had no intention of returning to Chicago. I could not bear to think of travelling side by side with Lily and Cliff and watching my baby swaddled and cared for inches away. Sarah had procured a wet nurse until baby formula could be purchased in Kingston. A local woman whose own child had been born dead was providing nourishment for my baby while my own breasts ached for her suckle.

I would leave as soon as I was able. I'd done my part. The baby was delivered, Cliff had his props of wife and daughter, Lily had her elevated status and freedom, and I would demand my compensation. I would travel to Kingston, board the train, and make my way to Saint John. I would impose on my Aunt Victoria and from there decide the course of my life. I would determine the next step in my life and never again defer to another human being.

Lillianne
1918

I could not convince Cliff or Cordelia to come with me on this beautiful moonlit walk. The January night was cold and crisp, the snow-covered fields illuminated by the full moon and vast array of stars. I couldn't imagine a lovelier place on earth and was filled with peace and well-being. For now, at least, my exhaustion had dissipated, and the worry and frustration that sometimes gripped me had evaporated.

Oh, how I wished Cordelia and Cliff would allow their heaviness to be lifted. Cordelia complained and griped about her condition and seldom let a good thought surface. Cliff was so weighed down in misery. At least his drawing gave him some pleasure, and the time he spent with Samuel helped to comfort him. Our last letter from Chicago had brought the terrible news of Charlie's passing.

On this island I felt so removed from the troubles of the world and the sorrows we would be forced to face when we left. Here in this peaceful place I was able to remember Charlie as he was during the months I knew him and not face his absence and the crippling grief that must be consuming the Randolphs. My job here was to keep Cliff and Cordelia cared for and to prepare myself for the next part of my role as Mrs. Clifton Randolph the Fourth.

The people on the small island were good and hardworking, and although they never refrained from reminding me I was from away, they embraced and welcomed us into their community. I was especially blessed with the friendship of Maggie Williston.

*

In late October, Cliff and I were walking by a house at the end of the Marshall 40 Foot Road when Cliff sat himself down abruptly on an upturned crate beside the mailbox. A very pretty young woman was making her way from the mailbox, and I saw her lift the edge of her apron to wipe a tear from her eye. I had seen her from a distance on previous walks but had not had occasion to speak with her. Samuel had informed me her name was Maggie Williston and that her husband was serving with the Ontario Regiment in Italy. I could tell from the bulge beneath her apron that she was quite far along with child.

"I hope we did not startle you."

"Oh, no, I often see you and your gentleman walking by from my kitchen window."

"His name is Cliff and I am Lily."

"Forgive me, Lily. I am somewhat preoccupied. I have not heard a word from my husband for nearly a month, and he has been so faithful in writing until now. My time is getting close, and I hate to think of birthing his child without so much as an idea of where or how he is. I'm thinking Prime Minister Borden has not given us women who wait at home much regard with his flowery patriotic speeches, which seem to tell us nothing about an end to this nightmare."

"Maggie, is it?"

"Oh, yes. Sorry for my rudeness. I can't seem to be civil these days. I am filled with anger at a war that takes a young man from his pregnant wife and his duties at home to fight across the ocean for God knows what."

"Cliff planned to enlist. He is an American and was anxious to do his part once his country joined the fight. Circumstances stood in the way, however. I can only imagine how you are feeling."

I looked at Cliff sitting, staring straight ahead, not seeming to notice our conversation, and I thought briefly of what I had tried not to let myself think in the last few days. Would it have been better for his family to have lost him to the horrors of war than to see him in this condition, barely able to show the least emotion or spark of life?

"Was he injured in some way?" Maggie commented as if able to read my thoughts.

"He has suffered a trauma, but I am hopeful that he will make a complete recovery." I tried to exude the optimism I was not feeling. "I see you are with child. Cliff's sister is with us. She, too, is expecting a baby. She will deliver in April."

"Would you like to come in for a cup of tea? I would love some company. The neighbours have been very good, but they have their own lives to attend to. My family lives in Ottawa, and James's family has passed on. His mother got away last winter before James signed up. Luckily she never had to see him head off to war and never had to feel the worry of not knowing, when all around you people are getting word of terrible injuries and deaths. I can barely stand to see poor Mrs. Willard, and her with five children to raise, Gladys the eldest and not yet ten years of age. Those youngest ones won't even remember their father. That is what I fear the most, that this child will never even be held by his own father." She paused. "Listen to me going on so. Not much wonder my neighbours don't break down my door to visit. The doom and gloom I go on about. Bring Cliff into the house and I'll steep the tea."

*

Our first visit began a friendship that became my saving grace. I rapped on Maggie's door, seeing lantern light still glowing in the kitchen.

"What brings you out on this cold night?"

"Just walking and trying to shed the burden of the day. I know I have no place to complain when you still face each day not knowing the whereabouts of James. My walk has served to lift my funk somewhat and I intended to turn around at your gateway, but I saw your light on and I thought you might like some company."

"I am always happy for your company, Lily. My time is getting close, and for some reason this baby will not settle tonight. I have had a burst of energy today, and the older ladies say that can be a sign. I sent word to Sarah that she might be needed soon. I am afraid, Lily. As much as I look forward to this baby being born, I can't help wonder if I have the courage."

"I expect you'll do just fine. No one really knows what they're capable of doing until they are forced to do it. As I've been telling Cordelia these last few days, women have been giving birth since time began and somehow get through it. I don't mind saying to you I'm getting quite fed up with Cordelia's dramatic ways. I knew these months would not be easy, but I find myself wanting to give her a good shaking."

"I take it she was sent here to have the baby to keep people from knowing? It must be difficult for her to know her condition is seen as shameful. She certainly wouldn't have the same feelings of anticipation and excitement as I do. Even without my husband here, I know my suffering will bring great joy. Does Cordelia plan on keeping the baby?"

"Cliff and I will raise her baby as our own. His family arranged our marriage and our stay here as part of the plan to manage Cordelia's pregnancy. She will be the aunt and we the parents of the child Cordelia births."

"No wonder she can find no joy in her situation. Does the father of the child even know?"

"No. It was a one-time indiscretion that resulted in her unfortunate state. An error in judgement and a night of carelessness have brought her such misery. My heart breaks for her."

"What about you? How do you really feel about what has befallen you? Your future has been impacted by her actions. Are you willing to take the consequence of it? I am thinking perhaps your struggle may be greater than you are letting on."

Maggie's words hit me forcefully. She had just voiced the conflict I'd been battling long before I stepped off the ferry onto this island. I had played a part in this, but had I truly considered the magnitude of what I'd done? I saw this arrangement as my path to a better future—but had I instead locked myself into a future I had absolutely no control over? What price was I paying for my release from being a housemaid and a person of no value? Was I not still in the employ of Marion Randolph?

"I cannot see any purpose in questioning my situation, Maggie. I was powerless before and now at least I have some security. As Cliff's wife, I will always have the comforts and assurance of a home and a place in society. As an orphan and a housemaid, I was at the mercy of whoever chose to dictate my circumstance. You must think me self-serving and greedy, but is it so wrong to want a future that gives me back what my past robbed me of?"

I began sobbing, and it was several minutes before Maggie spoke. "I am not judging you. I can only imagine your suffering after losing your parents and the years of misery you lived in the orphanage and in domestic service. My family was not one of means, but I always had enough to eat and felt their love and protection. Of course you're frightened by the thoughts of marriage and motherhood, but you will not be lost in it. You can build the future you desire. And please take comfort in knowing as you face the next months I will be a friend to you. But I fear this conversation needs to be cut short. The twinges I was barely feeling when you arrived have become quite strong. I am thinking perhaps you should go now to fetch Sarah Brown."

After summoning Sarah, I stopped at home to tell Cordelia I would be returning to Maggie's, where I would stay as long as I was needed. But my hope for a fast and uneventful delivery was dashed when the sky darkened the next evening and Maggie's labour still continued. Sarah was confident the head would crown soon. But in the wee hours of the morning there was no progress, and Maggie's pain was worsening with no end in sight. With each cry of anguish, I feared her stamina would fail and she would succumb.

"This is common for first deliveries, Lily. I have seen first babies take three days to come."

"How can you stand to see such agony, Sarah?"

"The travail of childbirth is the lot we have been given, and I have seen my share. In life we are given many hardships but in turn many rewards. Trust me: when this baby is delivered and Maggie holds her child, the pain and suffering will be transcended. It is the dark and light, the sorrow and joy, which are the very force of life that drives everything. At the darkest hour, all we can do is cling to the hope of dawn's awakening."

The awakening of which Sarah spoke came at 7:43 on January 25, 1918, in the form of a nine-pound, eleven-ounce boy whom Maggie immediately put to her breast and named James Clifton Williston. Tears streamed down her cheeks and I wiped her brow and assured her that, someday soon, James would return and proudly receive this amazing gift she had laboured so fiercely to deliver.

Lillianne
1993

I spent an hour absorbed in thoughts of newborn babies. I'd heard of women in seniors homes who sat and rocked dolls or stuffed animals, believing themselves to be once again nurturing a newborn child. I could not truly say I ever possessed such maternal cravings, but I carried out my duties as best I could. The first newborn I held was Maggie's boy, James. He was the most precious sight the morning I took him from Sarah Brown's arms and swaddled him. Poor Maggie was near death from exhaustion and was barely able to grasp the miracle of his birth. She briefly suckled him and then fell into a deep and well-deserved sleep.

I'd been away two full days and was worried about Cliff and Cordelia in my absence. But I returned to find them perfectly fine; I was not as pivotal to their well-being as I thought. From that day on, Cordelia left the house regularly, even staying for days at a time with Maggie. Perhaps seeing that Maggie had survived the birthing of a baby as large as James gave Cordelia hope for her own survival.

Clara was a beautiful baby, but her temperament was ghastly. Maybe the trauma of her birth and the abrupt break in the mother-child bond caused her poor disposition, as it wasn't until she was past a year old that she slept the night or began to show any signs of contentment. I was at a loss as to how to care for her. I was not neglectful, but I let Mavis assume most of the mothering in the first few years.

Perhaps my lack of involvement with Clara was reason for my obsession when it came to mothering Leah. She was a pleasant, delightful baby from the start, and I willingly took over caring for her when Clara was unable. If ever I felt motherly instincts, it was during the first five years of my precious granddaughter's life. My love for Leah was the closest I had to experiencing that wonderful bond. And then Hilary, of course.

Hilary was the most beautiful child I'd ever laid eyes on. She came into the world with a thick head of curly black hair and a face like an angel. I swear she smiled soon after she was born and spent her toddler years smiling and laughing. Her pleasant temperament was constant, and she rarely cried or showed displeasure. Her parents' devotion to her only intensified after the stillbirth of their son. Hilary was to be, as her mother and grandmother before her, an only child.

Single, adored children, just as Hilary's great-grandmother had been... though the difficult truth I was facing was that I wasn't actually related to any of them. Where would the telling of that fact leave me? It was much too late for Cordelia to take her rightful place in the family tree. She had been seen as the spinster aunt, the independent career woman, first a nurse and then an esteemed obstetrician, delivering other women's babies but never having her own.

She put on such a brave and noble front. We only stayed on Amherst Island for two weeks after Clara was born, and Cordelia had travelled to Kingston a week earlier. I did not feel she was strong enough, but she was determined and had decided she was never going back to Chicago. She got a drive to Kingston and left by train to stay with her aunt in Saint John.

Cordelia always claimed her choice to stay away was because of the anger and resentment she felt for her mother. She was heartbroken when she separated herself from Clara and transferred those feelings into hatred for a mother who could so effortlessly condemn her daughter. Cordelia found a confidante in her aunt Victoria, who harboured her own resentment toward her sister, firstly blaming her for the drowning death of their mother and then jealous of the privilege marrying Clifton Randolph provided Marion.

However unhealthy that alliance was, at first it helped give Cordelia the focus to make her way and become the successful woman she was. Years later, she was able to make her peace with her mother, but never saw her in person again.

Babies. All those babies Cordelia Randolph delivered in the forty years of her career. Did any of that make up for the one baby she couldn't claim because of the shame and judgement of the time and the society she'd been born into? How cruel would it be for me to now share the truth and allow Cordelia her motherhood, seventy-five years too late?

I picked up the phone and dialled Cordelia's number.

Cordelia
1918

I could barely grasp the fact I was still alive. Against Sarah and Lily's advice, I had taken a ride into Kingston on a truck leaving Amherst Island on the first of May. I did not expect the ride to be comfortable, but by the time I was dropped off at Hanley Station I was cramping and quite distressed. It wasn't until after I boarded the train and settled into my berth I noticed the bleeding. At first I was not alarmed, sure that some bleeding was natural. I lay down, thinking the pain would lessen if I attempted to sleep. I drifted off despite my acute discomfort but was jolted awake a while later. A spasm as terrible as my most difficult labouring forced me to sit up, and I realized the bed was soaked with blood. I rang for assistance but barely responded to the attendant who answered.

When I awoke I was in a bed in hospital surrounded by a cacophony that seemed foreign. From my limited knowledge I knew it was French being spoken. A nurse leaned toward me speaking broken English with a measure of compassion.

I understood "Montreal" and "surgery" in her string of words. In my addled state, I tried to shift in my bed to get a better look at my surroundings, which seemed a large room with several beds, but weakness and discomfort kept me still.

"I get doctor, mademoiselle," the nurse said.

It seemed a very long time before the nurse returned with

a tall middle-aged man. He was dressed in a doctor's white starched coat, but his looks were so similar to my father's I thought I was hallucinating. Tears came to my eyes and I choked out, "Daddy."

The man spoke technical words with precision and detail, not completely lacking compassion but with a matter-of-fact tone that left no room for the emotion welling up in my throat. I had been taken from the train and brought to the Montreal General Hospital in grave condition. I'd lost a huge amount of blood due to a postpartum hemorrhage. Emergency surgery was needed, which resulted in a complete hysterectomy.

The doctor must have realized the gravity of telling a seventeen-year-old girl he has had to remove her uterus and childbearing was no longer a possibility for her. His face showed the burden of this revelation, but I also detected judgement of a girl who had just given birth with no next of kin and no indication of a newborn nearby. I may have read this into his facial expression, but my shame and his declaration of my punishment were the messages I received.

I turned my head from the doctor's words. Perhaps death would take me from the depth of my despair and I could be buried and forgotten: an unnamed girl in an unmarked grave.

Hilary
1993

I closed the flaps of the last cardboard box and pushed it toward the back door. Colin had already left with one load. Thankfully we were able to store everything in his parents' basement. We let the apartment go, since neither of us was sure we were returning to Queen's in the fall. My parents were not happy with my decision to take a year off. A degree only half completed is as useless as no university education at all, according to them.

"Money for your education was set aside before you were even born. How many kids your age can say that? No student loans for a Randolph great-grandchild. You don't have to earn your own tuition. Why are you even planting trees?"

These had been Mom's arguments when we talked on the phone since I'd dropped the news that I was working in BC for the summer. I hadn't added the possibility of not returning to school at all. When she and Dad arrived last weekend and I dropped that piece of news, the arguments intensified.

"I can't believe you and Colin are throwing away what you already have. Once you stop you won't go back. You have no idea how sorry I am that I never finished my degree. What are Colin's parents saying? Wait until your great-grandmother hears about this."

I had written Gram a long letter explaining why I wasn't going back to university. She had not said very much when she wrote back to me, and she certainly hadn't reacted the way Mom was threatening she would. She said we would discuss it when I got to her house. As for the tree planting, I was not entirely convinced I wanted to spend my summer in the wilderness. I would much rather spend the time with Gram.

I mentioned this briefly to Colin last night, but planned on giving a stronger argument for staying in Odessa once we actually got there. I would lay on thickly how much my great-grandmother needed me once we saw her. Surely a ninety-three-year-old woman could elicit his sympathy. My time with her was running out. He could go tree planting by himself. It wouldn't be the end of the world to be separated for two months.

I had been struggling with my novel, and not just because of Professor Dunfield's harsh criticism. Why was I digging so deeply into a family story I barely knew anything about? My novel was fiction and hadn't started out as my great-grandfather's story, but somehow I could not shake the hold it had on me. It had been the remark Gramps made during the visit I'd had with him and Martin two years ago. We had gone to Toronto's gay pride parade. When we got back to their condo, Gramps broke down and wept before he was able to speak about his own experience. The emotion in his voice was intense as he compared society's tolerance and understanding of homosexuality these days compared to when he had been institutionalized to eradicate his condition. The few details he shared haunted me, and my novel began with the main character a patient in the New York State Psychiatric Institute in 1916.

And another comment he made that day stayed with me:

"Even the hoax Lily and Mother pulled off wasn't enough to prove to Chicago that Clifton Randolph the Fourth was not a freak."

Lillianne
1993

I could see a sliver of light under my bedroom door but turned from it, letting the deep darkness envelop me. I remembered the task of filling the oil lamps and trimming the wicks. I could recall the circle of light the lanterns gave off: a mellow glow just barely lighting the way as you walked through a dark house. Electric lights were harsher, more glaring.

I had never been afraid of the dark. Nights at St. Vincent in the dark shadows of our room seemed foreboding at first, but I soon realized it was not the darkness I feared. Darkness gave freedom, anonymity, refuge, and the time to remember the essence of who you were. During my days of domestic servitude I rose early and retired late, and darkness offered me rest. The darkness on my late-night walks during our months on Amherst Island was always a welcome gift. I never minded the hours in the middle of the night.

Those hours were more of a challenge lately, though. I welcomed sleep, but most nights I awoke with a jolt. Then for the next few hours I battled the same scrimmage I'd been having with myself for months. A light would not have diverted that.

I had so wanted Cordelia's approval. Had I known for months that time was running out for her to give me permission? Had I waited until I knew Cordelia would no longer be able to stop me? Had she ever considered telling the secret herself, claiming what was rightfully hers before it was too late? Had her silence been in consideration of me, Cliff, Clara, or herself?

We had all so carefully protected the truth, and had long stopped questioning the morality of it. Possibly we had never dissected it at all. We became deeply committed to the lie immediately, and no one broke the pact. Perhaps the guilt I felt, causing the burning desire to unload my burden, was fitting, since it had been me who started it all. And me who gained the most.

Cordelia lost the most the morning she laboured so valiantly to give us Clara. She had suffered greatly, and days later the hemorrhaging forced a complete hysterectomy. She almost lost her life. But we had already lost her when we accepted her beautiful gift and watched her leave.

She did not get to be present as her daughter grew, did not get to welcome her granddaughter or cradle her great-grand-daughter. She lost them all, and I got to stand in her place. I thought I wanted her permission to tell Clara the truth, but as I realized she wasn't able to give me that, I wondered if what I really wanted was for her to forbid me from telling. If I'd gotten strict instructions to leave well enough alone, I would have been forced to do so.

So learning that Cordelia no longer had the ability to discuss this with me came as a shock. At least I could no longer hurt her, but I had robbed Clara of the opportunity to truly speak to her mother. Also, I could not share the blame of so great a lie with Cordelia. Clara's anger could not be doled out equally. Would she even see Cliff as a guilty party? She had forgiven him long ago and accepted the choices he had made.

Cordelia had been an exceptional aunt. She was unwavering in her attention to her niece. She welcomed Clara often in her New Brunswick home and travelled around the world with her on many occasions. But Cordelia never visited our home and never returned to Chicago. She sometimes visited Cliff and Martin in Toronto, but she never saw her parents again after the day they left us at the Amherst Island ferry dock. Cordelia had not received any of the Randolph inheritance, which had been reduced during the crash. She did not benefit from the sale of Randolph Island, although a trust fund was established for the education of her descendants.

The Randolph name had been carried by Cordelia's daughter but ended with her. No sons carried it to the next generation, and possibly that was Cordelia's greatest revenge. Her parents lived without the shame of her mistake but didn't benefit from it either. Cordelia lived a life of accomplishment and service and now sat in a Saint John nursing home, no longer knowing her own name, let alone suffering the guilt and sorrow of giving up her daughter. It was too late to make amends, but, nevertheless, the truth was forcing its way to the surface.

I turned toward the bedside table and switched on the lamp. Sitting up, I reached for a photograph of my great-granddaughter. The lie would stop with her. Hilary would tell her children the story of their true genealogy. She would proudly claim Cordelia and reveal how a family had allowed the judgement of society to lead them into such deception and falsehood.

Lillianne
1934

"It is almost midnight, Clara. Mavis and I were becoming quite concerned. We were just remembering when you ran away from the Royal York and I found you at Union Station waiting for a train to Chicago."

"Oh, Mother. I was a just a child then. I did not run away tonight, I just stayed at Vivian's to listen to the Hit Parade on her radio. I knew if I came home, you and Mavis would be listening to Fibber McGee and Molly. It's bad enough I have to live on this godforsaken backroad. I can't be sitting around listening to boring radio dramas like some old lady."

"She thinks we're old ladies, Mavis."

"You know what I mean. I have no social life. Odessa is no hub of activity, but at least you don't have to walk a mile to see people your own age. I can't help it if you and Mavis are perfectly content to sit here night after night. I want more than that. As soon as I can, I am getting out of here."

"Well, I hope when you are ready to go, you will let us know you're leaving."

"You'll know. When I finally get out of here, I'm throwing a great big party."

As I watched Clara storm up the stairs, I thought back to this afternoon. Was I content? Did I want more? Mavis's trip into Kingston and Clara being at school had given Will and I some uninterrupted time together. It had been delightful. It was so difficult to find those stolen moments, and it seemed Will was becoming impatient. His parting words still echoed in my mind, and with Clara's angry words, I felt the urge to break into tears, but becoming emotional was not my way.

"I want more than this, Lily. I want to sleep by your side every night. I want to see your face across my supper table. I want to proudly walk down the street with you on my arm. I want to marry you and tell the world you are mine."

Will's words hadn't surprised me, but the tone with which he delivered them held a tension I hadn't detected before. For the last few years he'd seemed content with the way things were. It was difficult to hide our relationship, to sneak time together, to suppress our feelings for one another, but we had managed. We had a rhythm, and for the most part it worked. We saw each other almost daily, as there was always something to fix or a job to be done. He'd spent the summer building the gazebo.

Will knew my imperfections. I shared all my secrets with him and confided in him more than anyone. But would he be willing to accept the fact Randolph money kept me from divorcing Cliff and making a life with him? Odessa might tolerate an affair between the reclusive author on Millcreek Road and her handyman, but moving him in while still married was not acceptable. Would Will force me to make the choice, to give up one for the other?

Clara
1945

I didn't know whose reaction to the broken engagement was more difficult to take. The look on Joe's face still haunted me two weeks later, and I did feel guilty for leading him on so long. Mother, however, did not need to be quite so cruel in her blunt assessment of the situation. She said it had not come as a surprise, given what she described as my "romp through the bevy of available men" in the three years Joe had been serving overseas.

"You had no intention of marrying him, Clara, and did not even, or so it would seem, save your virtue for him any longer than it took his vessel to sail from the harbour, the day he set out on active duty. You took your own active duty very seriously, and it's a small miracle you didn't have a child or two to present him with on his return."

Mother took every chance to let me know that my social life was of a low moral standard. This from a woman who had lived the last twenty-five years in a reclusive state writing book after book, barely leaving her house. How could she possibly think that I would want the life she had in her brick fortress, stuck out in the middle of nowhere?

When I moved to Toronto and took my first apartment on Bloor Street, she was horrified that I would live alone in the middle of a busy city. Luckily I had my own access to Randolph money, or she never would have agreed to finance me in those months before I got employment in the mailroom of the *Toronto Star*. Father had always been much more supportive of my ambitions and had never judged me the way Mother did.

When I returned Joe's grandmother's sapphire ring and told him that I was no longer in love with him, he had been crushed. I felt very bad about that, but experienced such relief that I had not given into the euphoria of the passion we had found together in the weeks before he left for Europe, three years before. At the time it seemed like a hasty marriage might somehow ensure his safe return, and the fact we could not engage a magistrate to perform the ceremony in time was the only reason that I had not become Mrs. Joseph MacDougall before he sailed across the ocean. I had tried to remain loyal (longer than Mother said) and wrote regular heartfelt letters, not letting on my feelings had changed. It would have been cruel to break up with him while he was suffering the hardships of war.

Two weeks ago, I waited at the armouries for Joe's troop to return, and without fanfare broke off our engagement. I had considered not telling him in person, leading him along for the week, and then leaving him a note before I travelled to New York to take passage on the *Queen Mary*. That would have been the cowardly way out. I explained that to Mother, but her judgement remained harsh, and our last visit had not ended well.

*

I had started working at the *Toronto Star* two years before but never shared that fact in any of my letters to Joe. I spent the first six months doing menial tasks in the mailroom before getting the opportunity to apply to be assistant to the copyeditor. My last name, which still held some clout in the right circles, and my affair with the copyeditor Thomas Blackmore helped get me the promotion. But the affair, although entertaining at first, was not something I was willing to continue once Tom made it clear he wanted it to become permanent. His overinflated opinion of both his good looks and his importance at the *Star* were not enough motivation for me, and I ended it before he foolishly shattered his wife by terminating their fifteen-year marriage.

By the time our affair ended, I'd gotten my first photography assignment and was moving closer toward my ambition of becoming the *Star*'s first female press photographer. The first assignment, photographing groups of women knitting socks for soldiers in a Red Cross workroom, had not been exactly the news-breaking story of my dreams, but from that I went on to photograph women soldering airplane parts, and then I took a series of pictures of people waiting in long lineups to use their food stamps at Eaton's College Street store and other locations in downtown Toronto.

The opportunity to travel to Europe had come about when Terrance Kilfoil returned from the Canadian Army's Film and Photo Unit. Terrence was owed a favour, and the month we spent together helped to transfer that favour to me in the form of my current assignment: covering France's free election in October.

So after breaking my engagement, a short, unpleasant visit to Odessa, and a train trip to New York, I found myself aboard the *Queen Mary*, sailing to Southampton. I was very excited about the adventure before me. Not only would I get the opportunity to photograph postwar France, which could be very beneficial in advancing my career, I would get to visit Aunt Cordelia in London.

Aunt Cordelia's last trip back to Canada was in 1939, and I had missed her terribly. She had been so anxious for me to come, but up until now she'd been worried about my travelling overseas. This was a very troubling time to be in Europe.

When I wrote to Aunt Cordelia about my plans to sail on the *Queen Mary* she did not approve of my decision, but I was twenty-seven years old and neither she nor Mother had any say in how I chose to live. Brave Aunt Cordelia, who during the terrible war had continually risked her life with no regard for her own safety, was full of worry when it came to me. Mavis was always worrying about me, too, but I no longer had to consider her opinion, God rest her soul.

As far as Aunt Cordelia was concerned, the dozen or so troops on board the *Queen Mary* and the large crew and thirty passengers would provide me no security and could all potentially cause me harm. Her latest letter was a lengthy list of precautions I should take in every detail of my journey, from how I should walk through the streets of New York to how to fasten my cabin door securely and proceed from the train station when I got to London. She even suggested I disguise myself as an elderly woman for the entire trip, because, according to her, large numbers of young men just released from the responsibilities of battle were now waiting to ravage young women travelling alone. I assured her I would—for the first part of my journey, at least—be travelling with two *Star* reporters who would take the job of protecting my well-being (if perhaps not my honour) very seriously.

*

Mother set an example of independence for me, even if she did not always encourage me to live independently. She lived her life capably as an unattached woman. She also claimed to have set an example of celibate restraint, but it was common knowledge to Mother's friends and neighbours that Mr. Carlson, who used to carry out household maintenance and repairs, had spent part of his time looking after some of Mother's more personal needs as well. I wondered if she'd found another man to do so since Mr. Carlson's death.

We were midway across the Atlantic, and the last few nights had been spent in Gerald's stateroom instead of my own. Alfred showed no interest in me, supposedly happily married to his annoying bride, Ruby, for almost a year. Why, if Ruby was so wonderful, did he agree to take this assignment overseas?

"Don't think, Gerald, that I have any intention of keeping this up when we dock in Southampton. It is lovely to have the company on these boring nights at sea, but I don't want to be tied to you when I get to London."

"Oh, it's good company I'm providing, is it? You're a better actress than Lana Turner if it's only good company I offer. I thought maybe I meant something to you, but if it's only a warm body you need, I'll give you that as long as you want. I'm not looking for a wife, and I damn sure don't want to be a daddy."

"Don't you worry about that. I look after my own business. I don't trust my fate to a flimsy piece of rubber."

"Always the romantic, aren't you, Clara?"

Hilary
1993

I was preoccupied on the drive to Gram's. I'd done the short drive many times, but I didn't notice when Colin made the wrong turn. He kept saying he wasn't angry with me, but his outburst as I pointed out his error said otherwise. I'd meant to wait until we got to Gram's to tell him my change of plans, but when we stood in the outdoor outfitters store yesterday, I couldn't see the point of buying gear for tree planting if I wasn't going.

"Well, it was nice of you to finally tell me," Colin said as we left the store abruptly. "When did you decide this?"

"I have been thinking about it for a while. You know how close I am to Gram. She's almost ninety-four, for goodness' sake, and she's not going to live forever. What if I'm stuck in the middle of BC and she dies? Can they even call into wherever we're going?"

"Wherever *I'm* going, you mean."

"I really want Gram's help with my novel, too, Colin. I've lost my confidence, and maybe with Gram's guidance I can get back on track. You know the biggest reason I want to take a year off is so I can seriously get to my writing. You have been supportive of this. I just can't see wasting my summer when I could spend it with Gram and concentrate on my writing."

"Spending the summer with me would be wasting your time? Have we been wasting the last three years?"

"No, of course not. Two months apart won't kill us. You don't even really have to go, you know. I'm sure you could get a job in Kingston."

"I'm going. I've already committed, and we agreed the money we'd make in two months would set us up to make whatever choices we want in the fall. Now it's only going to be about half as much—but I suppose you can always fall back on Randolph money."

"You say that like it's a terrible thing. My trust fund has paid the rent for the last two years. So what if I don't want to break my back planting trees? You've always understood writing comes first with me."

"I didn't think it came before me."

"Now you're just being ridiculous."

Colin had barely said a word all morning. The drive was unpleasant, but even with the tension I was filled with excitement at the thought of sharing my manuscript with Gram.

Clara
1945

I packed several rolls of film securely in Gerald's kit for his return to Toronto. I knew by not returning to Toronto with Gerald and Alfred I probably would not get the byline on whatever photographs the editor chose to accompany Alfred's story on the French election, but I was not regretting my decision to stay. I'd spent frenzied days and nights enjoying everything Paris had to offer. The streets were teeming with American and Canadian troops. I had no intentions of going home yet.

This morning when I fastened my hair into its tight victory roll and applied my red lipstick, I looked at myself in the mirror. In some people's opinion I was bordering on being an old maid. There had been less condemnation of single women in the war years, when so many young men were away fighting. And my engagement to Joe had in some ways given me an acceptability, as I was spoken for, just waiting for my man to come home.

My looks were certainly an asset. I had been told many times how much I resembled Aunt Cordelia. She was still a very attractive woman. I never questioned her choice to remain unmarried. She made her own way, even choosing to do so without the security of Randolph money or the Randolph name. Dr. Cordelia Kingston was making her own way and never answered to anyone.

I had not gone without anything in my childhood, but Mother

was always very frugal and made a point of not spoiling me. Often she would use Aunt Cordelia as an example of what overindulgence could produce. Papa rarely spoke of Cordelia but always talked freely of his memories of my Uncle Charles, who died of polio at the age of nine. I always wondered if that was why Cordelia became a doctor, even though she chose to be an obstetrician.

My beautiful Aunt Cordelia spent the war years in the ravaged areas of London heading up a team of midwives attending to the poor of the East End. I wondered what she saw when she welcomed me off the train. Did she see a spoiled, self-centred woman only interested in advancing her own career? Was I the type of woman Mother said Cordelia had been so long ago?

The train deposited me along the right bank of the Seine and I walked by beautifully coloured wood-framed houses on the narrow streets. I moved on to Rue Eau de Robec and walked past several artisan shops. The October sun was warm and several artists were perched on stools in front of easels on the cobblestone sidewalks. One young man greeted me, his words lyrical and unmistakably flirtatious. He pointed to his easel, which showed a nearly finished figure of a scantily dressed woman. He seemed to be offering to paint a similar portrait of me.

An elderly woman came out the shop door and chastised the young man. She batted a straw broom toward him, letting loose a string of angry words, before turning to address me sweetly.

"*Mademoiselle, bienvenue! Chapellerie. Chapeau?*"

I looked in the shop window and could see that she was pointing to a large selection of women's hats. I followed her through the open door and let her direct me to sit at a mahogany counter displaying an ornate, oval mirror. She held an elaborate feathered hat.

"Une plume noir."

I allowed her to place what put me in mind of a large bird of prey on my head. She stepped back and started a long deliberation, which seemed to be an attempt to convince me that the hat had been made exclusively for me. I turned toward a more demure black felt hat with a large green taffeta bow and indicated that I would like to try that one on.

A few minutes later I was paying the woman for the black hat and a large-brimmed red one festooned with feathers and netting. As she placed them in hat boxes, I asked her if she might know Maurice Bertrand. Amid a flurry of French words that seemed to hold deep emotion for her, she attempted to speak a few words of English to explain to me where I could find Maurice.

"Bon homme! Bon homme! Il fait du bonnes travail! Il fait de bonnes actions! Fourth house, walk three... Rue Saint-Romain. White house, red door."

✻

I saw Maurice as I approached the tall stuccoed house the hat seller had directed me to, on the cul-de-sac at the end of Rue Saint-Romain. He turned when he heard me call his name, quickly setting his shopping basket on the stone step and rushing to embrace me. He looked pleased that I'd taken him up on his invitation to visit him in Rouen.

On Alfred and Gerald's last night in Paris we had gathered with other reporters at a busy Paris nightclub. Despite being surrounded by Canadian journalists, I'd caught the eye of a dashing Frenchman who spent the entire evening trying to get my attention. I finally relented, and as we were leaving I slipped him a matchbook with the number he could reach me. After his call we spent the next week in the throes of a passionate affair.

Maurice Bertrand was a painter, an amateur photographer, and if he was to be believed, a soldier in the French underground. I was caught up in the romance of our days together as he showed me Paris from a much different perspective. I held no illusions but allowed the pleasure of our time together to quiet the conflict I was juggling within. On our last day, Maurice carefully mapped out the route to Rouen, explaining France's rail system and urging me to visit him before returning to Canada.

I waited three days before leaving Paris, not knowing exactly what I was travelling toward but certain of what I was travelling from. Finding my way to Rouen took my attention away from the conflict I felt about what to do next. I desperately wanted to do something that might finally make Aunt Cordelia proud of me.

"Clara! Bonjour! By the look of what you are carrying, you were grabbed by Madame Dubois. I swear she can sense when a strange woman walks by her shop and within minutes has dragged them in and convinced them they need hats. You got away with only buying two. You must have sidetracked her somehow. *Bienvenue!*"

"I asked her if she knew you. Once I told her I was looking for you, she could talk of nothing else. She kept kissing and hugging me and crying. When she stopped embracing me she finally told me where to find you."

"Maria Dubois is a very passionate woman. She is quite fond of me—but there is time enough later to hear her story. For now, let me feast my eyes upon you. I trust you had no problems travelling."

Maurice enfolded me in his arms, kissing me in a manner that made my hours of travel fade from my thoughts.

"Clara, Clara, sweet Clara. Now that you are here, I may

never let you leave. I have fresh bread and wine, but I must go to the market again and get meat. I will make you my *blanquette de veau* for your welcome supper. You caught me unprepared, but I will go now."

Maurice quickly emptied his shopping basket on a table in the foyer and hurried out the door past me. "I will go to the patisserie, too, and get éclairs and tarts. You relax, my love. We shall have a feast tonight!"

*

We sat drinking wine after enjoying the delicious meal Maurice had prepared. Afterwards he showed me the studio in the attic garret where he painted and the small darkroom where some of his photographs were displayed.

"Tomorrow we will go to the seaside. It is still quite warm for October, and you must see the beautiful shores of Deauville. We will leave early and make a day of it. We have suffered such destruction, but the beauty of the seaside could not be destroyed, even though the beaches of the Normandy coast have seen so much bloodshed.

"This country and the whole of Europe have suffered so in this barbaric war, and many are still suffering," Maurice added. "Food is scarce, many homes have been destroyed, and families have had such terrible losses. The war is over, but there is still much we must do to help one another."

*

I sat speechless on the sandy shores of Deauville. The autumn wind kept the water roiling with whitecaps, and as Maurice told me details of the D-Day invasion, I could envision the thousands of troops storming the beaches. How had I been so oblivious to the horrors and magnitude of that invasion? Joe had joined troops in Normandy three days after the June 6 invasion, but when I heard about it I had hardly given it a thought. I received the news with a total lack of real understanding and only surface compassion for the soldiers who died. Joe had been spared from the slaughter of more than two thousand men.

Maurice wept as he told me of the American soldiers mown down by machine-gun fire on Omaha Beach. He told of the determination of 130,000 British, Canadian, and American troops that doggedly stormed these beaches, leading the way for the million that would come within the following weeks, finally liberating France in August 1944.

We walked by the impressive hotels and villas that had once been the heart of France's tourist hub. Those buildings had been occupied by German troops during the Occupation. The beaches that had seen such frolic and enjoyment by thousands of visitors over the years had recently witnessed such death and devastation. This seaside village was struggling to rebuild, just as much of France and Europe were doing.

*

Three nights later, Maurice's friend Anna, her daughter, Genevieve, and Madame Dubois joined us for a feast prepared by Maurice. How he could take small amounts of meat from the market and create such culinary wonder was impressive. Many of Maurice's neighbours could barely afford bread. From a garden in his backyard he harvested a large supply of root vegetables, which he generously shared.

Tonight Maurice made a beef bourguignon with a small cut of beef he'd haggled with the butcher over, offering a painting as payment. Anna and Genevieve had arrived by train yesterday from their home somewhere near the Belgian border. Maurice invited Madame Dubois to join us, and together we enjoyed the wonderful meal.

I took several photos of Anna. Her face held so much pain and courage. Genevieve, who had just turned sixteen, was the youngest of the five children Anna had brought out of Germany, hoping her husband would soon join them. The pain of never seeing him again and imagining the end he endured had etched her beautiful face with lines of suffering. She had raised her five children with the ever-present fear of their Jewish identity being revealed in a country unwilling to give her refuge.

Genevieve's face held the beauty of youth but was not without the stamp of worry and hardship either. I listened as they told me of their lives, which for most of the last six years had been spent in hiding, moving from one village to another, totally reliant on the compassion of others and the hope that their Jewish identity would not be discovered. Anna's accent was noticeably Austrian, but Genevieve had adopted the French language and accent easily, and for her it was easier to blend in. Anna described with anguish her uncertainty of the whereabouts of her sons, having not heard anything from them in more than four years.

"It is my prayer the boys made it to England. I expect someday soon I will see them, now that it is safe to return. I cannot think God would take them from me. Is not my sorrow deep enough, with the fate of my beloved Wilhelm? I held on so long to the hope he would find me and the children, but I have had to face the grim truth. Surely my sons are safe and happy in a country that allows them to be themselves. My other daughter, Yolanda, is married and now has a French husband and name and is able to live safely enveloped by a large French family on a farm outside of Rennes. I allowed her to be there and have not gone near so as not to put her in any danger. Her colouring and features never spoke loudly of her heritage, which I thank God for, though I must also ask his forgiveness for doing so. I could not let my baby go, and in my selfishness have kept her close to me. But surely now we are free."

Madame Dubois crossed the room and held Anna as her tears fell. This woman who whisked me off the sidewalk on my first day had made every effort in her broken English to communicate to me, and I found myself so drawn to her. She treated Maurice as if he were a grandson and embraced me as a granddaughter.

She had not seen her son Armand for several years. Armand had been in the Marquis, which actively sabotaged and attacked German troops during the occupation. They were also instrumental in creating a network to assist grounded Allied airmen in escaping. Armand had gone undetected for a long time, until he made the mistake of trusting an infiltrator. Knowing his life was in danger, he had gone into hiding for weeks before successfully escaping France. The story of his hiding was the bond that so solidly formed the love between her and Maurice.

Two days ago, Maurice lifted a trap door hidden by sod squarely in front of the rose trellis, showing me the large underground room hidden beneath. The solid timbers created a watertight room with space for several bunks, a small table, and a few chairs. A small wood-burning stove was attached to a flu that distributed its smoke through the house's chimney so it would not give away the hiding place, which he told me had given refuge to at least fifty people during the Occupation.

Armand Dubois spent four weeks and six days in that dank hiding spot, dependent on Maurice for food, water, and his very life. Almost four years after his escape, Madame Dubois had received a letter with proof of his successful escape. Armand was now living in New York with an American wife and a six-month-old baby. Madame Dubois proudly showed me a photograph of baby Maurice Dubois.

"I will go to New York someday. Someday I hold my *petit-fils*," she said in her broken English as tears streamed down her cheeks. "Maurice: *bon homme, bon homme!*"

❋

The sun streamed in through the narrow window. I did not want to disturb Maurice's peaceful sleep. I watched the rise and fall of his chest, wishing I could simply stay and allow this amazing man to fill my empty soul. I travelled to him to escape the gnawing desire to be more, to do better, and to achieve something important. He had shown me so much and opened my eyes to what I had ignored. I was no longer the self-absorbed, vain, arrogant woman who had come to Rouen on the train two weeks before.

Reluctantly I would leave this wonderful man and use my camera to tell the difficult stories that needed telling. I would go back to London and try to find a man named Richard Jenkins I'd met there who was working for *Life* magazine. He'd told me of the group of photographers he'd recruited for the magazine to travel to Germany to photograph the displaced persons camps. Such an assignment did not interest me then. After taking the grainy prints of Anna, Genevieve, and Maria from the developing liquid in Maurice's darkroom and staring at eyes holding such beauty and courage, I could see my calling. I had to document the women and children of this war-torn continent. Maybe I could convince Richard that a North American magazine should publish such photographs.

Lillianne
1993

I'd only read the first few pages when I set them down on the coffee table. I looked through my tear-filled eyes at Hilary sitting across the room from me.

"What, Gram?" Hilary asked hesitantly.

"Did your great-grandfather tell you those things?"

"No. He told me he was sent there, but I researched the details."

"I cannot even imagine the horror of that place. I always knew the toll it took, but he never spoke of it. Barbaric treatment and so damaging. It took him years to recover."

"How could his family have sent him somewhere like that?"

"They knew no better. It was his mother's doing. She was horrified with Cliff's lifestyle. She believed he was ill and needed the drastic intervention the New York hospital provided. I think afterwards she realized how cruel it was. She chose a much gentler approach the next time she felt the need to have him hospitalized. But even Maplewood was wrong in thinking homosexuality was a condition that could be reversed with therapy. Your poor great-grandfather suffered years of anguish because of the narrow-minded thinking of the time. Thankfully, he weathered that misery to live the life he found through his art and with Martin's love."

"Am I doing the wrong thing writing about this, Gram? Maybe I'm struggling with the writing because it isn't my story to tell. I think about the misery the family has suffered, your parents dying when you were so young, Great-Granddad's experiences, my grandfather murdered by a mob, Mom and Dad's experience in Munich. So much suffering, but none of it is mine. I have lived an entitled and sheltered life. What gives me the right to tell a story of suffering that is not mine?"

"I understand what you are saying, but we don't always have a choice about what we write. In fact, I don't think we ever have a choice. That would sound ridiculous to a non-writer. But a writer knows that the real gift of writing comes when you allow a place deep within you to govern the story you tell. Anyone can choose the easy way and write something that doesn't grip them, doesn't stretch them, and doesn't make them go somewhere they are desperately afraid to go. Whatever you run from is probably the story you most need to tell."

"But am I betraying my family if I tell their story, even if I mask it in fiction?"

"No. If you tell it honestly and craft it well, you are doing the opposite. You are honouring their suffering and giving it a voice. It is not easy and does not come without its share of pain and anguish, but pushing it away or denying it is a more enduring and deeper pain. It is a burden the writer must accept and not apologize for."

Hilary picked up the next page of her manuscript and began reading it aloud to me.

I stared at the water stains on the ceiling. Strapped to the bed, I could only turn my head slightly, but I felt the starkness of the small, grim room. I'd been restrained for hours and was fighting the desperate urge to give in and urinate. Surely someone would come in soon. I was hoping it was the younger of the two. It had taken two nurses to strap me down, and the younger one seemed kinder even in the fastening of the straps. As she buckled each one, she voiced concern about the tightness and offered apologies. The other tightened the straps roughly and without regard while continuously ranting about my depravity.

"An abomination, unnatural. A sodomite. Your buggery and evil acts are crimes against nature. Don't think your high-and-mighty ways and family money count for anything here. Sodom and Gomorrah, this world is today. You should all be turned to blocks of salt."

I felt the warm gush. Nurse Fire and Brimstone was not going to take kindly to that. I closed my eyes and willed myself out of this narrow dim room and back to the banks of the St. Lawrence. They could strap me down and treat me like a depraved animal, controlling my body, but I still controlled my thoughts and the depth of my soul.

Clara
1946

Right after my first meeting with Gabe Pasternak, the January weather turned frigid and my time outside was limited to short, hurried trips between our accommodations and whatever building we went to investigate life in the camp for articles and photographs. When going about my business, I found myself hoping my path would cross with the man who had left a memorable impression on me.

Given the mass of people crowded into this place, it was not unthinkable that during my time here I might never again run into Gabe Pasternak. So after three weeks of keeping watch for him, I had resigned myself to that fact and made plans to leave Feldafing on the third of February with the team and continue to the next camp on our itinerary.

The day before our departure we were photographing staff, students, and the patrons of the hair-dressing school teaching young men the fine art of haircutting and styling. The school had recently been set up in the basement of one of the brick buildings that had formerly been a part of the Nazi school. White-coated young men stood at a line of sinks and mirrors behind occupied chairs, where they were practising their barbering skills. I focused my lens on the back of a man whose face was lathered generously with shaving cream, and I was startled as the man's head turned and his voice addressed me by name.

"Clara, the Canadian! If you give young Benjamin here a few

more minutes, your camera can take a picture of a handsome, freshly shaven, and clean-cut Pole."

Somehow the few hours I spent later that day with that clean-cut Pole were enough to persuade me to let the team go on without me when they left for Fochrenwald the following day. Gabe asked three young women to cram another make-shift cot into their already crowded room, and it was there I took up residence. Miriam, Esther, and Ruth welcomed me and introduced me to what life was really like in Feldafing. I joined in their labours, which included preparing three meals a day at the school.

*

"Where are you taking me?" I asked Gabe as we stumbled through a field farther from the camp than anywhere I'd ventured in my month there.

"To the lakeside. The moon is bright, and if we walk briskly we will soon find the shelter of a stone wall, which will keep the wind from freezing us."

Every night as I anticipated meeting Gabe I was filled with giddiness and excitement. After greeting one another in front of my barracks, we would find a quiet corner somewhere we would not be bothered and talk for hours on end. A kiss or long embrace would be our only physical contact, and I always parted longing for more.

We walked the considerable distance to the stone wall, which ran along the shore of the lake. We chose a spot, and, indeed, as we sat protected by the wall, the cold wind subsided. The water was illuminated by the moonlight and I snuggled closely in the crook of Gabe's arms and gazed up at the night sky. The drab buildings and barren landscape, along with the hardships of our daily existence, faded under the splendour of the deep blue-black sky dotted with the flickers of a multitude of shimmering stars and the glowing full moon.

We sat speechless under the beautiful canopy for several minutes before Gabe spoke, cradling my face in his work-worn hands. "You are my angel, Clara. It is for meeting you that I lived."

This was not the first time Gabe had spoken those words. Each night during our time together, he shared more and more of his horrific story, and in the telling of the gruesome facts he repeatedly said he had survived such horror to meet me. I had no such stories of suffering, but each night in his arms, I felt I, too, had been brought to this place to find the love of Gabe Pasternak. I had never in all of my encounters felt anything like what I was feeling with him. I, too, told my story, and if Gabe judged me for taking the comfort and privilege I had been blessed with for granted, he did not voice that condemnation. He held me as I wept and I held him as he told me the horrifying details of the monumental injustices and terrible losses he had endured.

Gabe was born in Warsaw, Poland. His father was a tailor and had established a good business that provided well for his wife and six children. Gabe was the third child, with brothers Moshe and Henryk being older and his beloved sisters, Sarah, Rivka, and Leah, younger. Their comfortable life as a well-to-do Jewish family abruptly changed in 1940, and the hardships of living under the scrutiny of an anti-Jewish regime soon took its toll. The harsh winter of 1941 brought bitter cold and deep snows. The Judenrat would daily round up the young men and force them to shovel the snow from the railroad tracks.

During that hard winter, Jewish families were being stripped of their possessions, and while Gabe was away shovelling in late January, the Judenrat demanded gold and furs from his mother and oldest sister as they walked along the street. Gabe returned that night to discover their bodies. His mother had told the Judenrat that she had no such possessions, and they shot both her and Sarah as they stood in the street.

A year later, Gabe's father was shot in the back when he went to buy bread from some children who had smuggled it into the ghetto. Shortly afterwards, the girls were sent to one location and the boys to another. Gabe was singled out and separated from the others.

"My parents and Sarah were spared what came next. It is the fate that Rivka, Leah, Moishe, and Henryk met that gives me nightmares," Gabe sobbed. "My own hell I know, but the hell they were led to I know nothing of, and the imaginings are what haunt me. I pray they survived their hell and that I may someday embrace them again."

*

For two more months, not a night went by when I didn't rush to meet Gabe, and somewhere in the confusion of that place we searched out a corner where we could be alone. In Gabe's arms I felt safe and hopeful, but I always came away from our time together anxious to be able to take our love further. In my past, any relationship I had with a man, however long it lasted, had always very quickly become sexual. With Gabe, despite our physical attraction to one another, this had not yet happened.

Gabe treated me like I was made of china, too precious to handle. I had never experienced this before, and even though I was frustrated by our lack of intimacy, when he wrapped me in his arms I felt a kind of intimacy that was entirely new to me.

One night our passion rose and it seemed like his restraint was faltering. I was ready, and despite our tenuous meeting place in the back of a large truck in the machine shop, I was certain it would be the night we would give in to our desire.

But at the height of our passion, Gabe gently pulled me to my feet and led me to the edge of the tailgate, jumping to the ground and helping me down. He led me to the lamppost and then knelt in front of me.

"My angel Clara, I humbly ask you to be my wife. It is in your arms I long to spend the life I have been granted. I come to you a poor and damaged man, a man who has been beaten and marked with the ink of hatred and suffering, but if you will be my wife, dear Clara, I will do my best to spend my days giving you the life you deserve."

Through my sobs I shouted yes, and Gabe rose to his feet, scooping me up into his arms.

*

Miriam brought yards of bandages from the infirmary, and together we sewed the gauze to make a bridal veil that in my mind would rival anything created by wedding designers in New York. I wore a white dress that Ruth borrowed from her cousin who had been married the month before. I carried a bouquet of blackthorn branches, the small white blossoms making a beautiful arrangement as I walked through the small group gathered to watch the marriage of Clara Elizabeth Randolph to Gabriel Aleksander Pasternack on April 8, 1946.

*

"Our honeymoon continues, my love."

We were spending another moonlit night by the lake, this trek offering a warm breeze that gave relief from the sweltering heat wave that had been upon us during the last week of May.

"Don't be such a prude, Clara. You are a married woman, and it is only your husband who will see your beauty in this moonlight."

Gabe had completely removed his clothing and was standing naked on the shore, urging me to do the same. I'd never been accused of being a prude, but I was reluctant to bare myself and even more reluctant to dip in the lake that for so many months had seemed foreboding. Comparing it to the waters off my beloved Randolph Island, I felt no affection for Lake Starnberger.

"I guess you will need some coaxing," Gabe teased as he pulled my loose dress over my head and unclasped my brassiere. I slipped my underpants to my ankles and stepped ahead quickly, finding courage and running into the water.

The cold water instantly took my breath away, but I plunged under the rippling waves. Gabe dove in a few inches from me and we both surfaced at the same time. Gabe wrapped his arms around me as I sputtered and flung my wet hair back from my face. He cupped my breasts. In that moment I realized how full and tender they were and thought about the fact that our nights of pleasure since our wedding night had not been interrupted by my menses. The realization that I may be carrying Gabe's child heightened the passion I felt as we stumbled to the shore, where we made love atop our crumpled clothing under a vast and beautiful moonlit sky.

Leah
1972

"You've been looking for a Jewish guy to fall in love with for as long as I've known you," my friend Roxanne said the night I told her about meeting David Jacobs. The night of the opening ceremonies had been a blur of activity, and I'd met so many guys at the after party, but meeting David Jacobs had me bursting with excitement when Roxie and I got back to our apartment.

"Well, I couldn't ignore those muscles, could I?"

David was a personal trainer to wrestler Gord Bertie, and his very fit body was certainly not difficult to look at, but there might have been something to Roxie's observation of him being Jewish adding to the attraction. Just from our brief conversation, I found out David was born and raised in Montreal, but that his family was from Poland. I couldn't help but feel the connection of a shared history, a history that I only recently had a strong desire to explore further. I'd already decided I would travel to Poland before returning to Canada after the games were over. I felt the need to travel to the place my father was born—and the place where he was killed.

Now, only eight days later, the falling in love part seemed to be a possibility. David and I had spent every available moment together and were already discussing a plan to travel to Poland after the Games finished, visiting Warsaw, where both our fathers were from. Yesterday, the last day of the swimming events, was full of excitement as Leslie earned silver in the four-hundred-metre individual relay, and what started out as a small crowd turned into a pretty big party. As the celebration wound down, David and I snuck out and for the first time had an opportunity to be alone.

The next morning I was taking great pleasure in sleeping in, and after waking up was still lazily lying in bed when Roxie burst in the room.

"What time did you get in last night?"

"None of your business."

Roxie sat on the side of my bed, and the look on her face scared me into sitting up. "What's wrong, Rox?"

"Were you with David? Did he walk you back? Were you in the building where the wrestling team is staying?"

"What? What's going on?"

"Terrorists!"

Before the Games, we'd been given long briefings about security, practised evacuation drills, and discussed every possible scenario concerning violence and terrorism. The organizers had gone out of their way to create an atmosphere of goodwill and harmony, trying hard to reflect the current government of Germany's tolerant and progressive ideas with hopes of banishing the ghosts of the Nazi-controlled 1939 games.

"Terrorists have taken Israeli athletes hostage. They took over the wrestling team's building, Leah. People have been killed. The whole village is locked down."

"David walked me back and then was going right back to his apartment. Oh my God, Rox. What time did the attack happen?"

"They aren't telling us anything except that we need to stay in our buildings. Bob was out running early, and he was the one who told me what was going on. He heard at least one person is dead. It's a standoff. They have the building surrounded.

He said some people got out at the very beginning, but the terrorists are holding hostages."

Rumours ran rampant all day. Nobody knew what exactly was going on, but the village was packed with police and media and lots of stories spread in the hours before we were told that the terrorists and hostages had been transported to the Munich airport. At one point, it was going around that all the terrorists had been killed and the hostages were safe.

✳

I broke into tears of relief when I answered a knock on the door almost twenty-four hours later and David was standing there. His face was ashen and expressionless. Roxanne quickly left us alone.

"I saw them, Leah. I was crossing the yard on my way back. They were in tracksuits and had duffel bags. I didn't even think anything of it. I just figured they were getting back late and didn't want their coaches to see them sneaking in. I passed a couple of them once they climbed the fence and they seemed drunk to me. I spoke to them briefly and went to my wing. I didn't hear another thing until a couple of guys came to my door around eight in the morning and told me we were to stay in our rooms. They told me there had been a terrorist attack on the Israeli team."

David sobbed as I held him and assured him he hadn't done anything wrong.

"I should have told somebody. Why would guys have a duffel bag with them out for a night on the town? I should have known something was wrong. Eleven guys are dead, Leah. They were good guys. They targeted them just because they're Jews. Lambs to slaughter, Leah. Again, Jews are just like lambs to the slaughter."

Hours later, I sat beside David at the sombre memorial service the authorities quickly organized after deciding against cancelling the remainder of the Games. Eleven Israeli athletes and five terrorists were dead. The Olympic flag and country flags, except for a few Arab countries, were flown at half-mast. Emotions ran high and the tension, anger, and fear were evident. Sitting with some American swimmers, I was told that Mark Spitz, who had already finished competing, had made the decision to leave Munich and return to the States.

"He's a Jew, you know," his teammate explained. "He was afraid he might be kidnapped or a target of anti-Jewish hostility."

"We are Jewish, too," David replied loudly with an edge of defensiveness. "Imagine, a Jew at risk in Germany," he added sarcastically. "This makes me sick. A heartfelt memorial won't change what happened."

"Yeah, really," a Dutch athlete who was sitting in front of us replied. "Why didn't they put more money into better security? They just hopped a fence and walked right in. They should have known the PLO would take advantage of that and pull off an attack."

"I can't stay here, Leah." David stood up and I followed him as he made his way through the crowd and out of the stadium.

"It's okay, David. We can go back to my room and sleep. Your next events don't start until Sunday. We can stay away from all this until then."

"No. I mean I can't stay in Munich. I just want to get out of here, and I don't want you staying here without me. The swimming events are over. The party is over as far as I'm concerned. Staying here and pretending like this didn't happen is disrespectful to the guys who died and the families left behind. They should have shut this farce down and shown some solidarity with the Israeli athletes. What if it had been our country they'd targeted? This isn't right."

"Okay, I'll leave with you, but let's not hurry back to Canada. My mother's friend Maurice lives in France. Let's take a train to Rouen and stay with him for a few days. Then we can decide what to do next. Maybe we'll still want to go to Poland before returning home."

After quickly making arrangements to leave, we walked past an illuminated blue sun at the Olympic Village entrance. The symbol of *Die Heiteren Spiele*, "The Happy Games," seemed so macabre now, and we silently got into the cab and made our way through the streets to the train station to catch the midnight train to Paris.

The days spent in Rouen were among my happiest ever. David and I enjoyed exploring the northern coast of France. Maurice and his wife, Annette, welcomed us into their home, lavishing us with good food, good wine, love, and acceptance, helping us to recover from the terror of Munich. We both took the vacation being at Maurice's provided, and during that time the love that began in those first days in Munich grew stronger, surprising us both with its intensity.

On October 10, after spending more than a month with Maurice and Annette, David and I prepared to board another train, this time heading for Poland.

Our plan as we hugged Maurice goodbye was to spend some time exploring the region of Poland where our fathers were both born and then return to Paris, where Maurice and Annette would witness our marriage. We hadn't told either of our families; we didn't want to hear anyone's opinion on the length of our engagement.

Two days later, we found the name *Moishe Pasternak* by just looking in the Warsaw phonebook, which seemed too good to be true, and made our way to the address beside the name. I was prepared for the disappointment that the man would not be my uncle but just a man with the same name. But the man who opened the door to us hugged me tightly when I introduced myself as Leah Pasternak, daughter of Gabe Pasternak.

We were welcomed warmly into his home, meeting his wife, Berta, and seeing pictures of their six children and two grand-children. He told his story, one of suffering in Auschwitz then Mittelbau-Dora and his liberation in April 1945 by American troops. Against all odds he had survived, and after spending time in several DP camps, he and Berta returned to Poland in September 1946. He'd looked for family members but had not found any evidence of any of them having survived.

"Leah, beautiful Leah. The namesake of my beloved sister, the daughter of my dear brother. You are a gift to us. The pain, the evil and death, have not won. You live and Gabriel lives through you."

It was with the strength of love, foundation of place, and a sense of peace that David and I left Poland two weeks later after finding the house his father was born in, and the street where my father was killed. We placed a marker in his memory in a Kielce graveyard. In Paris we stood before a magistrate with Maurice and Annette as witnesses and recited our vows of marriage, overjoyed with the possibility I was carrying a child who had been conceived in the homeland of our fathers.

Clara
1993

The 401 was especially congested, even taking Mother's advice. I'd found the first part of the drive pleasant enough, having put in a Kate and Anna McGarrigle cassette and listening to the entire thing twice. Perhaps it was the melancholy lines of "Mother Mother," but even with the anticipation of seeing Bud and the boys, Leah, David, Father, and Martin, and the excitement of my exhibit, I couldn't shake thoughts of Gabe and those dark days when I wanted so desperately for Mother to take my hurt away.

After realizing I was pregnant, Gabe and I decided we would make arrangements to leave and get to Canada before the baby came. Gabe was certain we could make a better life and give our child more chances in Canada, with the support of my family. He wanted, however, to make one last trip to Poland. He felt compelled to go back and see if any of his siblings had survived. He joined a group of men who were repatriating to an area south of Warsaw and left by train on June 30.

Gabe arrived in the town of Kielce, Poland, July 3, unaware that a simple lie would seal his fate. A nine-year-old boy, in an effort to escape punishment for not returning home on time, made up a story of being kidnapped and kept hostage in the local Jewish Committee building. It was in this building that

Gabe had taken shelter, looking for any trace of his siblings before making his way to Warsaw.

Police investigated and quickly disproved the boy's accusations, but a large crowd of over a thousand angry millworkers had gathered outside the building. Polish soldiers and policemen entered the building and called on the occupants to surrender. A shot was fired and the killing began. The angry crowd viciously beat those who were fleeing the turmoil inside. By the end of the day, forty-two Jews had been killed. Gabe had lived through four years of hell in the Mühldorf Mettenheim labour camp; had found a temporary home in the DP camp of Feldafing; had met and fallen in love with and wed Clara Randolph of Odessa, Ontario; and was just about to embark on a new life on a new continent. He was facing a future that might begin to erase the suffering of his past. But, instead, he was beaten to death on the street in his homeland.

Tears streamed down my cheeks. Even forty-seven years later, I felt the deep pain of Gabe's loss. Bud was a wonderful husband, and I had so many blessings, but my heart always went to thoughts of what might have been. On that July day, the love of my life was murdered. Gabe was not given the chance to hold his precious daughter or find a life free from hate and fear.

Coming up behind a van with licence plates from New Brunswick, I recalled the trip I made to visit Cordelia five years after Gabe's death. Mother thought some time in New Brunswick with Aunt Cordelia was what I needed. I was still barely functioning and certainly not mothering Leah as I should have been. Cordelia had bought a cottage on the Saint John River, and I ended up staying the whole summer.

That summer was a turning point for me. Day after day, I sat on the shore of that river and watched Cordelia swim out into the deep water. I barely put a toe in, but would watch her every day run into the water and submerge herself minutes after we arrived on the beach. One of those days she lay on the blanket after getting out of the water and began the speech that somehow turned my life around.

"Did you know my grandmother died right here? She was saving my mother, who had slipped under the water trying to retrieve the stick she was playing with. My mother was only three years old but recalled the day with haunting clarity. She had a deathly fear of water and forbade us from swimming. It didn't stop us, though. I was drawn to the water for as long as I can remember. Even now as I swim into the deep water, I feel a tug toward something I don't even understand.

"The deep water envelops me and gives me the same gifts every time. It fills me with happiness, with purpose, and with a self-assuredness I can't even explain. How is it the same thing that took my grandmother's life and shaped my mother so deeply keeps me alive and believing in the power of hope? Untimely and tragic death marks us. It changes who we are. But it does not defeat us unless we allow it to. You must find your deep water, the place you can go that brings back what Gabe's death took from you. Nobody can find that for you, but once you have found it, nobody can prevent you from diving into it."

I considered Cordelia's words for a long time before realizing photography was deep water for me. I returned to Odessa in September, and through my camera lens I returned to myself and to my daughter. I felt guilty it took me so long. The strong relationship with my aunt never lessened despite distance and the time between visits, but the gap between Mother and I was always present. Why had I never felt the same connection to her that I felt to Aunt Cordelia? Perhaps the photographs in my exhibition were my last-ditch attempt to close that gap.

Soon I would lose both of the women I loved so dearly. They

had lived long lives, but I was not ready to let them go. I turned up the radio and focused my attention on *Quirks and Quarks*. In less than an hour I would be at Dad's. A hug from him would perk me up, as it always did.

Lillianne
1956

Standing on the sidewalk in front of Saint John's Union Station, I looked up and down at the row of parked vehicles, looking for a Ford truck with a wooden box on the back. Cordelia said a man named Ernie Nagle would be picking up Leah and me. Mr. Nagle would squeeze us into the cab of his truck, and chances were we would have to hold some boxes on our laps during the drive out of the city. Picking up supplies at the wholesalers was the reason Mr. Nagle was in the city and able to give us a drive to Cordelia's cottage on the Saint John River.

Cordelia had her own vehicle but had arranged our transportation with the local storekeeper.

"Once I get to Bedford Wharf and settle in for my month, I refuse to leave. I count the days to get here and do not leave this paradise until my vacation is over."

Four winters ago, regular letters began coming from Cordelia. Our correspondence up until then had been sporadic. We both had busy lives—mine slow-paced and solitary, hers more frenzied and altruistic. I could only imagine the stresses and demands of an obstetrics practice. Christmas and birthday gifts had always arrived for Clara, and then for Leah, but visits seldom occurred. Cordelia had very deliberately distanced herself, and after taking her nurse's and later doctor's training in Montreal, had made her life in Saint John, New Brunswick, excluding the rest of us for the most part.

Her first letter was filled with the details of purchasing the house her mother had once worked in. It seemed odd that a woman so determined to cut ties with her mother was finding such pleasure in the ownership of a house with that history. It was where Marion Kingston had first met Clifton Randolph the Third.

> *It is on the shores of the most beautiful river I have ever laid eyes on. The years have taken their toll on the structure, but its bones are strong, and with a bit of work it will make a lovely summer retreat again. I feel as drawn to this house as I once was to the house on Randolph Island. I have found my paradise, Lily, and it will not be ripped from me.*

The following summer, Clara spent July and August at Cordelia's cottage, and when she returned in September, the change was evident immediately. I was overjoyed that Cordelia had been able to break through Clara's deep and debilitating sorrow. It was with mixed emotions, however, that I handed over the mothering of Leah. The healing I'd prayed for had come about, but with it would come the eventual separation from my grand-daughter. Sooner or later, Clara would decide she needed a life somewhere other than under my roof.

Cordelia's most recent letter, dated Clara's birthday, contained the invitation for us to visit the Kingston Peninsula. Clara was too busy with her lucrative photography studio and had also committed to several wedding shoots, so Leah and I travelled by train to Saint John to spend three weeks with Cordelia at her Bedford Wharf cottage.

"Mrs. McDonough? If you are she, then I am Ernie Nagle. Well, I suppose I'm Ernie Nagle regardless. But if you are Mrs. McDonough, then it is you Dr. Kingston has sent me to fetch."

"Please call me Lily. And this is my granddaughter, Leah."

"Then follow me, Lily and Leah. My apologies for the lack of room and any discomfort. Ella's list was long today."

Hilary
1993

For three days, I sat across from Gram and read my work aloud. In the reading I discovered some of what I guess Professor Dunfield had been trying to tell me. Gram hadn't said what she thought my writing needed, but when I returned to it and rewrote the places she said lacked clarity or the intensity I was so sure I had written into it, I felt the manuscript taking shape.

"There has been a lot of suffering, hasn't there?" Gram said yesterday after hearing Chapter Seven. "Stranger than fiction, they say. Generation after generation our family has endured sadness, loss, and heartache. Even money could not keep us from suffering."

*

"Have you been up long, Hilly?" Gram walked into the kitchen and sat at the other end of the table.

"Not too long. Can I get you some coffee?"

"Tea, please. I never developed a taste for coffee. Many a cup I served in my day, but I never took to it myself. Tea and two slices of toast. Been starting my day with that for a very long time. Set in my ways, I am. Your grandmother wouldn't put it that kindly, I'm sure. *Stubborn old coot* might be more her description."

"Grammie took some beautiful photos of you. If you want, I could drive you to Toronto to see them. The gala is over, but the exhibit will be at the gallery for a month."

"I think I'll pass. She showed me some of them, and somehow they don't make me look as old as I feel. I am perfectly content to stay put. I'm so pleased to have you here with me, Hilly, but I don't think Colin was too pleased about it, was he?"

"He'll be fine."

"I had a man once, you know. I miss him still."

"Gramps, you mean?"

"No. I never really had your grandfather. Wasn't his fault, of course. It was mine for thinking he was someone he wasn't. I thought briefly he was my knight in shining armour. I was just a silly girl. By the time I met the man I could love and who could love me back, I was much older and wiser. Not wise enough to keep him, though."

I passed Gram her cup of tea and waited for her to tell me more.

"His name was Will. He wanted to marry me, but I refused. I needed the money your great-grandmother enslaved me with. Again, not her fault, but mine for letting her. She paid for the truth she wanted, and I played right into her hand. Like a divorce would have made the reality of her son's sexuality any more evident. By the end of her life, Martin lived with Cliff right under her roof. I could have married Will then, but it was too late."

"Why?"

"He was dead. He probably wouldn't even have signed up if I'd agreed to marry him. He was too old to enlist when the second war came, but they took him as a tradesman and the ship he sailed on was torpedoed."

"Somehow I seem to have been exempted from suffering, Gram. I feel so privileged sometimes. Even being Jewish isn't difficult these days. My generation is so entitled."

"That doesn't mean the past hasn't affected you. I'm glad you haven't suffered, but you are young. None of us knows what is ahead. There is a veneer of acceptance, but society still judges, still pigeonholes, still does damage. You are a writer, my love, and you must bear witness to suffering, to the human struggle, and to the power of love."

Gram got up and set her cup and plate in the sink. "We don't send jolts of electricity through young men anymore trying to eradicate their base desires, but society still tramples individuality. We don't shame the unwed mothers, but we still keep secrets."

The phone rang in the middle of the night. Four rings, then Hilary's voice answering. I could not hear her exact words, but I sensed the tone. Of course a call at this time would be bad news. I lay still, wondering what the news would be.

Hilary sat at my bedside without turning on a light. She reached for me, checking if I was awake.

"I heard the phone. Who has died?"

"It is Great-Aunt Cordelia, Gram. It was Grammie on the phone. She hadn't meant to call until morning but dialled your number by mistake. She told me not to wake you, but I figured the ringing woke you up. I didn't want you worrying about who might have been calling this late. Grammie was very upset."

"I knew I'd waited too long. How will she ever forgive me?"

"Who, Gram?"

"Your great-grandmother has died, Hilary."

Hilary leaned in to console me as my shaking and sobbing began. She was probably certain my grogginess was causing my confusion and the ridiculous statement I'd just made.

"I need you to turn the light on and help me into my robe. We will go downstairs and put the kettle on. God rest her poor, dear soul. Our darling Cordelia took the secret to her grave, but I will not do the same."

*

Hilary drove me to the Pearson Airport, parked, and walked

me to the Air Canada departure area. Clara and I spoke briefly on the phone yesterday and agreed right away that we would fly to Saint John together for Cordelia's funeral. Martin's health was preventing Cliff from attending. Leah and David were vacationing, and I'd assured them there was no need to rush back. Hilary had offered to accompany me, but I'd talked her out of it. My reasons sounded trivial even as I offered them. I hadn't wanted to come right out and say it, but I sensed she understood the trip to bury Cordelia was one I needed to take with only Clara.

"I don't need a wheelchair," I snapped at the perky Air Canada employee. "I am perfectly capable of walking, thank you very much."

"Gram, I think you should take her offer," Hilary interjected. "Once you get through security it may be quite a walk to your gate, and Grammie isn't here yet to help you. You might get overtired or disoriented. Let the airline staff assist you in whatever way they can."

"I suppose you are right, Hilary. And for the price of airfare I should take whatever extras they offer me. God knows there will be no decent meals or pampering of any kind. Now train travel—that was style and comfort in the day."

"We will take that wheelchair after all," Hilary said, motioning to the girl behind the check-in desk.

I could blame my irritability on my nervousness about seeing Clara. I had no intentions of blurting out my confession as soon as I saw her but was worried I would not be able to keep my emotions under control. She would no doubt attribute any show of emotion simply to Cordelia's passing. I would feign exhaustion and stay quiet on the flight and wait until we reached our hotel room before I faced the daunting task of telling my daughter she was not my daughter, and that the aunt she was mourning was the mother she'd been prevented from having. I slumped into the wheelchair, thankful I no longer had to support the weight of my own worn and weary body.

*

The cab driver pulled up in front of the Hilton Hotel. A uniformed staff person opened the door and directed me to a wheelchair, then quickly began wheeling me up a ramp at the side. Again, I would let my age earn me care and attention. I wasn't sure I could muster enough energy to walk up the stairs and into the lobby. My moment of dread was getting closer, and with each minute my courage and stamina were waning. I would allow the hotel staff to transport this old lady safely to her room. There I would stretch out on a double bed and let the fireworks begin.

*

By the time I finished my staccato of sentences and finally turned toward Clara to gauge her reaction, I was shaking and almost breathless. She stood up from the wingback chair where she'd been sitting across the room and started toward me. I feared she might strike me, or even worse, storm out of the room in a cold, angry silence.

"When I was a little girl, I felt so guilty for the longing I felt to be Cordelia's daughter. I cried myself to sleep so many nights with her photograph clutched in my fingers, praying that I would wake up and it would be Cordelia I called out to when I said, 'Good morning, Mommy.' As I got older, my guilt changed to fear, knowing that the love I had for Daddy would be erased if his own sister were my mother. Anger replaced my guilt and fear. I always felt I wasn't who I was supposed to be.

"But my biggest shame is my cowardice. I made a choice and fell into the charade as solidly as you, Father, and Cordelia did."

"What do you mean?" I stammered.

"It was a brief encounter, one I'm sure Cordelia dismissed and never knew I paid any mind to. Spencer Hitchcock was my father, wasn't he?"

"How do know that?"

"My life's work has been looking at faces and reading emotions. When I was sixteen I saw his face in a crowded ballroom, and when he looked at me, his expression evoked an intimate recognition. Then her face spoke loudly of fear, embarrassment, shame, and flickers of desire and regret. Seems like a heap of emotion to see in two quick glances, but I read it all. It seemed the room went silent and I felt the tug between them that my presence created.

"Later, Cordelia denied knowing the man we'd met and her voice faltered as she made weak attempts to disguise her emotion and I took note of the name. Not a very nice man, it turned out. A cad and a cheat and not worthy of any of the heartbreak my mother endured."

"Where do we go from here, Clara?"

"Where is there to go? You talk about the plan that orchestrated the charade, and I do resent being the child who was moved around like a piece on a damn chessboard. But my anger fizzled long ago. I know I was blessed with the love of two mothers, and at this point anger and resentment change nothing. We all suffered. The only thing I ask is that the lie stops now. Tomorrow I will stand in the church and eulogize Cordelia and claim her as my birth mother. I will bear witness to her life and tell every aspect of its truth. We will find our way from there."

Clara sat on the edge of the bed and wrapped her arms around me.

"And is time for you to forgive yourself, Mother. Forgiveness can be dealt to whomever and in whatever measure we see fit. I have a daughter, a granddaughter, and if I am blessed will see great-grandchildren. They will all know our truth and find their place in it."

Hilary
1995

The night we'd gotten the news of Cordelia's death, Gram and I sat for hours as she told me the truth. She told my grandmother the truth when they travelled to New Brunswick for Cordelia's memorial service. They brought back Cordelia's ashes and placed the urn on Gram's mantel in Odessa. Almost a year later, within a two-week period, Gramps and Martin passed away and their ashes were combined in an urn and placed beside Cordelia's.

Mom and Grammie had been telling me that Gram's health was failing. When I arrived in Odessa a week ago, Gram was just recovering from a bout of the flu, and for the first couple of days I blamed her slow movements on that; but as more days passed, I realized she was indeed slowing down.

After *Beyond Wind and Whitecaps* was rereleased, she had declined all invitations for readings and public appearances.

"Nobody wants to hear this old woman read, Hilly," she said when asked about her refusal to make public appearances. "Just getting to the stage would take me half an hour and the room would clear out, waiting."

On this trip I'd brought copies of *Beyond Wind and Whitecaps* with me to have her sign them for several of my friends, and she still voiced disbelief in the interest surrounding her first book.

"I can't even believe my publisher even bothered with it. Nobody cares what Lillianne McDonough has written anymore."

"That's not true, Gram. My professors at Queen's used your work as a measuring stick all the time, and the university bookstore carries most of your books."

"Oh, I'm a legend all right. Just wait until I kick the bucket. Then I'll get really popular. Hilary, I'm so proud your book will soon be joining mine on bookstore shelves. I just hope I live until September to see it. Does your publisher not know how old your great-grandmother is? You'd think they could have stepped things up a bit so the old lady who wrote the blurb for the front cover would actually be able to hold it in her withered old hands."

Gram seemed to be talking about her death a lot lately. It was definitely not something I wanted to even think about, and, in attempts to cheer her up and get her mind on something besides her declining health, I suggested Mom and Grammie meet us in Kingston so we could all take a Thousand Islands cruise. After convincing Gram she was up to the outing, I booked it.

It wasn't until last night I realized the real reason Gram had consented to the cruise.

"We're taking them home," she announced, pointing to the urns on the mantelpiece.

*

I helped Gram out of the rented Toyota.

"I can walk on my own," Gram snapped as I tried to take her arm and help her onto the dock. "Take this bag from me, please. Cliff would not want me to stumble, break their urn, and have them blow through the cracks between the timbers before we even get to our destination."

A tall man in a white captain's uniform extended his hand and welcomed Gram onto the deck of the boat. Mom, Grammie, and I followed after them.

"Good afternoon. Welcome to the *Island Queen*. We are happy to be your hosts on this lovely day for a tour of the beautiful Thousand Islands. Is this your first cruise with us?"

Gram curtly replied that yes it was her first cruise with them but that she had sailed on these waters long before he was even born.

The captain turned to us, hoping, I am sure, for a more cordial response. "I hope you ladies have a lovely time."

"Could you just show us inside, young man? This wind is biting," Gram snapped.

I gave him an apologetic smile and followed him into the dining room, where a server seated us to start our meal before the actual tour of the islands began.

"I hate how people speak to me now as if I haven't an idea left in my head. They seem to think if the body slows down, the brainwaves stand still, too."

"He was just being polite, Gram. Part of his job is to greet the passengers. Do you want a glass of wine?"

"Yes, that would be lovely. Maybe with a drink I can stomach the sugar-sweet gestures of these people doing their *jobs*. I would have been happier chartering our own boat and going directly to where we can give Cliff, Martin, and Cordelia their proper send-off. But there is probably some law against it."

"Gram, let's just enjoy the cruise. Mom and I have never seen the islands."

"Oh, right. I forgot we sold the island before Leah was born. Randolph Island was such a part of Clara's life, but I forget you and your mother never even got to see it. I wish we did have our own charter so we could go to shore when we get there and Clara and I could really give you a proper tour. Maybe next year we'll do that, and bring the men with us. I remember every inch of it as if I was there yesterday. Are they going to bring that wine, or do I have to get it myself?"

Gram settled a bit and seemed to be enjoying the food, which even she had to admit was delicious. The tour began with a recorded blurb about the history of the Thousand Island region. Gram interspersed the facts with some corrections and critical comments.

After the recorded segment, a girl about my age approached our table and said she would be our guide for the afternoon. She focused her attention on Gram, raising her voice slightly to accommodate an assumed hearing deficit. Her tone held a sugary sweetness that was sure to annoy Gram.

"I will be giving you a little bit of information about each island as we pass by them this afternoon. The cruise sails through the maze of smaller and larger islands, and we will also see the famous Boldt Castle. Feel free to ask me any questions and I will attempt to answer them."

Gram refused to look at her and turned to us instead. "I could tell them a few things about a few of these islands and some of the uppity residents who inhabited them."

Grammie reached out and put her hand on Gram's arm. "Mom, settle down and relax. You don't have to educate this poor girl on the real history. Just let her impart the truth as she's been told it."

The hostess spoke again. "There are many uninhabited islands, some not much bigger than this boat. Some of the islands have light beacons located on them that have guided sailors for hundreds of years. Have a look at the chart on the lower deck showing the many wrecks in the waters of Lake Ontario and the St. Lawrence River.

"They see shipwrecks as some romantic story, and have no idea the tragedies that occurred and the destruction that lies below. Look at these self-indulgent people who don't for one minute understand the devastation a storm on these waters can bring. They would not be so smug if the wind whipped up and tossed them out of their chairs."

"Gram. You are wound up today. Try not to piss everyone off on this cruise. Our server is already avoiding our table."

The hostess picked up her microphone while pointing out the starboard window. "This island was owned by the Windsor family of Philadelphia. At one time, it was a very grand house, but it has fallen into disrepair. It has just been purchased by a company with plans on restoring the mansion, turning it into a resort."

"The Windsors lost the place during the Depression. Served Robert Windsor right for all the profit he made during the war. He got greedy and overextended himself and the crash came as a severe blow to him. Well, at least if they turn it into a resort, the place will finally show some hospitality to the people who visit, unlike the days when Geraldine Windsor was receiving guests there."

Gram continued her commentary on just about every island our guide spoke about. Mom, Grammie, and I chatted amid her comments, enjoying our meal, letting Gram have her say—not that we could have stopped her. The hostess moved far away from our table, no doubt trying to be out of earshot of Gram's grumblings.

"Help me with my coat please, Hilly. We are getting close and I want to be ready to go out on the deck. You know, I was very seasick the first time I sailed here, and your great-grandfather was such a gentleman."

I could see Gram's eyes fill with tears as she continued telling me about how Clifton Randolph the Fourth had been her knight in shining armour as she vomited over the railing on her first trip.

"He was very handsome. Tall and muscular, like your young man. I was so young. I had no idea what was ahead. The years go by so quickly, Hilly. I cannot begin to tell you how fast the last seventy-seven years have gone."

Gram carefully reached for the canvas bag at her feet. Grammie picked up the bag holding Cordelia's urn and we all moved toward the door just as the tour guide started her facts about Randolph Island.

Out on the boat deck, we could still hear the guide's words transmitted through the speaker above our heads.

"This is Randolph Island," the guide began. "The mansion was built by the Randolph family of Chicago in 1905. This is a fair-sized island, one of the region's largest, with some lovely buildings, including a gazebo and bath house. The house is still lovely and has been maintained by the Emerson family also of Chicago, who took possession of it in the late 1920s, and it still remains in the Emerson family.

Gram gripped the railing and looked toward the island. Grammie moved toward her, passing me her bag so she could completely enfold Gram in her arms.

"Stanley Emerson was more than happy to buy the island in 1929. Got it for next to nothing, the bastard. Took advantage of the family's faltering finances and Clifton's poor health. We shouldn't have let it happen."

"It's okay, Mom. The island was never lost to us in our hearts. We are bringing them back today. It's all right, Mom. Everything is all right."

Gram's tears streamed down her cheeks and I reached out to her. She leaned against me and removed Gramps's urn from the bag. Grammie leaned against the railing, taking the bag back from me and removed the urn holding Cordelia's ashes.

"Clifton was a good man, Hilary. He was caught in a time and a society that would never have accepted him, and his only escape was the one he took. He was always a wonderful father to Clara and loved your mother and you deeply. He and Martin had a wonderful life together, and his art gave him great pleasure. He began sketching right here, captivated by the beauty of this place, and now his paintings can be found in galleries all over the world. Today Martin finally joins him in the waters surrounding his beloved island."

I hugged Gram tighter, feeling the urn pressed between us.

"Will you take the urn and lift the lid, Hilary? I want you to face away from the wind and upend the urn to distribute the ashes."

"Don't you want to do it?"

"I want you to free him and allow him to finally find rest in the waters off his beloved Randolph Island."

Gram reached for Grammie's hand.

Clara spoke, her voice clear and her eyes firmly cast on the approaching island. "I want to give my mother, his little sister, that rest as well, as her ashes mix with his and disperse in the waters she loved so dearly."

"Forgive me, Cordelia," Gram whispered as she leaned toward the railing.

The band providing the entertainment segment of the cruise began playing their first song. The strains of Bette Midler's "The Rose" seemed a fitting serenade for what was about to happen. *"Some say love, it is a river..."*

I took the urn and carefully removed the lid as Grammie lifted the lid of the other urn. Holding them out as far as we could, we tipped them up and released the fine ash. The light breeze whirled them briefly skyward before the ashes cascaded down toward the swirling waves. I returned the urn to the canvas bag and slipped my arm around Gram's stooping shoulders. Grammie turned from us, not taking her gaze from the island.

When the island was almost completely out of sight, Gram released herself from my embrace, let go of the railing, and walked to the door. She turned slightly, taking one more look, then gripped the door handle. She pulled it open, stepped over the threshold, and went back inside.

Rivers
2004

"Why do they call it 'skinny dipping,' Nanny?"

"I'm not sure, sweetie. I guess because we strip down to the skin before we run in and dip in the water."

"Is that why we do it after dark when there are no boys around?"

"That's why I do it after dark. Your Great-Grammie doesn't seem to care what time of day it is or who her audience is. I'm sure she'll continue skinny dipping regularly this summer when she gets to the cottage."

"Did Mom call me Rivers because of this river?"

"Maybe. I'm not sure. She named your little brother after my father, I know."

"Why did Gabe's twin die?"

"You're full of questions tonight, aren't you? I don't know why your sister died, sweetie. She wasn't strong enough when she was born, I guess. Thankfully your brother was, so your Mom and Dad didn't lose both babies. Gram, my grandmother, always said, 'Into each life some rain must fall.'"

"Is that why they named her Lillianne Rain?"

"Maybe. I don't know. You'll have to ask your mommy."

"I had two great-great-grandmothers, the one who lived in our house and the one who lived here at the cottage."

"You are a lucky girl. I don't think you can ever have too many grandmothers, great-grandmothers, or great-great-grandmothers. I loved Gram a lot, but I never got to meet my babcia in Poland."

"Great-Grampy Bud's mom lived in Poland?"

"No, my dad, Gabe, was your grandfather, too, remember. He died before I was born, and his mother died years before that."

"And what about the lady you said used to live in that house where we stopped to buy eggs yesterday? Who was she to me?"

"She was your great-great-great-grandmother. Her name was Marion Kingston."

"Papa always takes us to Kingston store for ice cream. Did she own the store?"

"No. Kingston is where the store is. Kingston was also her last name. Not quite the same thing."

"We go to Costco at the Kingston near us. How come there are two Kingstons?"

"Are we going to go skinny dipping or stand around shivering while you keep asking questions?"

"Race you in, Nanny."

"You can try, Rivers Cordelia Thompson. You can try."

Acknowledgements

I begin with a huge thank you to Terrilee Bulger and Acorn Press. And a special thank you to Penelope Jackson who worked her magic again in what seemed like an effortless process. She is so patient and kind and so forgiving of my bad habits. Thanks to Matt Reid for his design expertise.

Thanks to my friend Barb who read the very first draft of many. Her sharp reading eye and keen mind jarred me into working harder to tell this story. Always find first readers who don't let kindness get in the way of honesty.

I must acknowledge the beautiful region of our vast country that inspired this book. Kingston, Ontario and the Thousand Island Region are places worth visiting. I love my home province and the beautiful Kingston Peninsula, NB but for the first time I allowed my writing to travel further. I did however feel the need for one character to be born there and other characters to find their way to the peninsula as the story unfolded. Who knows where I'll travel next.

My husband Burton remains my biggest and most supportive fan. His encouragement and adoration have always propelled me to keep going. Thanks to Meg, Cody, Emma, Paige, Ashlie, Chapin , Brianne, Anthony, Skyler, Bella, and Caleb for your love and support. Love you and miss you Zac.

Susan White was born in New Brunswick and as a teenager her family moved to the Kingston Peninsula and she only left long enough to earn her BA and BEd at St. Thomas University in Fredericton. She and her husband raised four children and ran a small farm while she taught elementary school. Since retiring she is grateful to now have the time to work on her writing and the freedom to regularly visit her grandchildren in Alberta. She is the author of *Waiting for Still Water*, *Maple Sugar Pie* and five middle-grade novels, including the Ann Connor Brimer Award winning novel *The Year Mrs. Montague Cried* and *Headliner*, which is nominated for The Mrs. Dunster's Fiction Book Prize.